3

A LUKE TREMAYNE ADVENTURE

MURDER
IN THE
MAGHREB

AN ISLAMIC INTERLUDE NORTH AFRICA 1657–8

GEOFF QUAIFE

Order this book online at www.trafford.com
or email orders@trafford.com

Most Trafford titles are also available at major online book retailers.

Print information available on the last page.

ISBN: 978-1-4907-8585-1 (sc)
ISBN: 978-1-4907-8584-4 (hc)
ISBN: 978-1-4907-8583-7 (e)

Library of Congress Control Number: 2017917714

Trafford rev. 11/22/2017

 www.trafford.com

North America & international
toll-free: 1 888 232 4444 (USA & Canada)
fax: 812 355 4082

The Luke Tremayne Adventures

(In chronological order of the events portrayed)

Major Characters

Luke's Men

Luke Tremayne, Sir (Maj. Gen.)	Cromwell's top agent, now ambassador
Ralph Croft (Capt.)	master and navigator of the *Cromwell*
John Neville (Lt.)	naval gunnery expert
Bevan Stradling	Luke's former sergeant, now equerry
Miles Oxenbridge (Capt.)	commander of soldiers on the *Cromwell*
Simon, Lord Stokey	royalist and papist peer
Ninian, Lord Fyson	brother of a kidnapped toddler

Benbali Authorities

Murat	pasha, sultan's representative
Sharif	pasha's doctor
Ahmed	dey, elected ruler of Benbali

Yusuf (Commander)	controlled internal policing and taxation collection, "chief of police"
Gamal (Colonel)	Yusuf's deputy
Hasan (Admiral)	commander of the fleet
Nasim (Admiral)	former fleet commander
Osman (General)	commander of the janissaries and governor of the citadel
Ismet (Colonel)	janissary officer seconded to Luke, Osman's deputy as governor of citadel

English Residents

Ambrose Denton, Sir	English consul
Rose Denton, Lady	Ambrose's wife
James Goodrich	merchant and religious extremist
Lucy Goodrich	James's wife
Gregory Applegarth	Denton's partner
Patience Applegarth	Gregory's wife
Jethro Chatwood	new arrival
Chantal Chatwood	Jethro's sister
Rowland May	lawyer
Silas Sweetlace	bookkeeper
Peregrine, Lord Morton	escaped war criminal
Elizabeth Scarfe, Lady	survivor of a massacre

Other Benbali Residents

Nour	alleged enslaved English toddler Anne
Wasim	Benbali merchant, adopted Nour
Elif	companion and confidante of the pasha
Jan Claasen	chaplain to the Dutch residents
Lorenzo Battista	chaplain to Genoese residents and chief negotiator for the freeing of Christian slaves
Kareem	hostile bargeman
Ali	friendly bargeman
Ashar	hostile jihadist Arab/Berber sheikh
Ibrahim	friendly Arab sheikh

Others

Nicholas, Conde de Varga	governor of the Spanish enclave of Oran y Verganza

Referred To

Gerard, Marquess of Fyson	eldest brother of Anne
Nanny Squibbs	nursemaid to baby Anne
Viscount Thames	relative of a key figure

Real Historical Personages

Oliver Cromwell	Lord Protector
John Thurloe	Cromwell's chief minister and head of intelligence
John Stokes (Captain, later Admiral)	commander of Mediterranean fleet
Charles Stuart	exiled claimant to throne

Benbali is a fictitious city created from circumstances and events involving the seventeenth-century Islamic states of Tripoli, Tunis, and Algiers—to differing degrees, semiautonomous provinces of the Ottoman Turkish Empire.

Prologue

The government of Oliver Cromwell flexed its muscles in the Mediterranean to protect English merchants, modify the threat of Islamic piracy from the Maghreb— Algeria, Tunis, and Tripoli— and compete with Venice, the papacy, Genoa, France, Spain, the Dutch Republic, and the Ottoman Turks for control of the sea. Its assertive stance was spearheaded by the navy, initially commanded by Robert Blake, but supplemented by its diplomats and agents who negotiated secret treaties, double-crossed their overt friends, and maintained indefensible friendships with sworn enemies.

Into this complex and volatile world, Cromwell sent his most effective military agent, Luke Tremayne—now knighted and promoted to general, in command of England's newest frigate, the *Cromwell*—as the government's ambassador-at-large to the Islamic states of the Maghreb—known to contemporaries as the Barbary Coast. Luke must save English shipping and trade from Muslim attack, free English slaves, and reform the English trading community in the sultan's westernmost territory of Benbali.

Solving these major issues are complicated for Luke by divisions and murders within the English community, the death of a friend, unauthorized attempts to free an abducted Englishwoman, and efforts to find a stolen golden Madonna and to uncover the assumed identity of a war criminal who had escaped the Tower of London on the eve of his execution a decade earlier. His mission is constantly threatened by the byzantine nature of local politics manifesting itself in a series of coups and countercoups, a possible foreign invasion, and a rampaging cult of jihadist assassins.

Luke is provided with pleasant but potentially fatal diversions in his relationships with three women: Elizabeth, a damsel in distress; Elif, the pasha's adviser and concubine; and Patience, sensual and unhappily married.

1

Luke did not foresee—as he made his way to a routine meeting with England's ruler, the Lord Protector Oliver Cromwell, and his senior ministers—that the events of the next hour would dramatically change his life. As head of military intelligence, making his weekly report, he expected to outline his concerns and achievements and receive the usual mixture of criticism, plaudits, and new instructions.

As soon as he entered Cromwell's chamber, he sensed that all was not as it should be. There were no ministers, no secretaries to take notes, and none of Cromwell's personal attendants. Luke was alone with England's powerful ruler, who immediately addressed his loyal colonel. "Luke, you and I have served together for over fifteen years. You were a brilliant cavalry commander, a most effective bodyguard, and a loyal and successful secret agent, troubleshooter, and investigator. I am about to send you on a mission very different from your past service. It requires a major change to your status and activities."

Luke was completely unprepared for what followed. Cromwell continued. "You are appointed as ambassador-at-large to the Islamic states of North Africa. To carry out that role, you will need to reflect the appropriate status. Consequently, although you have refused it in the past, I am promoting you to major general. And as of this moment, I bestow on you a knighthood. You entered this room as Col. Luke Tremayne. You will leave it as Maj. Gen. Sir Luke Tremayne."

An astonished Luke could only mumble, "If that be your wish."

"There is worst to come." Cromwell chuckled. "After a lifetime as a cavalry officer, I am transferring you to the navy and putting you in command of our newest frigate."

Luke finally found his voice. "Sir, I am greatly honored by what you suggest, but I must protest against my transfer to the navy. I know nothing of ships."

"You do not need to. You will command the *Cromwell,* which is the fastest and best armed vessel in the fleet. It has the latest in lightweight, long-range, rapid-fire cannons. You are in overall command and responsible for the political and military activities of the ship, but the master mariner-navigator will be responsible for the running of the ship and be your overall deputy. A specialist gunnery officer will manage the *Cromwell*'s immense firepower."

"What happens to my old intelligence unit?"

"Your former deputy, Sir Evan Williams, is already in command and, as we speak, organizing the movement of the whole company to York to investigate possible subversion of high-ranking officers and local gentry."

"Can I keep some of my old comrades with me in this new role?"

"Only your sergeant, who can act as your equerry. You will have a half company of infantry on board who have experience in the areas where you will be sent."

"What exactly is my mission?"

"Follow me, Luke, and the situation will become clearer." The two men entered an adjoining antechamber, where Cromwell introduced Luke with his new title and rank.

Luke was surprised to find that the room contained several men whom he knew. Two sailors he had worked with on the Medway a few months earlier—Ralph Croft and John Neville— stepped forward as Cromwell announced, "You know both of these gentlemen. Captain Croft has been persuaded to rejoin the service after wasting a few years as a harbormaster. He will be master of the ship, responsible for its functioning, and above all your navigator. Lieutenant Neville will be your gunnery officer, capable of turning the *Cromwell* into a formidable weapon of war." Luke embraced his old friends, who congratulated him on his knighthood and promotion to general.

Cromwell continued his introductions. "This army officer, resplendent in the red jacket we are now issuing to our troops, is Capt. Miles Oxenbridge. He will command the half company of troops aboard the *Cromwell*. Miles has spent a decade soldiering in the Mediterranean and is fluent in both Arabic and Turkish. He will be an essential element in the success of your mission, acting also as your interpreter."

"A mission that you have yet to explain to me. I do not—" Luke was stopped midsentence as yet another old acquaintance entered the room.

"I do not need to introduce your senior companion on this mission. Simon, Lord Stokey—with his Catholic beliefs, social status, linguistic skills, and royalist connections—will be an ideal partner for you in dealing with the confused and volatile world of the Catholic and Islamic Mediterranean."

"Where we are to do what?" reiterated Luke, impatient for the details of his mission.

"Let me explain," replied Simon. "In the 1630s, when Islamic pirates had a base in the Bristol Channel, they consistently raided the coasts of Somerset, Devon, and Cornwall and abducted hundreds of English men, women, and children into slavery. On one such raid, the estate of Erasmus, Marquess of Fyson, was attacked. Fortunately, the family was absent in London, except for the youngest daughter, a two-year-old toddler who had been left behind in the care of a nursemaid. The toddler was taken, although the family has preferred to think that she was murdered during the raid."

"It is so long ago that the child could long be dead or, if alive, a slave in the harem of any of a thousand Barbary Coast households. Why has the matter suddenly been raised?" asked an unimpressed Luke.

"A few months ago, our fleet under General Blake sought provisions from Benbali. The ruler refused, and Blake threatened to bombard the city if they failed to supply our ships. The Benbalis pointed out that they did not have the victuals to sell, but as an act of good faith and to avoid Blake's cannonade, they offered to free thirty English slaves, which they did," interjected Cromwell.

He continued. "Among those slaves was an elderly woman who had been baby Fyson's nursemaid. When she returned to Cornwall, she confronted the current marquess—Gerard, the baby's eldest brother—and explained what had happened. Baby Anne and her nursemaid were bought as slaves by a wealthy Benbali merchant who has treated Anne as his own child and has not yet permitted her to marry. Gerard, a Royalist, has pleaded through Lord Stokey with both Charles Stuart and now me to rescue his sister before she is married off to some infidel."

"Surely, the normal approach would be for our consul in Benbali to pay a ransom to the merchant concerned," commented Luke.

"Not possible in this case," answered the Lord Protector. "No one in Benbali is aware of Anne's aristocratic background. If this became known, the Benbali rulers might take Anne from her household and ransom her at an incredible price. Also, the nursemaid affirmed that the merchant is a kind man, besotted with his adopted daughter, and is in no position to sell her as he freed her from slavery years ago. Consequently, her real identity must be kept secret, even from our consul and, until the last minute, from the man who adopted her."

"And there is a far more serious obstacle to the success of our mission," added Simon. "According to the nursemaid, Anne Fyson knows nothing of her English and Christian background. She has been brought up a Muslim, speaks only Turkish and Arabic, and believes herself to be Nour, daughter of the merchant Wasim. She will see us as kidnappers, not rescuers."

"Then why are we embarking on such an impossible task to help a royalist peer?" asked a still unimpressed Luke.

"As always, there are other issues, some of which I am not privy to, but the Lord Protector will enlighten you on your major agenda," confessed Simon.

"I want you to assess the worthiness of our consul in Benbali. Is he loyal? Does he advance the interests of our resident merchants in the city? Does he do his best to ransom the many English slaves in that jurisdiction?" said Cromwell.

"This does not need Simon's assistance. Why is Simon really part of this project?" asked Luke suddenly.

"Years ago, when you and your then deputy Harry Lloyd worked with Simon in France, he was trying to relocate a vast treasure that had been hidden from its rightful owners," Cromwell explained.

"Are we to steal some vast Islamic treasure trove from our Barbary Coast corsairs?" half joked Luke.

"Something like that," answered Simon. "When Fyson first approached me, I was immediately suspicious of his stated motives. When the monasteries were dissolved a century and a quarter ago, much treasure belonging to the church disappeared. One such object was a two-foot-tall solid gold Madonna and Child encrusted with every conceivable precious stone. It disappeared without trace from the abbey of Witherham. It is well-known in Catholic circles that it was in the possession of the Fysons and probably stolen by the corsairs on the night they abducted Anne. I suspect Gerard is more interested in recovering the Madonna than his long-lost sister."

"Another impossible task. The infidel melts down Christian objects of worship. The representation of the deity is anathema to their faith," declaimed a pompous Luke.

There was a knock on the door of the chamber. Cromwell's chief minister and head of intelligence, John Thurloe, entered with a young man who—by the reaction of the group—was unknown to all of them. "What is it, John?" asked the protector.

"This young man is Ninian Fyson, brother of the kidnapped girl. He has convinced me that he has intimate details of the then baby and other family matters that would be of immense help to Lord Stokey and General Tremayne when they confront the girl. In addition, he is an able swordsman and an accomplished linguist. He speaks Arabic. I strongly recommend that he go on the mission with them."

Luke lightheartedly commented, "You have forgotten this lad's strongest asset. Like myself, he is a Cornishman." He turned to Ninian. "How did you become fluent in Arabic?"

"My uncle was a consul in Aleppo, and when our civil wars began, Father sent me there."

Simon was more probing. "Why do you wish to come with us? You hardly knew your baby sister, and you also have been away from your own family for a long time."

Ninian was a typical Cornishman in appearance. He was tall with olive skin and jet-black hair worn long in the manner of the cavaliers. He did not seem to be put off in the presence of the Lord Protector and answered Simon confidently, "True, I was only three when Anne was taken, and our family deliberately wiped her existence from our memory. Father put it about that she had been murdered during the corsair raid, and apparently, a requiem was said. There is a plaque in the family chapel commemorating her short existence."

"If that is the case, why are you determined to join us?"

"When Nanny Squibbs came to the house and told her story, my brother Gerard was over the moon—but not with any thought of recovering Anne. His only concern was to find the missing Madonna. I want to ensure that the recovery of that item does not get priority over finding and rescuing my sister."

Intuitively, Luke was convinced. Sensing the positive reaction of Luke and Simon, Cromwell issued his orders. "Gentlemen, the officers will take up their positions on board the *Cromwell,* currently docked at Greenwich a week today. When she is ready to sail the troops under Captain Oxenbridge and our two aristocratic passengers, the lords Stokey and Fyson will board."

Before he left the meeting, Cromwell handed Luke a sealed letter. "These are your most important orders. Open it as soon as you leave English waters."

Luke and Simon walked away from the meeting together. Luke was blunt. "Why do Charles Stuart and Oliver Cromwell trust you with regard to the Madonna? Your past record was to stop the treasure from falling into the hands of either government. If you get your hands on the Madonna, it is certainly not going into the coffers of the English government or into those of Charles Stuart or into the greedy paws of the Marquess of Fyson. You will return it to whom you conceive as its rightful owner—the Church of Rome."

Simon smiled and said gently, "To be more precise, it belongs to the Cistercian monks of the mother church who relocated to Spain. I am sure you have been chosen as my companion in this enterprise to prevent such a thing from occurring."

Luke had a serious personal issue to resolve before he left. He had remained unmarried despite his love for at least two women in his past. In recent months, he had been captivated by the newly widowed Lady Matilda Lynne, and both she and his circle of friends anticipated an imminent announcement of their betrothal.

Once again, after reflecting on the nature of his latest mission and his new status, he convinced himself that marriage at this time was not appropriate; but after spending five days in the company of Matilda before embarking on the *Cromwell*, they reached a decision. On his return from North Africa and having allowed considerable time to elapse since the death of her husband, Lady Matilda Lynne and Sir Luke Tremayne would announce their betrothal.

2

As the *Cromwell* approached Lisbon, a large Dutch fleet blocked their passage to the south. Ralph was alarmed. "Will they try to stop us?"

John Neville remained calm. "The Dutch are now our allies. We gave them a good thrashing three years ago. They won't risk upsetting us at this time."

Miles disagreed. "Don't be too sure. On many occasions when I served under General Blake, the Dutch did not hesitate to confront us. I will ready my men in case they attempt to board."

Luke agreed. "The government of the Dutch Republic *is* our ally, but it has trouble controlling its fleets. Each maritime province has a fleet of its own. While those of Holland are well disciplined, those of Zealand are less predictable. In addition, there have been several cases of rogue Dutch captains having a commission from another power to attack our shipping. John, ready your guns! Ralph, increase our speed!"

The *Cromwell* prepared for action. Ralph informed Luke, "By our treaty with the Dutch, they are required to lower their colors and to fire a salute, to which we must respond." The first Dutch ship approached the *Cromwell* with its gun ports open. Was this to deliver a salute or a damaging broadside?

Luke began to perspire profusely. He faced his first major decision as the overall commander of the frigate. Would he risk a damaging broadside or even worse, or should he fire first into the Dutch ship—a major breach of maritime law?

At the last moment, the leading Dutch ship veered away, firing a reluctant salute, to which John Neville responded with an impressive cannonade. Ralph quickly maneuvered the *Cromwell* to depart at an increased speed in the opposite direction. The Dutch ships were soon out of firing range and accelerating away toward two merchantmen who had appeared on the horizon—an easier and much more valuable prize than an English frigate.

Ralph increased sail and hugged the Spanish coast. This course soon provoked from the Spanish coastal castles a series of cannonades that fell well short of the ship. Nevertheless, their noise alerted Spanish naval authorities to a possible danger; and as the *Cromwell* neared Càdiz, three war galleons appeared, guarding the approaches to the harbor. Luke signaled Ralph to put farther out to sea. He had no intention of provoking trouble.

Out of sight of the Spanish coast, the lookout alerted Luke to a flotilla of Portuguese merchantmen in the distance. It soon became clear that the laggard in this Portuguese fleet was under attack from a ship whose colors were not immediately visible.

Luke summoned his officers. "Gentlemen, apart from my specific orders regarding Benbali and the rescue of Anne, Lady Fyson, I also received the general orders issued to all English naval commanders in this region, one of which is to assist our new ally, Portugal, on every occasion possible." He shouted up to the lookout, "Can you make out the attacker's identity?"

"Yes, it's a Dutch-built ship but flying the privateering flag of Dunkirk."

"Great, a Spanish ally," declared John, anxious to test his gunners.

Ralph was also enthusiastic. "A great chance to test the speed and maneuverability of the *Cromwell* in battle conditions."

Miles was more cautious. "Don't engage in an unnecessary loss of ammunition and risk damage in a matter that need not concern us. If the ship being attacked was not an ally but a neutral, we could claim it as a prize, having saved it from the Dunkirker. In this case, we cannot claim as a prize a ship we have saved as part of a treaty of alliance. There is no gain in this adventure. Also, the Dunkirker is attacking the laggard of the Portuguese fleet. The rest of the merchantmen are not reacting. These Portuguese merchantmen are usually well armed. They could have turned around, and their combined efforts would have overwhelmed the attacker. If the Portuguese commander does not see it as important enough to save one of his ships, why should we? You will have plenty of opportunity once we sail into the Mediterranean to test the capabilities of this frigate—and pick up prizes."

Simon suggested a compromise that immediately appealed to Luke. "Why not use a bit of bluff. If we sail full speed toward the Dunkirker and fire a few cannons so that our range can be appreciated, its captain should immediately conclude we can outrun and outgun him. He will turn and run."

Simon's prediction was accurate. The Dunkirker fled. The merchantman fired a short cannonade in appreciation, and almost simultaneously, the rest of the Portuguese reappeared, returning to assist its partially disabled companion.

Benbali was the westernmost North African town under the nominal control of the Ottoman Turks. Towns farther to the west were part of the kingdom of Morocco. It was a thriving city whose wealth came from the paradoxical activities of privateering and victualing the very ships that they may or may not seize for their intrinsic value—the value of the cargo—and for prisoners who may be sold into slavery, transferred to their own ships, or ransomed. Along with Tripoli, Tunis, and Algiers, they were the Barbary Coast corsairs—Islamic pirates who preyed on the Christian merchantmen of the Mediterranean.

Benbali was blessed with a deep harbor that was protected from the elements by a long breakwater that narrowed access to the half-moon-shaped inlet and from its enemies by a citadel that stood high above the town and overlooked the narrow entrance to the port. Towering on a hill in the south of the city was a magnificent mosque whose pure white color stood out against the cloudless azure sky. Its two minarets were incredibly tall, giving the muezzin a perfect position to call the faithful to prayer—and to spy on the community. Miles pointed out that in some communities, because of this possible breach of privacy, the position was held by a blind man.

The call to prayer, which could be heard well out to sea, indicated that it was close to noon. As the *Cromwell* approached the entrance to the Benbali harbor, a single shot was fired from the citadel in its direction. The inexperienced Luke was troubled. "This is not a very friendly reception. The cannons of that castle could do us serious damage."

"No worries, General!" said Miles. "That is simply a greeting that implicitly asks who you are and why you here—are you friend or foe?"

"And how do we respond?" asked Luke.

"You send someone ashore to inform the authorities of your identity and intentions."

"And who are the authorities? Is this a semi-independent military republic or a loyal province of the Ottoman Empire?" questioned the fast-learning commander.

"A bit of both. The representative of the Turkish sultan is the pasha, who simply legalizes the decisions of the real power—the dey. The dey is elected by a ruling council made up of competing factions, and his hold on office is tenuous, given the changing balance of power among these factions," explained Miles.

"Playing politics at home is confusing enough. I trust it is not complicated here. I had hoped to complete our mission without having to become too involved in local affairs."

"Benbali is not as complex as the other Barbary states. There are three factions—the elite Turkish troops, the janissaries, who control the citadel and are responsible for the defense of the state; the corsairs: captains and sailors, who bring in much of the city's wealth and who are predominantly Christian renegades who have converted to Islam; and the followers of the city's commander, an official responsible for internal policing and the collection of taxes and who, over time, has developed a force of his own made up of Arabic-speaking locals. He has close links with the general populace of the city and the rural sheikhs."

"Lower the longboat! Let us pay our respects," declared Luke.

"To avoid confusion, Luke, remember that the Turks do not use family names. In place of these, they add their titles to their given names. For example, the top men in Benbali are Murat Pasha and Ahmed Dey."

"What are you going to tell them?" asked Simon. "Any mention of the golden Madonna or of a specific slave would be dangerous. These people are basically concerned with making money."

"Don't worry, Simon. As ambassador-at-large, I will be the perfect diplomat, concerned with signing a treaty to stop Benbali corsairs from attacking English ships, negotiating for the release of English slaves, and anxious to reform the resident English traders."

"I will come with you," announced Simon.

"So will I," echoed Ninian.

"No, only Miles and I will go ashore. Until we discover the attitude of the Benbalis, the rest of you will stay here, well out of range of their guns. And, Ralph, if any of their ships approach the *Cromwell*, you are to forget us and use your superior speed to escape. Simon and Ninian, as English aristocrats, are potential objects of hefty ransom demands. Until their safety is guaranteed, they will remain aboard."

As the longboat approached the narrow entrance to the harbor, a small galley emerged to block their path. "Our official welcome," uttered Miles. "Did they know that we were coming?"

"Thurloe sent letters to our consul here asking him to inform the authorities that the English government would be sending a high-powered ambassador to negotiate with them," answered Luke.

As the longboat reached the galley, a white-turbaned officer rather short of stature with an olive skin, deep brown eyes, and a very short black beard announced in Turkish, "Welcome to Benbali! Are you the expected English ambassador?"

Miles replied in the same tongue, "My companion is Maj. Gen. Sir Luke Tremayne, ambassador-at-large, who seeks permission to discuss a range of issues with your government."

"I am Colonel Ismet, deputy governor of the citadel and designated by the pasha to escort the ambassador to His Excellency. Come aboard. Your sailors can return your boat to their ship."

Luke and Miles landed on the eastern shore of the harbor and were led by Ismet and a small detachment of elite janissaries along the waterfront toward the palace of the pasha that dominated the western edge of the bay. Ismet explained to Miles that they would be accommodated in the palace and that he would arrange meetings for them with the dey and his council, the city's commander, and the resident English community as required by Luke.

After some time, one of Ismet's men began and continued what became an increasingly heated argument with his colonel. Luke eventually asked Miles, "What is his problem?"

He replied, "The soldier wants to know why Ismet landed us at the eastern side of the bay when our destination is at the opposite end of the harbor."

"An interesting question. I wondered about that myself. What is the colonel's answer?"

"That the pasha is unable to receive you immediately and that it was more courteous to you, as a visiting dignitary, to take the time arriving rather than cool your heels in an antechamber of the palace."

"That does not appear to have satisfied the complainant. He is still harassing his commanding officer."

"Yes, he now has a second concern. He is worried about crossing the plaza that runs to the water's edge in the center of the port. It is market day and full of unruly rural Arabs who have no time for the Turks."

Ismet hoped to take advantage of the midday prayers, which had momentarily stopped trade and created a silence, broken only by the chanting of the imam and the responses of the faithful. It was not to be. Prayers ended as the group entered the plaza. The market burst into noisy and unruly activity.

Ismet's critic confronted his officer. Miles reported, "He wants Ismet to stop here and either return to the galley or call for reinforcements. As we approach the market, you can see several brawls erupting."

"I take his point—six skilled janissaries against dozens of belligerent Arabs. Not good odds," commented Luke.

Ismet ignored his man's request but suggested to Miles that he and Luke should be ready to draw their swords in case of trouble. He led his group to the water's edge to avoid the sprawling brawlers, but one group deliberately crushed against the janissary guard, who retaliated, provoking more of the rioters to direct their attention toward Ismet's group.

Suddenly, one of the assailants pushed a janissary aside and ran at Luke with a dagger whose blade gleamed in the hot sunlight. Luke struggled to get his sword into a defensive position.

3

Luke was saved by Ismet, who—with one swing of his scimitar—decapitated the advancing attacker. His querulous off sider did the same to another of the advancing group, forcing the rest to quickly retreat into the main body of the fracas.

Luke nodded his thanks to Ismet, who—as soon as he had moved his group some distance from the trouble—had a long conversation with Miles. Miles explained, "Ismet apologizes for the assault but is very concerned by what happened. It is contrary to both Arab and Berber customs to attack a stranger and a man of obvious importance. He thinks you were singled out and that the whole riot was staged to cover your assassination."

Luke was shaken—but unconvinced. "Ridiculous! There was no time to organize such an event. From the moment we entered the harbor until now is but half an hour, and who among such people would know who I am? It was like any brawl in an English alehouse. In the end, many an innocent bystander becomes involved. And often, an unsuspecting passerby becomes a victim. We had a lucky escape from being in the wrong place at the wrong time."

Miles disagreed. "General, one group did know you were coming, a group that, upon seeing an English warship off the coast and the use of the pasha's galley to bring you ashore, would rightly assume you were the promised ambassador—a group also aware of the local protocol in receiving visiting persons of eminence."

"And who would they be?" asked a skeptical Luke.

"The English community. You have the authority and force to completely reorganize their existence here. Some must be terrified that you will curtail or even end their activities. Merchants don't care about right and wrong, Cromwell, or Charles Stuart. Profit rules—and you are a potential threat to it."

"In that case, I must interrogate the English as soon as possible," replied Luke, trying to lighten the conversation.

"Ismet suggests that you have a bodyguard at all times. He will seek the pasha's permission for me to disembark enough of my men for this purpose."

As Luke and Miles were talking, Ismet's talkative subordinate was in earnest conversation with him. A grim-faced Ismet relayed the latest conversation to Luke through Miles. "Ismet is now firmly convinced that you were the target but unsure of who organized the assassination attempt. During the fracas, one of his men heard a loud voice identifying you as the target and urging the locals to persist in their endeavors. The man was not a native Arabic speaker, revealing an accent that many Europeans develop in grappling with the language.

"On the other hand, the attackers may have been Arab or Berber fanatics who hate all foreigners. A group of these jihadists gather from time to time in the forecourt of the Grand White Mosque, which you can see on rising ground just behind the market square. The mosque authorities and the city commander usually keep them under control. Today they may have just left midday prayers and witnessed your arrival. Even with so little pomp, it could have infuriated the more unhinged of the group. They wish to remove all unbelievers, and even fellow Muslims who do not share their beliefs, from North African soil."

Luke's audience with the pasha, Murat, settled immediate issues and laid the basis for later negotiations with the dey and with the English community. Luke was surprised. Expecting an ethnic dark Turk, he was confronted by a man taller than himself and of pale complexion and a broad graying beard.

Miles whispered that Murat was an ethnic Croatian. He explained that very few of the administrators and generals within the Ottoman Empire were Turks. They were Christian boys from the Balkans who were enslaved, converted to Islam, and given an education that far surpassed anything in Christian Europe. The best graduates from this education became the sultan's administrators, including the current chief minister, the grand vizier. The present occupier of the position was Albanian. The vast Ottoman Empire was ruled locally by other top graduates, such as Murat Pasha. The same educational system provided the elite corps of the sultan's troops—the janissaries, which included Colonel Ismet, the dey, and the garrison of the castle.

Murat invited Luke to berth the *Cromwell* at the western end of the harbor adjacent to his personal galley. Luke diplomatically refused the offer and explained that his ship would anchor in the inlet next to the Benbali harbor, conveniently out of range of the castle's guns.

The pasha permitted Miles to land a dozen of his men as a bodyguard for the ambassador and seconded Colonel Ismet to the English mission to liaise with local authorities. He advised Luke to inform Commander Yusuf, who controlled the internal policing of the city, of any intended movements within Benbali. Luke nodded compliance.

The pasha hoped Luke would bring to the negotiating table an offer of several English ships to join the Ottoman fleet or at least to allow the Benbalis and the Ottoman Turks an opportunity to buy the faster and better armed frigates of the *Cromwell* class. Luke smiled and thanked the pasha for his suggestion.

Finally, the local potentate encouraged Luke to reorganize and reform the local English community provided that none of his changes impinged on relationships with the local authorities. In any moves he should make in this regard, both Ahmed Dey and Commander Yusuf should be informed.

Luke thanked Murat Pasha for his welcome and stated, if it was acceptable, that he and Miles would move as soon as possible from the palace to the English quarters. The pasha was not impressed and suggested that Luke and Miles enjoy the pleasures of his palace at least for some days while he found them accommodation suitable to their status.

The first pleasure of the palace arrived into Luke's palatial temporary apartment soon after Miles left for the *Cromwell*. He was to collect a dozen of his troops, Strad, Stokey, and Fyson and to instruct Ralph Croft to move the ship to the adjoining inlet. Ismet also departed to consult the dey regarding a meeting with Luke.

A veiled and lavishly dressed youngish woman entered the room, followed by an array of servants bearing platters of fresh fruit, enticing sweet meats, and jugs of iced mint tea. The woman was tall with flowing black hair, sparkling deep green eyes, and sensuous lips. Her body was adorned with gold—a bejeweled golden necklace, thick golden bracelets on both wrists, and long delicately wrought golden earrings.

Luke was at a loss on how to respond to this beautiful and richly dressed woman in the absence of his interpreter, Miles. He nodded his approval to the servants bearing food and drink but was confused about how to react to the attractive woman who began to stroke his hair.

Confusion changed to amazement when the girl spoke to Luke in English with a slight West Country accent with which he was very familiar. "My lord sends you the repast, and myself to meet whatever requirements you might have. In addition to these private needs, I am to act as your interpreter until your captain returns. I am Elif Iqbal, slave to the mighty Murat Pasha."

Luke, feeling more secure in the presence of someone who spoke English, asked, "You are one of the many English slaves captured in Benbali raids on the Devon and Cornish coast?"

"Yes, Your Excellency. In a past life, I was a dairymaid, Abigail Stanton. Now I am a leading member of the pasha's household."

"I will arrange with your master for you to accompany me back to England at the end of my negotiations here. I will buy your freedom no matter how much it costs," announced a humane but naive Luke.

"Sir, you do not understand. I have converted to Islam and have no desire to return to my previous life, in which I was physically abused by my parents, my master and his son, and my fellow workers. Fortunately, probably because of my very young age at the time, this never amounted to sexual abuse, so I remained a valuable prize and was selected by the pasha as his share of the raid that captured me and countless others."

"Where are the others?"

"If they became Muslims, many have a similar life to mine in the homes of wealthy local officials or merchants. Some have even married their master and obtained their legal freedom. Those who remain Christian lead a more difficult life, subjected to all the abuse that an evil master might choose to apply. Many have been raped and several killed."

"These women would welcome my attempts to have them freed. It is one of the reasons I am here—to rescue English slaves."

"I cannot comment. I have no contact with those unhappy souls. The only other English girl in the pasha's household has similar views to me. She would resist any attempts to return her to England. But there is one group that does need rescuing—the men who have been condemned to row our Benbali galleys. My cousin is one of them. But if you try to free these men, you will confront the might of the corsair commanders, who with the janissaries are the real powers in Benbali. You would need to offer them a fortune to give up such vital manpower."

"I have just the perfect bargaining tool—an English frigate. By converting from oar to sail, there is no need to maintain a vast army of rowers," Luke suggested.

At that moment, a large African entered the room and addressed Elif, who turned to Luke and asked, "The Dutch chaplain wishes to see you."

"The Dutch chaplain. How would he know that I am here? What could he possibly want?" asked a surprised Luke.

"I don't know, but he is a friend of the pasha, and their weekly game of chess was postponed with your arrival. Do you wish me to find an interpreter?"

"No. The only language I speak other than English is Dutch, although I did not expect to find a need for it in Benbali."

"I will leave, but a Nubian servant will stay by the door, and if you need anything, just signal to him, and he will fetch me." Elif showed the Dutch cleric into the room and departed.

Luke recognized the visitor. "Jan Claasen! It must be twenty years since we last met."

The two men embraced, and the pastor commented, "Yes, it is two decades since you saved my life. You have certainly climbed the military ladder. Then you were a young trooper serving in the Dutch cavalry, and now you are a major general and ambassador for the mighty Oliver Cromwell."

"My rescue of you was my first mission as a soldier. The Spaniards overran your village, burned your church, and had you, as pastor, tied to the stake, ready to burn as a heretic—a warning to all Dutch protestants. Your parishioners were herded into the village square, and once your pyre was lit, they were to be shot."

"I never saw you coming. I had my eyes shut and was in prayer when your troop broke through the Spanish defenses and decimated their musketeers in the square, which enabled my flock to flee. You cut me free, scooped me up, and carried me to safety. I was very surprised to discover that my rescuer was a young Englishman."

"They were great days. How did a bright young pastor of the Dutch Reformed Church finish up in a North African Islamic backwater? Have you been here long?"

"I've been here for five years. My wife died ten years ago. I had a few disputes with the church authorities. When the government insisted that, in return for their paying for a consul here to assist the merchants, they had to provide a chaplain for the Dutch community. I offered my services, hoping in some way to discover the whereabouts of one of my flock taken by Benbali corsairs. There was nothing to keep me in the Netherlands. What brings you here? Or is that a state secret?"

"Not at all. I am to negotiate a treaty to prevent the Benbalis from attacking English ships and to free as many English slaves as possible. I am also to investigate the activities of our consul and the general situation of our English merchants."

"Not before time. Dealing with the Benbalis will be much easier than your own people. Ambrose Denton, your consul, is a dangerous piece of work as you will soon discover. Watch your back. Do not believe a word he says."

"Tell me more," asked a concerned Luke.

4

"Denton is an autocrat who dominates a very unhappy community. He uses his position as consul solely to advance his own commercial interests and destroy his rivals. He maintains his power through his manipulation of local factional leaders. Your timing may be perfect. Denton and the former commander of the corsairs were very close and both staunch allies of the current equally corrupt dey. Two weeks ago, the corsair admiral, Nasim, was replaced by Hasan, who also plans to overthrow the roguish Ahmed Dey and replace him with an honest man more sympathetic to the sailors and the Arab population," explained Claasen.

"What can you tell me about Colonel Ismet, who has been assigned to me as a guide, bodyguard, and interpreter? Where does he stand in the local power structure?"

"You are receiving the treatment—first Elif and now Ismet. He is not simply a janissary officer. He is deputy commander of the garrison in the citadel and was seconded to the pasha when news of your imminent arrival was first reported. It is rumored that he was close to the sultan before his transfer here, but I do not know where his first loyalty lies in Benbali. Is it the pasha, the dey, or the general of the janissaries? Or is it to Colonel Ismet alone? He is an influential figure in his own right and would be a good ally. His suspected close connections to the sultan's court give him an influence and status above his current rank and position. There are rumors that he has been meeting lately with Hasan."

"What else can you tell me about the English community? How many people do I have to deal with?"

"Not many. To survive here, an English merchant needs to be closely allied to Sir Ambrose or to one of the local faction leaders. There are only three merchants— Ambrose and his partner, Gregory Applegarth, and James Goodrich, who deals with the native population in local goods and has strong ties with the city commander, Yusuf, and the rural Arab interests. There are two senior employees. Rowland May is lawyer to the English community in general but is also employed by Denton and Applegarth to run their warehouse. Silas Sweetlace is everybody's bookkeeper but, in his spare time, assists Goodrich. Jethro Chatwood is a recent arrival and has both the English community and the local authorities concerned. He is not a merchant, and his arrival from Constantinople with the latest detachment of janissaries has given rise to rumors that he is a spy for the sultan."

"An interesting group," muttered Luke.

"Your desire to free slaves will not be welcomed. It will create enemies, which will jeopardize other aspects of your mission. Treat the freeing of slaves as a purely commercial transaction, if you want any hope of success."

"What is the procedure regarding the release of slaves?"

"For centuries, all negotiations have been carried out by papist priests belonging to the Order of Mercy."

"Surely, our Protestant consuls can act on our behalf?"

"No. The Turk does not distinguish between nationalities or religious divisions within Christendom. The current priest in Benbali is Fr. Lorenzo Battista. He is chaplain to the Genoese community. There are only three European communities here— representatives from the Dutch Republic, England, and Genoa."

"That may explain why the English government encumbered my mission with two Catholic aristocrats who may bring a more sympathetic attitude to this issue."

"I hope you have also brought a fortune with you. The Benbalis will not give up their slaves. You will have to buy them out. And quite a few of the personal slaves will not want to be freed.

Concentrate on the galley slaves, where a gift of an English warship or at least a massive amount of arms and ammunition would work wonders. Talk to Admiral Hasan, and offer him personal sweeteners before having any formal discussions with the dey."

"That sounds like the very corruption I have been sent to stamp out. It is clear that I will need your advice throughout my stay. I want to move into the English quarters as soon as possible, but the pasha has other ideas."

"He probably fears that isolated in the English quarters, Sir Ambrose Denton will have undue influence over you. Get rid of Denton, and the pasha will be your friend for life. How many troops do you have to enforce your decisions within the community?"

"A half company of musketeers, some of whom must remain on board the *Cromwell*."

"You will also have Ismet and his men, and if in the city, Commander Yusuf's police will probably shadow you for your own safety. Always keep Yusuf and his deputy, Gamal, informed of your plans. Yusuf is the most amenable and honest of the local officials and Gamal one of the most competent."

"Any other advice?"

"You are at a disadvantage. Local Turkish authorities expect ambassadors to come with a large entourage bearing expensive gifts. You have come alone with a potentially menacing warship that refuses to accept Benbali hospitality and enter its harbor. It is an inauspicious beginning. You will have to do better, Luke," commented a smiling Jan Claasen as he left the room.

Luke turned to a platter of dates and figs, but before he could indulge, Elif reentered the room. "The English consul wishes to see you."

Sir Ambrose Denton was a very small man and, despite the local climate, wore his mousy brown hair to his shoulders. His oblong pale face sported a narrow mustache, a short compact beard, and bushy eyebrows—all a nondescript mousy brown. His elaborate cuffs and collar suggested to Luke that the consul was deliberately flaunting his royalist sympathies.

"I am glad you have come. I will need you to accompany me or other members of my party when we negotiate with the authorities. I must also talk to the English community as a whole and put them in the picture regarding the purpose of my visit," announced a diplomatic Luke.

"And what is that purpose, General?" asked an obviously uptight and suspicious Ambrose.

Luke had taken an immediate dislike of the man and would have preferred to have replied with a simple "I am here to replace you with an honest and loyal servant of the English republic." Instead, he answered carefully, "To negotiate a treaty to exempt our shipping from Benbali raids and to free English slaves. In addition, I am to report on the state of our community here and your achievements as our consul. I will discuss all of these matters with you tomorrow, but my immediate priority is finding accommodation for a dozen to thirty men within the English quarters." Luke gave the consul details of his requirements and stated his soldiers should arrive at any time.

Ambrose left immediately to reluctantly make the necessary arrangements. Luke would enjoy clipping the wings of this arrogant merchant.

The pasha insisted that Luke stay in premises suitable to his status. He made available a large complex on the edge of the English quarters but within his own palatial compound—a minipalace. Luke was joined in this mansion by his equerry, Strad; the aristocrats, Stokey and Fyson; his interpreter, Miles Oxenbridge; and Ralph Croft, his master navigator. John Neville remained on board the *Cromwell*. The land-based English soldiers were accommodated in part of Ambrose Denton's extensive warehouse.

A detachment of Ismet's men guarded the ambassador within his new residence. Luke was a little uneasy that his personal guard consisted of Turkish janissaries and not English musketeers, but as a diplomat, it was unwise to upset the pasha.

The next day, Luke—accompanied by Simon, Miles, and Ismet—began negotiations with Ahmed Dey, the elected ruler of Benbali, in a large room within the citadel. Ahmed was tall, of olive complexion, of muscular and bulky build, and carrying the largest scimitar that Luke had ever seen. Luke was immediately disconcerted by his piercing brown eyes and penetrating stare that created unease in its recipients.

Ahmed was not alone. Ismet introduced another tall but incredibly thin turbaned figure as General Osman, commander of the Turkish troops and governor of the citadel. Osman was brown skinned with blue eyes and displayed no facial hair.

A smaller paler-skinned figure next to him, wearing a bright red scarf as a headdress, identified himself as Hasan, admiral of the corsair fleet. He welcomed the visitors in English. "On behalf of the dey and the authorities of Benbali, I welcome you and hope our discussions will lead to outcomes beneficial to us both. I am English born. I once served in your navy, became a privateer, converted to Islam, and only a few weeks ago was elected to command the entire Benbali fleet."

Luke put forward his conditions—an agreement that Benbali ships not attack those of England and that all English slaves be set free. The dey indicated that the first would be readily agreed to, but he would like more detail on what England would offer in return before signing any treaty. The release of slaves was a much more difficult issue and may not be possible.

Hasan explained, "Most government slaves can be released at a price, but any freedom to galley slaves, where most Englishmen are deployed, would depend on what effect the loss of this manpower would have on our fleet. Although we are slowly replacing galleys with sailing ships, the former are still vital to our survival."

Luke realized, as Jan had suggested, that he should talk to Hasan alone on this matter. The dey made clear that the release of slaves owned by Benbali residents was not of government concern but that the English should pay a fair price and that they must negotiate with the owner, using the Genoese chaplain, Father Battista, as the mediator.

Ahmed suddenly toughened his position by suggesting that, as an act of good faith, the *Cromwell* move into the harbor and Benbali authorities be permitted to inspect it. Luke ignored the first request but responded that an inspection of his ship would be welcomed, but he would like to discuss the details first with his naval officers.

Back at his residence, Luke referred the matter to Simon, Ralph, and Miles. "How do we respond to the dey's requests?" Luke asked.

"Unless the *Cromwell* is full of priceless gems and gold ingots, we have brought little to bargain with," commented Miles.

Luke smiled. "I do not have gems or gold, but there is enough silver aboard to enable me to dispense reasonable bribes and sweeteners and to buy slaves, but it may not be enough to satisfy the apparent greed of the local hierarchy. Nevertheless, I have something I suspect the Benbalis want more than gold, silver, or gems. I have authority to offer them a ship of the *Cromwell* class that is near completion in our shipyards—at an inflated price."

Ralph was dumbfounded. "Surely, the protector is not prepared to arm the infidel with such a ship. Their fleet, reinforced with just one fast and well-armed frigate, could wreak havoc among our merchantmen. Any treaty we sign is just a piece of paper that the Benbalis will ignore when it suits them. It is too high a price to pay for what may be an unenforceable treaty."

"What do you suggest we offer instead?" asked an impressed Miles.

"Nothing. General Blake showed us the way at Tunis. If a single English ship is attacked, threaten to bombard the city, and sink the local fleet. Reprisal, not access to the latest naval developments, should be our only offer. The English Mediterranean fleet is in the area. Summon it here to emphasize our naval superiority."

"Clearly, Ralph, you would not bring the *Cromwell* into the Benbali harbor?" concluded Luke.

"What about the slaves?" asked Simon, deliberately changing the subject.

"Talk to Father Battista regarding slaves in private hands, and I will speak with our fellow Englishman, Admiral Hasan, regarding the galley slaves."

Elif entered the room and handed Luke a note. He announced, "We are all invited to a welcoming banquet this evening by the English residents at the home of Gregory Applegarth, Denton's partner."

"Why not at Denton's own residence? He is the consul," asked Miles.

Before Luke could answer, he was informed that Hasan was without and needed to speak to him urgently. "This is a surprise—and most unusual. Normally, visiting officials have to wait to be summoned," said Miles. Luke cleared the room, apart from Miles.

Hasan entered alone. He spoke directly to Luke in English. "I need your advice and some help."

"What's the problem?"

"One of our coastal vessels has just reported a large English fleet headed in this direction. Does it come as a friend or enemy? Is it coming to enforce your demands? Is General Blake about to do to us what he did to Tunis?"

Luke was about to confess that he had no idea when he caught Miles's eye. He should give nothing away. He would create the impression he was in full control of the situation.

5

Luke lied, "The fleet's arrival is earlier than I expected. It is to give substance to our requests and be in a position to retaliate, if I should be attacked. As neither has happened, its commander will assess the situation and, with my advice, move on—but remain on station in the western Mediterranean, from where it can return if needed."

"Ambassador, would you join me to greet your fleet?" asked Hasan.

Luke was silent for some time and finally answered, "I have a better idea, Admiral. Come with me aboard the *Cromwell*, and we will meet the fleet well out to sea so as not to alarm your people. You can put your concerns directly to its commanding officer."

Two hours later, Luke was in the cabin of the English fleet's commander, while Hasan was shown over the flagship by its officers. The commander introduced himself. "I am Adm. John Stokes and, until a day ago, a mere captain and deputy to General Blake for our southern fleet, part of which sits off the Iberian coast, and the half I command directly patrols the western Mediterranean. Yesterday a frigate from England brought me news that General Blake had died and that I, never being a soldier, was promoted to the traditional rank of admiral. I was also informed of your presence in Benbali and the general purpose of your visit. I was ordered to assist you, if needed. Here I am."

"Congratulations, Admiral. I am sorry to hear of Blake's death. I served under him in the early days of the Civil War. I could use your presence as a bargaining chip to put a little pressure on the Benbalis, but it is still too early for me to define any precise action."

"Who is the infidel who came aboard with you?" Stokes asked.

"He is one of the powers within the Benbali government and of particular interest to both of us. He is the commander of the Benbali fleet—and he is an Englishman by birth."

"Why is he here?"

"Overtly, he wanted us to meet out of sight of Benbali so that his people would not become unnecessarily alarmed, but I suspect he has other motives. He has only recently been elected commander of the fleet, and his faction may be looking for some help from us. Treat him as a potential ally."

Hasan and an English officer entered the cabin. After introductions, John Stokes was direct. "The ambassador suggests that we naval officers arrive at some sort of agreement that our respective governments could then endorse. Do you have any specific proposals?"

"I am sorry to hear of Blake's death. He was a formidable opponent, although in recent times he became too predictable. I will have to adjust to your tactics in due course, but in the meantime, I believe we can help each other to achieve mutual ends."

"What precisely do you want of us?" asked Luke.

"Your assistance in toppling Ahmed Dey."

"That might be possible if Admiral Stokes stayed here with his fleet and we bombarded Benbali into submission, but neither of us has permission to use force unless attacked," lied Luke once again.

"I am not suggesting any great overt display of support for our coup—rather a subtle undermining of the current regime by suggesting that you might be more generous if you were dealing with other leaders."

"I need a brief lesson in Benbali politics before I can commit," replied Stokes.

Hasan obliged. "The dey is elected by a council that balances out the Turkish interests of the janissaries that occupy the castle, the captains and sailors of the fleet, and the local Arabs represented by the city's commander. At the moment, the dey represents a corrupt faction within the janissaries, which has allied itself with equally corrupt elements in the merchant community, the worst of whom is your consul, Sir Ambrose Denton. They are lining their own pockets to the detriment of the fleet and the locals."

"Have you anyone in mind to replace Ahmed?" asked Luke.

"Yes, the dey is traditionally an officer of the janissaries elected by his fellows. The leader of a reformist faction among these elite soldiers is the deputy governor of the citadel and now the leader of the unit attached to you—Colonel Ismet. He is our candidate."

"Where does the pasha stand in these factional maneuverings, and what reaction would you expect from the sultan?" asked Stokes, concerned with the wider issues.

"Overwhelming support for us. We are the westernmost outpost of the Ottoman Empire. The sultan has poured replacement janissaries into the country and equipped us with ships that are the latest produced in Constantinople. In return, every season, we sail east and join the sultan's grand fleet against the Venetians and their Italian and Spanish allies. Algiers, Tunis, and Tripoli are no longer reliable in the sultan's eyes. Consequently, the pasha here exerts more influence than in other North African cities. There are rumors that Ahmed and his faction seek to make Benbali independent of the Ottoman Empire or, even more bizarrely, part of Algiers."

"How will the Arab populace react to changes in the local administration?" asked the astute Stokes.

"The urban Arabs are well controlled by Commander Yusuf, although some of the rural tribes remain on the edge of rebellion. Those who border Algiers to the east and those close to the Moroccan border in the west show little loyalty to Benbali."

"But where exactly do they stand regarding your proposed coup?" reiterated Stokes.

"They know the income of Benbali comes from two sources— their agricultural and pastoral activity and the wealth the corsairs obtain in captured goods and ships. They resent that many of the profits from both activities are siphoned off by local officials in league with corrupt European merchants led by the English but closely followed by the Genoese."

"Not the Dutch?" asked a surprised Luke.

"No, the Dutch play by the rules and, as such, are undermined by Denton and his fellow rogues. Until your arrival and the prospect of you cleaning out the English parasites, I was negotiating through a Dutch-born captain of one my ships to seek Dutch intervention."

"So what exactly would you expect me to do, should we decide to assist you?" asked Stokes.

"Over the next few weeks, the ambassador should clean up corruption within the English community and refuse to deal with any official guilty of malpractice, which he—in unraveling Denton's crimes—will identify as the dey himself; the general of the janissaries, Osman; and my predecessor, Nasim, commander of the fleet, who still lives in luxury in the citadel rather than in its prison."

"What role would you expect the English fleet to play?" asked Stokes.

"After I return to Benbali on board the *Cromwell*, sail your fleet past the city, firing a salute to the citadel. I will argue how I have, with the ambassador's help, negotiated your peaceful passage through our waters. It will give both of us increased bargaining power."

Stokes readily agreed. "I will leave behind one of my frigates, the *Wild Fire*, to support the *Cromwell*. It can be used to get a message to me should the return of the whole fleet be required. That is a threat that both of you can use to achieve your ends."

Luke, Simon, Ninian, Ralph, Miles, and Strad were received on the rooftop garden of the merchant Gregory Applegarth. They were immediately offered platters of assorted pickled and fresh vegetables (onions, peppers, celery, cucumber, and eggplants), fish (anchovies, sardines, mackerel, and sea bass), fresh fruits and nuts (dates, almonds, and olives), and small lamb sausages to be consumed with a sweet chili sauce. All this was to be eaten with the aid of pieces of wheaten bread coated in sesame seeds and washed down with red Italian wine.

Simon hoped such concessions to local cuisine would not extend to the main courses. He was overheard by a petite blond woman who, in the stifling heat, wore little to hide the conformation of her well-endowed body. A large pendant drew further attention to that part of her body. It was in the shape of a heart and studded with three columns of precious stones—emeralds, sapphires, and another of emeralds. Across the top were three rows of diamonds.

"I am Patience, wife of your host. Do not worry, my lord, the main courses are typical English fare—mutton, lamb, beef, and chicken—although they may be enhanced with local spices. At least I have saved you from the local mint tea and insisted on some excellent Italian wine obtained from our Genoese neighbors."

Simon blushed. "My apologies, Mistress Patience. I had no desire to offend."

Luke came to Simon's assistance. "I am Sir Luke Tremayne, ambassador-at-large, sent to uncover any problems within your community and to effect any consequent reforms. Can we have a quiet chat tomorrow so that I might have your views on the situation?"

Before Patience could answer, Sir Ambrose Denton moved in between them. He was clearly irate. "What ails you, sir?" asked an annoyed Luke.

"I have just received orders that the English community must remain within the English quarters until notified to the contrary. If we do leave for business or personal reasons, we must be accompanied by a Benbali guard after receiving permission from a local authority."

"Is that unusual?" asked Luke.

"Only regarding the source of the order. From time to time, the dey—and more often the city commander—concerned with local unrest, confines us to our quarters for our own protection. This order came from Murat Pasha, and the guard who has surrounded our enclave is part of that allocated to the pasha himself. When I questioned one of the guards, he told me that the order had been requested by the English ambassador. Is that so?"

Luke had not made such a request, but it suited his plans. "I did not make such an explicit request, but I did indicate to the pasha and later to the dey that I needed to interview every member of the community. The pasha has obviously decided that my task would be helped if you were all confined to these quarters for a day or two."

Ambrose became slightly less aggressive. "Sir, as in any community, there are troublemakers and gossips who, if listened to, could create a completely false picture of the situation. Patience is a dear friend whom I trust implicitly, but there are others out to destroy me. Do not believe everything you hear."

"Ambrose, I may be a novice ambassador, but I am well aware of protocol. As consul, you will be the first person I will formally interview, and you can give me a picture of the community as you see it—but not tonight. I will visit you at nine in the morning."

"Nine may be good English time, but here in Benbali, we start work much earlier. How about seven? The call of the locals to prayer will have you awake long before that." Luke, suitably rebuked, nodded his agreement. He disliked this man.

As Ambrose moved away, Luke's attention was drawn to a rather solid and almost plump man with long locks and no facial hair and dressed in somber brown who was berating Patience. His almost comical appearance was manifest in a large round face, small reddish nose, and large ears. Miles whispered to Luke that the newcomer was their host, Gregory, who was obviously uncomfortable at his wife revealing so much flesh in company. "Or wearing such a valuable jewel" was Luke's less romantic comment.

Their discussion ceased as Patience led her husband toward them. Gregory apologized that, as host, he was not present to receive his guests but had been called away on an emergency. "Not a real emergency but a panic by Ambrose concerning some order to remain in our quarters," explained a somewhat flustered husband.

"Enough, dear, the ambassador does not want to hear about our petty disputes."

6

Luke was cross that Patience's intervention may have inhibited Gregory from revealing scandal about the English community. He contradicted his hostess. "Exactly the opposite, Mistress Applegarth. I have specific orders to understand the workings of this community and what may be done to improve its representation of English interests in the area. I will return here tomorrow at nine to ask you a few questions."

"We would both be ready to answer your questions at nine," responded Gregory.

"That is not quite my method. I want to get an official picture from the leading merchants and later probe the more intimate issues with the wives. I would like to interview you separately."

Gregory did not seem pleased, but Patience purred, "I will eagerly await your summons."

Luke joined Ninian, who was talking to a young man about his own age. "Luke, this is Jethro Chatwood, who has only been in Benbali for the last few months."

Luke went straight to the point. "I have already heard that newcomers are not welcomed by the established traders."

"That *is* an understatement," announced a fiery redheaded young woman who appeared from behind a potted palm.

"This is my sister, Chantal," explained a slightly embarrassed Jethro.

"I would like to hear more about your difficulties. Sir Ambrose is already staring at us with disapproving, if not menacing, eyes. I will send a janissary to escort you both to my lodgings for a meal around noon tomorrow," said Luke.

"In the interim, don't believe a word you hear from this nest of vipers," whispered Chantal as she left Luke's company.

"That is the second time within minutes that I have been given that advice," he muttered to himself.

The welcoming banquet took place in a large room on a lower floor. Protocol had obviously bothered Ambrose in arranging the seating. Lords Stokey and Fyson, as aristocrats, should have taken precedence but have been seated on either side of the host, but at the last minute, the pragmatic Ambrose rearranged the seating and placed the head of the English delegation, Ambassador Tremayne, in the preeminent position at the head of the table, flanked by Lady Denton and Patience Applegarth, who in turn were seated next to their husbands.

Luke was delighted with the range of hot lamb dishes—some replicating good English culinary delights and others altered by the discreet use of various spices. As he ate, he reflected on the local social hierarchy as defined by Denton's table placements. The Chatwoods were at the far end of the table with Luke's equerry, Bevan Stradling, and his navigator, Ralph Croft. Miles was further up the table with May and Sweetlace as was James and Lucy Goodrich. Next to Ambrose and Gregory sat the peers Simon and Ninian on opposite sides of the table.

This assessment came to an end as he pondered whether Patience Applegarth's knee brushing against his under the table was an accident or invitation. She could be an unexpected problem. For the wife of a somber Puritan merchant, she was exuding a sensuality clearly aimed at him—or so he, the serial womanizer, thought.

He ignored the contact and turned to Rose, Lady Denton, who looked considerably older than her husband. She was withdrawn, and Luke's attempts to engage her in conversation seemed to increase her level of anxiety, which she relieved by staring at her platter or making small talk only with her husband.

Eventually, Ambrose made a short speech of welcome and indicated that, in their discussions with Luke, the members of the community should put its interests first and not indulge in petty complaints.

Chantal Chatwood's loud response to this remark was heard by all. "The man cannot stop intimidating the community."

Luke replied to Ambrose's speech with an even shorter address outlining the purpose of his visit—to improve English trade.

Just as Luke finished, a goblet fell from a drinker's hand, bounced along the table, splattering those it passed with red wine. The gobletless drinker slumped to the table, his head making a resounding thud. There was a moment of absolute silence.

The collapsed diner was Ninian. Miles moved to his assistance. After a brief examination, he announced, "Ninian is still breathing but just."

"Does he have a history of fainting?" asked Luke of Simon.

"I don't think fainting is the problem. Look at the color of his lips. He's been poisoned," replied Simon.

Luke turned to Miles. "Have your men secure this room." He turned to the gathered guests. "No one is to leave. Ambrose, is there a doctor nearby?"

"The Dutch community has a physicist, but the best medical man in the whole city is the pasha's doctor, Sharif. He is also the nearest."

Miles sent a message by one of the janissary guards to ask Colonel Ismet and the pasha's doctor to come to the home of Gregory Applegarth—an English aristocrat had been poisoned. Miles commented to Luke, "The death of an English aristocrat will greatly embarrass the Benbali authorities. They will want the matter cleared up as a matter of urgency."

"Ninian is not dead yet, and this attempt has been made within the English community. The local authorities may not wish to be involved," countered Luke.

Ismet and the doctor arrived within half an hour, and Miles explained to them what had happened. Ninian had been carried to a soft couch, where Chantal Chatwood had been administering emetics to the comatose peer under Simon's supervision.

The turbaned doctor examined Ninian and, after smelling his breath, was jubilant. Miles translated for Luke. "Ninian has been poisoned, but the doctor has arrived in time to save him. It is a slow-working poison whose toxic repercussions can be reversed by the antidote that he has given Chantal to administer progressively over the next hour or so."

Luke, Miles, Ismet, and Dr. Sharif gathered around Ninian's vacated place at the table. Luke asked, "How was the poison administered?"

Sharif's reply created further problems for Luke. "It comes in liquid form and could easily be added to soups, stews, and salads." Yet the whole meal had been taken out of large pots or communal platters. How was it that Ninian alone was poisoned?

The doctor, after listening to Luke's dilemma, indicated another possibility. "The poison could have been smeared on an individual platter, spoon, or goblet that was for the victim's use only."

Miles was skeptical. "But the settings were in place when we came to the table."

Simon was less cynical and commented, "The exact location of who should sit where at the middle to the bottom end of the table was not clear until the last minute."

The doctor took up the goblet and, after smelling it, announced that it had been smeared with the poison as had Ninian's small plate, on which he rested his food.

Ismet and the Sharif left, and Simon and Ralph joined Luke and Miles in a corner of the room. "Why would anybody try to kill Ninian?" asked Simon.

"Who was he sitting next to at dinner?" asked Luke.

"He sat between Sir Ambrose and Lucy Goodrich," replied Miles. "He also talked a lot with May and Sweetlace."

"I wonder if May accidently also took some of the poison," said Strad.

"What do you mean?" asked Luke.

"When Ninian collapsed, May became incoherent for while, slurring his words. I assumed he had drunk too much, but Sweetlace says he does not drink alcohol. Maybe he was also poisoned."

"He seems to have recovered now," remarked Luke as he moved to question Lucy Goodrich.

"Mistress Goodrich, did Lord Fyson talk about anything that might have aroused the jealousy or fear in others?"

Lucy Goodrich was the epitome of the hardworking Puritan wife of a hardworking Puritan merchant. She dressed completely in black with tiny cuffs and collars. She was a tiny wiry person with graying hair and a tight-fitting bonnet. "Yes, I thought what he said might cause trouble. He had us all intrigued, particularly Mr. May and Mr. Sweetlace and even Sir Ambrose, with his tales of a priceless golden Madonna that had been stolen from his family decades ago."

"Foolish boy," Luke muttered to himself. He thanked Lucy and returned to Miles, Simon, Strad, and Ralph.

Strad was direct. "The talk of the Madonna can have nothing to do with the attempted murder. What would the murderer gain? He would want Ninian alive to tell him more. In addition, the poisoner would have had to work very fast. I cannot see any opportunity for someone to have smeared his utensils with poison after Ninian had revealed information on the Madonna."

"I agree," replied Simon. "Those utensils were poisoned before the meal started, and in that case, Ninian may not have been the intended target."

"Who was then?" asked Ralph.

"Luke, you were originally to be seated in that position," said Simon. Luke looked apprehensive.

"Don't fret. I doubt that you were the target, Luke. At the moment, everybody wants your support, and your death would bring instant retribution from the large English fleet just off the coast," added Miles.

"If the target was not Ninian or Luke, who was it?" asked Strad.

"The guest who could create the most trouble for Ambrose and the local authorities," suggested Ralph.

"From what I heard tonight, the Chatwoods would fit the bill," replied Luke. The others agreed.

"And of all the men in the room who look a lot younger than the rest—Ninian Fyson and Jethro Chatwood. Someone had orders to poison the young man in the room, not realizing that one of our entourage was also a youngster," surmised Miles.

"Excellent deduction, Miles. I will confirm a few facts with Patience."

Luke found Patience alone in an adjacent room and asked bluntly, "You organized the table placements. Was there an initial placement that you had to alter?"

"Strange that you should ask that question. I had a table setting organized for a day or more, but at the last minute, I moved the Chatwoods, knowing how Ambrose detests them."

"Which Chatwood was originally allotted the place ultimately taken by Lord Ninian?"

"Jethro."

Ninian was carried to Luke's new residence, where two women skilled in nursing and the medicinal use of herbs were sent by the pasha to implement the doctor's orders. Sharif, who had initially accompanied the women, explained that Ninian might open his eyes within the hour but would not gain control of his muscles or speech until the antidote had taken maximum effect, which might take a day or two.

After speaking to Sharif and his helpers, Luke entered his own reception room to find Elif, several other women, and two giant African servants. "My master, the pasha apologizes for his lapse in hospitality. He provided you a house but little more. I am now here to run your household, and those with me are servants to assist in the task. Under your direction, I will administer your affairs within the house, and Colonel Ismet and his men will provide external security. The pasha desperately hopes that the attempted murder in the English quarters was not an attempt to disrupt your mission. Will you accept this offer from the pasha?"

"I will be delighted to have your assistance," purred Luke.

When he told Miles, Simon, and Ralph about it the next morning, he explained that his joy was not derived from any possible sexual relationship but from a potential source of great information within his own household. Simon echoed the general unfavorable response. "Equally, the Benbali authorities now have a spy within our ranks. Be careful what you tell the beautiful Elif."

7

As arranged, Luke and Strad returned to the Denton residence. They were led by a servant through one wing of the house, across an expansive inner courtyard, and through the opposite wing to an adjacent large warehouse.

Luke marveled at the range of goods that were methodically stacked throughout the edifice. He recognized cotton from Egypt, bales of wool from Spain and England, and open bags of brightly colored spices, the aroma from which permeated the whole building.

The servant steered the men toward a semienclosed room in the far corner, which contained a large unglassed window looking back into the building. Ambrose welcomed them. "Forgive the long walk, but there is less likelihood of us being overheard here than in the house, and I wanted you to see as you traveled through the warehouse the range of my activities. From this small room, you can see the goods in the factory and, through the outer window, the ships from which we derive our livelihood."

Luke looked at the three ships at anchor in the river that led into the bay and that divided the Dutch from the English community. He noted a Portuguese galleon, a Maltese frigate, and a Roman merchantman—all victims of Benbali piracy.

Ambrose sensed Luke's mild surprise. "Ambassador, I make my money by receiving a commission from the sale of the prizes captured by the Benbali privateers. I made a deal with the former commander of the fleet and the current dey to give me a monopoly of this trade in return for a proportion of my profit. Either I sell the captured ships, crews, passengers, and goods on behalf of the corsairs and receive a commission or I buy the prizes outright and sell them on—a much more profitable approach."

"Don't the authorities already, by law, receive a designated cut of the prizes?" Luke asked.

"Yes, but everybody wants more," replied an unfazed Ambrose.

"This monopoly must put you in a position of some influence within Benbali," commented Luke.

"Undoubtedly. At the moment, the city would starve without me. The current drought has destroyed the crops, and Benbali is short of wheat. The cargo on board the papal merchantman, which you see out of the window, was entirely wheat. This is not the prize that your average corsair sees as the most profitable, but in the current circumstances, I will sell to the local authorities at a massive profit. The dey will get great satisfaction in saving his city with wheat intended for the chief infidel, the Roman pope."

"What happened to the crew of these vessels?" asked Strad.

"The Benbali navy first takes those sailors it needs to man its ships. Officers are usually ransomed, and the rest I sell on the open market."

"As slaves?" queried Luke.

"Of course. Benbali has a thriving slave market, one of the best in the Mediterranean."

"And the passengers, especially females?" continued Luke.

"The corsair captains initially decide their fate. I sell those who are not taken directly by the seamen or the authorities."

"Including Englishwomen?"

"Yes, it's all business."

"Have you ever bought Englishwomen yourself with the aim of freeing them?" Strad probed.

"Never. Englishwomen bring a premium. The idea of freeing slaves is a misplaced emotion. God has placed each of us in a certain situation. It is not up to us mere mortals to try to alter that. Only that meddling Italian priest maintains a constant campaign for the Europeans to waste money to buy out the slaves of their own nationality."

"What is your position now that the admiral of your fleet has changed?"

"The change is only temporary. The dey, Ahmed, still rules, and the former naval commander, Nasim, is under his protection in the citadel. Nasim will be reinstated in the next few weeks. Your visit has temporarily, if accidentally, delayed the government's reinstatement of the former commander."

Luke smiled to himself. Should he get involved and warn Hasan of this counter plot? His instructions were clear. Unless he could make a case that his interference in domestic affairs was to England's advantage, he must remain neutral.

"Thank you, Ambrose, for the frank account of your activities. You may be lucky. If I had come on this mission five years ago, you would have been dismissed as consul and sent back to England in irons. Only two appointments of the late king remain in place—the ambassador to Constantinople and you, the consul in Benbali. There are elements in the current government and in the city of London who want you replaced by one of their own persuasion. However, the Lord Protector is drawing many former Royalists into his camp, so your initial royalist appointment will no longer be held against you. Consequently, if I am satisfied that the current English government has benefited from your time here, I will not report adversely. Denton and Applegarth are doing very well. If similar benefits have flowed to English trade and power in the region in general, I will be content.

"Enough of the high politics. I would now like your views on the members of the English community. Let's start with your partner, Applegarth."

"Gregory is a hardworking and loyal member of the community. When I first came here as consul, he was the only English merchant in the city. He was a bit of a mystery. He had capital but no idea how to put it to good use. I, as consul, had power to develop useful contacts and considerable financial and commercial know-how. We formed a partnership in which the profits are equally shared but in which I make all the decisions."

"Gregory does not share in the special commissions you receive from various quarters?"

Ambrose smiled at what he thought was a ridiculous question and continued. "He is socially boring and has no interests outside his horses—and trying to control his much more adventurous wife."

"Yes, I gathered that from the reception last night. Her behavior upset him."

"He was very cross. The silly woman wore that incredible pendant. I have never seen it before. It should remain locked away. It is worth a fortune."

"Has Patience's lively behavior upset many in the community in the past?"

"No. Don't get me wrong. In terms of social protocol and Christian morality, she never puts a foot out of place. At times, her forthright comments and her occasional brief attire can be taken out of context. Gregory is forced to soothe ruffled feathers and, more often, correct unfortunate misconceptions."

"I imagine she could irritate James Goodrich."

"A very godly man. One of those extreme Puritans I thought I would be rid of coming here. He refuses to have any contact with the Papists in the Genoese community and refuses to negotiate with visiting Catholic merchants or ships. His wife, Lucy, is even worse. Both create trouble by trying to convert the local infidel to Christianity. They invited those fanatical Quakers to stop off here on their way to convert the sultan in Constantinople. Despite such prejudices, he has never bad-mouthed Patience."

"With such attitudes, how does he survive financially in this environment?"

"He concentrates on numerous small transactions with the locals and has built a reputation for being an honest trader. This low-profit margin means that he spends most of his time buying and selling. Our paths hardly cross. He has little time for my methods and has denounced me more than once as the spawn of Satan."

"So I can expect him to give me an interesting view on your activities."

"He won't be the most extreme. I can appreciate James's reaction to me given his views. The dangerous man whom I implore you to disregard is Jethro Chatwood."

"Why?"

"He is a man of mystery. He refuses to discuss his background. He spends more time in the native quarters of the city than he does within the community. What worried me the most was that when I complained to the dey that an Englishman had been admitted to the city without consulting me, I was told that Jethro had support at the highest levels and that I was never to raise the issue again."

"The highest levels—who would that be?" asked an intrigued Luke.

"If the dey, who is the effective ruler of Benbali, was overridden or ignored in that decision, it must have come from the combined pressures of the pasha, the admiral, the city commander, and the governor of the citadel or from an order of the sultan himself. Chatwood does not trade. What is he up to?"

"And his sister, Chantal?"

"She has not been here long enough for me to form an opinion, but she shows signs of being a troublemaker in flaunting her opinions—and her charms. Poor old James has already cast her as the scarlet woman."

"That leaves the two bachelors, who—given their mannerisms and behavior last night—are a homosexual couple. Surely, James would have taken steps to have them removed?"

"No, his wife, Lucy, is so virtuous that she does not believe that such relationships exist—and he is strangely quiet on the issue."

"Rowland May is a lawyer. Does he practice his craft here?"

"Yes, he is quite busy dealing with the commercial contracts. He has developed some expertise in maritime law, especially concerning which prizes are legitimately taken by privateers with a commission from a state or illegally captured as an act of piracy. This distinction is vital to our business."

"What does Silas Sweetlace do?"

"May is employed by me as consul. Sweetlace works for all the merchants. He is a superb bookkeeper and prepares all our returns to the local authorities so that they, in turn, can take their percentage from our trade. It could be a dangerous occupation if the authorities thought that the books presented by Sweetlace did not tell the true story."

"And do they?"

Ambrose smiled again. "The authorities have never questioned them."

"We have mentioned everybody except your own wife, Lady Rose," commented Luke.

"Rose is very unhappy. She is my second wife, whom I met and married in Italy. She is depressed by a feeling of an inexplicable guilt."

"I am sorry to hear that. Finally, I wish to raise with you last night's attempted murder. Who do you think was the intended victim?"

"I just assumed it was Lord Fyson," answered Ambrose.

"Some have suggested it was me. You changed the seating on the day of the banquet. Others think the target was Jethro Chatwood, one of two young men in the room. From what you have told me this morning, however, May or Sweetlace could also have been possible targets."

"I confess I would like to see Jethro gone, but for him to be killed in the English quarters and during your visit would be most inappropriate and politically stupid. If I wanted to rid myself of that troublemaker, I would employ a professional assassin to act when Jethro is wandering the old city. I fear Lord Fyson put himself into danger by raising the story of the golden Madonna. There are tales among the old sailors of many a rich prize being brought here, but their current location is never known. In truth, the infidel has no time for images or icons. The rule of the corsairs is that all precious metal belongs to the sailors. If this Madonna made its way to Benbali, it would have been smelted down and the gold shared among the sailors."

"If this is the case, is young Fyson still in danger?" asked Strad.

"Any tale of treasure attracts the most unsavory characters. These treasure hunters will follow Fyson wherever he goes and may abduct and torture him to find out more. A foolish boy."

8

Luke next met with Gregory Applegarth and diplomatically explained, "As Sir Ambrose was appointed by the late king, there are many in the current English government who would want him replaced simply because of this. Fortunately, the Lord Protector is more tolerant. And if my report is favorable, I am sure your partner will receive confirmation of his position as consul. What should I know about him?"

Gregory appeared to relax a little after Luke's reassuring remarks about his partner and commented, "Ambrose is a very successful merchant and has made considerable money for us in his shrewd and hardheaded negotiations over prizes. The corsair captains trust him to give them a good deal as do the Benbali authorities. You must take Ambrose with you when you negotiate with the dey. They are very close."

Luke saw this as a potential weakness and asked, "Is Ambrose *too* friendly with the local authorities?"

Gregory recoiled at Luke's negative interpretation of his previous comment. "No. Ambrose's relationship with the local administration is to the advantage of the English community and therefore indirectly to the English government. You, because of Ambrose, will have easier access to the dey than other foreign visitors."

Luke realized that Gregory would hear no criticism of his partner. He moved on. "Tell me about James Goodrich."

"I do not know how he makes a living. He deals in small everyday items and almost exclusively with the local population. There would hardly be a profit in most of his transactions. He is a retail shopkeeper rather than a merchant."

"Yet he does survive?"

"Only by working himself and his wife into an early grave. He rises before dawn with the local's call to prayer and trades into the night."

"The populace sees him as an honest man who offers his goods at prices below all others," commented Luke.

"Certainly, in the few areas where we compete, he is considerably cheaper than us," admitted Gregory.

"Because of his honesty and low-profit margins, his wife is forced into working beside him?" commented Strad.

"All the wives assist their husbands. This is not an English gentry estate. It is a hardworking English trading community. However, you are right. Given James's approach, Lucy works longer and harder than any of the other spouses."

"Does their religious extremism trouble the community?"

"In the short term, the rest of us are largely unaffected. There are people of similar views within the Dutch community with whom the Goodriches socialize. However, their views do alarm our Genoese neighbors and some local authorities. They try to spread the gospel to the local population, which will eventually bring the wrath of the Benbali establishment and Muslim religious leaders down on them and then onto us. Stop their provocative missionary work. If anybody in this community threatens the long-term interests of the English government, it is James and his wife."

"Ambrose implied that any immediate problems in your community would stem from Jethro Chatwood. Do you agree?"

"To be honest, Ambrose is obsessed with Jethro. He originally thought Jethro was a secret agent of the English government sent to spy on him as a precursor to your visit. However, we never see him. During daylight hours, he is within the old city dealing with small traders or out in the countryside negotiating who knows what with the nomadic Arabs. He has no warehouse or place of business."

"Ambrose says he has the secret support of someone in authority. Do you know who that might be?"

"Ambrose is right. Jethro was admitted to this country without consultation with him as the consul and apparently against the better judgment of the dey."

"Surely, the dey is *the* authority. Can anybody overrule him?"

"Nothing has happened here since my arrival years ago without the dey's approval. The only power that can overrule him is the sultan, who has recently shown some unease with the local authorities by sending new detachments of janissaries to Benbali who are not as supportive of the dey as the troops being recalled. And he has offered some of his latest warships to the Benbali corsairs on their recent change of commander—a man who does not support Ahmed Dey and who, everybody suspects, is planning a coup against him."

"Jethro Chatwood seems a most unlikely character to be an agent of the sultan or even deserving a favor from the Grand Turk himself, yet he arrived on the same ship from Constantinople as the new troops. He is certainly not an agent of the English government," remarked Luke.

Luke then had second and private thoughts about his last comment. He had had enough experience of the workings of Cromwell's chief minister and spy master general, John Thurloe, to realize that he often sent multiple agents into the same field without informing them of each other.

Gregory commented, "I am sure that Ambrose's fears are misplaced. Jethro is more likely to be a threat to the local authorities than to the English community."

"Any views on Chantal Chatwood?"

"I met her for the first time last night. I have no views of her, although Ambrose thinks she is a potential femme fatale who might disrupt marital relationships in the community."

"I am surprised at that comment. James Goodrich is so moral that he would not be tempted. You are happily married. Ambrose must be talking about himself. His wife seems somewhat aloof from the rest of the community."

"Ambrose has had a difficult time with Rose. She is unhappy, but I don't know why. I have suggested many times that he send her home to England."

"May and Sweetlace complete your small community. Any useful information?"

"May is brilliant. His knowledge of the law of the sea and the validity of privateering commissions has helped make us rich. The one worry Ambrose has is that, given his sexual predilections and the high percentage of similarly inclined young men in the local community, he might desert us for the infidel in pursuit of his lust."

"And Sweetlace?"

"He knows too much. He is privy to all our commercial secrets."

"Was he the target of last night's attempted murder?"

"Quite possibly. He may have threatened to expose any one of us."

"Or equally, his homosexual activity may have created a rejected lover who sought revenge," muttered Strad, who had silently taken notes throughout the interview.

Luke thanked Gregory for his help and asked that his wife, Patience, be summoned. Gregory smiled and bounded away, singing to himself in a high-pitched voice. Strad commented, "Strange. I did not think your questioning had put him under such pressure that its conclusion should create such a marked personality change."

Patience was the first person whom Luke had questioned that morning who exuded any sign of warmth. She was completely relaxed—unlike the two males before her. "So you want all the gossip about our little community," she pouted.

Luke smiled. "I would like to understand the relationships within it. For a start, it must be rather boring for you. Lady Denton is not well and Mistress Goodrich a religious extremist. And Chantal Chatwood has only just arrived. You must be starved of female company."

"Yes, there is no one within our merchant enclave to whom I can readily relate, but I have befriended Lady Elif, who dominates the pasha's household and is now running your own. The pasha likes the women around him to be highly educated. I began by teaching Elif to read and write her native tongue and later other English girls who have entered his household. Unlike Lucy Goodrich, I do not work in the warehouse with my husband. Ambrose, Gregory, and those creatures May and Sweetlace have everything under control."

"As you spend so much time in the pasha's residence, you must gain an insight into Benbali politics."

"Yes, but Elif knows a lot more. She is a very bright young woman and a clear favorite of the pasha. I have noticed in the last week or two that the new commander of the corsairs, also English; Elif; the pasha; and your escort, the relatively recent arrival, Colonel Ismet, meet regularly."

"There must be a limited number of girls to whom you can teach English. How do you justify your constant presence in the pasha's palace?"

"In return for my assistance with English, the pasha permits me to sit in with the women of the household to learn Turkish."

"Surely, Arabic would be more useful."

"All Turkish officials here speak both, but within the pasha's residence, the language is Turkish. Admiral Hasan is at a disadvantage with local authorities because, apart from English, he speaks only Arabic. That is probably why he is friendlier with Commander Yusuf, who I think is a locally born Arab, than with the dey or General Osman."

"Tell me more about Ismet."

"He is more important than his rank as colonel, and his secondment to the pasha and you suggest. He was a top graduate of the sultan's school and immediately sent here just a few months ago."

"Did the dey send him to the pasha, or did the pasha select him for his current role in supervising my visit?"

"I don't know. Is it important?"

"Yes, I would like to know whether Ismet is a spy for the pasha, keeping an eye on the dey, or a spy for the dey, watching the pasha. Maybe he is primarily a spy for Benbali watching me. What about the males of the English community, starting with your husband?"

"Gregory could not be happier. He is a born follower, intensely loyal and hardworking. Ambrose takes the risks and determines our activities, and my husband is happy to execute whatever plans are advanced. We both enjoy the financial benefits that the alliance with Ambrose has brought us."

"There must be some areas of difference between you and your husband."

"Differences between husband and wife are not an area that a government official needs to probe," replied a teasing, rather than annoyed, Patience.

Nevertheless, Luke changed the direction of his questioning. "Are you both happy to stay here until you are aged?"

"It is strange that you should ask that question."

"Why?"

"I wish to return to England eventually, but I have not lived in England for decades. I met and married Gregory in Italy. But such a move never entered Gregory's head until a week ago. Ambrose raised the possibility that the partnership might work more effectively if Gregory headed our operations in London as he intends to trade directly with England."

"How did Gregory react to such a suggestion?"

"That was strange. He seemed to display two opposed personalities. Initially, he was delighted and talked incessantly of meeting old friends. Then later that evening, he reversed his approach, expressing a reluctance to return to such a hostile environment while the Lord Protector ruled. He was further upset by the reaction of Sweetlace, who had overheard Gregory's discussion with Ambrose and immediately offered himself as a replacement partner for the English position if Gregory was not interested."

"You dislike Sweetlace?"

"He makes me feel uneasy. The thought of him with another man makes me sick. I do not trust him. He knows too much and could use the slightest indiscretion to blackmail any one of us."

Luke suddenly saw a simple explanation to the problems within the English quarters. "Do you think Ambrose, your husband, or James Goodrich is being blackmailed?"

9

Patience was silent for some time but finally commented, "I have considered the possibility. Everybody probably has skeletons in their cupboard, but I do not know for certain."

"If they were victims, who would you suspect as the blackmailer?"

"Sweetlace. He is best placed to uncover secrets."

"If Sweetlace is a blackmailer, it might explain the attempted murder last night. He could have been the intended victim, rather than young Lord Fyson. Let me move on. The Goodrich couple— they seem to live in a different world."

"True. They live within their kingdom of God on earth and only have an interest in the local Arab population. They are being very foolish. It is a capital offense to attempt to convert any Muslim to Christianity."

"Why don't the authorities act?"

"The Turks adhere to a more moderate interpretation of the laws relating to Christians. I am sure that the city commander, Yusuf, and his Arab supporters who follow a more fundamental approach will ultimately force James and Lucy to desist under threat of expulsion or death. The Turks prefer a fine to physical punishment, unlike the more fanatical Arabs and Berbers. Despite their desire to spread Christianity, the Goodriches remain popular among the local population."

"Are there any fanatical locals who might endanger the English community? Ismet believes one of them tried to kill me on my arrival."

"Yes, there is a small cult of Arabic-speaking Berbers led by Sheikh Ashar who wage a holy war against all Christians and all Muslims who do not agree with them. Their immediate aim is to remove the Turkish occupiers and rid Benbali of all foreign residents, but I cannot see how your murder would assist their cause."

"Simply, if I were murdered, the English would attack Benbali and destroy the local institutions and authorities. Out of the anarchy, Ashar would emerge and create an Islamic caliphate. Rowland May?"

"Rowland is very popular within the European communities. He has saved Ambrose and Gregory a lot of money by avoiding the many legal pitfalls that involve the capture and sale of prizes. If Gregory accepts Ambrose's offer to return to London, I am sure that he will offer Rowland a partnership to replace us here."

"Lastly, there is the mysterious couple, the Chatwoods."

"They are simply mysterious because they have only recently arrived, are clearly not merchants, and have received special treatment from the authorities."

"So which of the rumors concerning them do you believe?"

"That Jethro Chatwood is a spy acting on behalf of either the sultan to assess the local authorities or the English government to supplement your activities. Others think, given his purchases and times spent in the local bazaars, that he is a jeweler seeking precious metals and jewels who will give local authorities a share of his finds. Young Ninian's outburst last night already has people suggesting that maybe Jethro is sent by some important person to find the missing golden Madonna. A few view him as a scholar who may be seeking important manuscripts. He apparently speaks several tongues."

"Thank you, Patience. I will be talking to the Chatwoods this afternoon."

Elif had the servants prepare a lavish midday meal for Luke and the Chatwoods. The appointed time came and went. They failed to appear.

Luke sent Miles to inquire into their nonarrival. He was back within half an hour, accompanied by Ismet. "Trouble, Luke," an excited Miles proclaimed.

"What do you mean?"

"The Chatwoods have disappeared."

Ismet gave an explanation, which Miles simultaneously translated. "Yusuf's men escorted the Chatwoods to the bazaar as they have done every day for the last few weeks. They entered a shop, and when they did not emerge for some time, their escort entered the premises. They were told that the Chatwoods had been bundled out the back door by two large Nubian men who informed the shopkeeper they were acting for Commander Yusuf—a not unusual event in that part of town. Yusuf's men knew that the Nubians had not been sent by their commander, whom they immediately informed. He began a search."

"Two Europeans traveling with two giant Nubians would be an unusual sight," added, Ismet.

He had hardly finishing speaking when an Arab soldier entered the room and spoke to him. He informed Miles, who explained to Luke. "A convenient witness confessed to Yusuf, for a price, that he had followed the Chatwoods and their captors out of town through the agrarian areas and into the mountains. He assumed that they have been taken from there down into the desert. Yusuf considers this evidence unreliable as no one else has come forward to confirm even a small part of the tale. Nothing can be kept a secret in the souk, and Yusuf's generous rewards for information should have borne much more fruit than it has."

"What is Ismet's view?"

"That you begin an investigation from within the English community, and he will liaise with Yusuf."

Luke thought for some time. "In the circumstances, I will continue my interviews. The Goodriches will be very busy during the day. I will surprise the interesting Mr. May."

May worked out of a small annex attached to the Denton-Applegarth warehouse. He was neither surprised nor apprehensive about Luke's arrival. "Greetings, Ambassador. I did not think it would take you this long to question the black sheep of our community."

"Surprisingly, in the eyes of your neighbors, you are one of the few people who have received overwhelming praise. Given your obvious talents as a lawyer, I can only surmise that you have exiled yourself here because of something you did either as an attorney or as the result of your sexual predilections."

"A bit of both. I was blackmailed because of my sexual habits by a fellow lawyer, and when I could no longer pay him, I absconded with a large sum of money I held in trust for a client."

"I'm not interested in your past but in your views of this English community. Let's start with the women."

"Ambassador, you reveal your prejudices. You think that, because of my sexual orientation, I will have a different view of the women to heterosexual males." Luke accepted the reprimand with good grace.

Rowland's answer was blunt. "They are a sorry lot. No one should bring their wives to such a place. Lady Denton is sick in the mind as well as body. Lucy Goodrich sees me as Satan's agent but prays for me many times a day. Patience Applegarth is a normal, bright woman who unfortunately is married to the most boring man I know. Gregory has no mind of his own. He carries out the orders of Sir Ambrose as if they were divine commandments. Yet he is content. Patience would leave him if there were any viable options. Her friendship with the pasha's women may create that opportunity."

"I hear that if Gregory returns to England, you will take his place here."

"You have been asking the right questions. I will only accept the offer if I share his plethora of special agreements," was the honest reply.

"Chantal Chatwood?"

"Apart from the reception last night and my admiration for her quick thinking in assisting the stricken boy, I have had no contact with her."

"Concerning that episode, one of my men thought you may have also taken some of the poison. You appeared drunk, yet I understand you do not drink alcohol."

"Did I appear drunk?" asked Rowland, showing the first sign of concern.

"To be more accurate, after Ninian collapsed, you began to slur your words."

"That is true. I have a slight deformity of my tongue. When I get very tired or stressed, I do speak as if I have drunk too much. The shock of what happened shook me up."

"Regarding Chantal, she and her brother have just been kidnapped," Luke announced, hoping to gauge Rowland's reaction.

He expressed great alarm. "I fear for her brother. She is a pale-skinned Englishwoman. Lucky she is not a blonde. The local Arabs cannot get enough of light-skinned women but are particularly obsessed by fair-haired wenches. I know from the work I do regarding the prizes. English and Scandinavian women, especially blondes, bring the best price when sold to Arab dignitaries in the interior."

"Why do you fear more for her brother?"

"Unless he is extremely wealthy and can bring a huge ransom, he will be sold into slavery and taken across the desert and into black Africa."

"That is a pessimistic view. The local authorities are not convinced that the Arabs have taken them. They have politely suggested that their disappearance may have its motivation from within this community."

"The allure of Chantal Chatwood, despite her red hair, would still bring a good price." Rowland continued.

"I hope you are wrong. Any views on Sir Ambrose?"

"An efficient, ruthless merchant and a brilliant maker of deals. He has built a network of corrupt officials and compliant rivals who allow him to dominate the commercial life of Benbali and exert considerable influence on its politics."

"That must be a dangerous game."

"Especially at the moment. The janissaries are stirring, and half the garrison has been replaced by a new detachment from Constantinople, and the corsair captains have overthrown their longtime leader and elected the Englishman Hasan in his place. The pasha and the city commander have done nothing. Ambrose is terrified that if they stay on the sideline, his friend and partner Ahmed Dey will be overthrown by his own men and the navy. Ambrose hopes he can use your presence, and the threat of the English fleet, to resettle local politics to his liking."

"James Goodrich, I believe, is also treading a dangerous path. There is no place for Christian missionaries of his extreme kind in any Muslim country."

"True, but James's reputation as the most honest man in the city who always gives his customers the best price keeps him popular with the Muslim crowd, and the current dey follows a tolerant Turkish approach to this proselyting problem. A new dey could be more fundamentalist, and James and the whole English community would then be in trouble," Rowland observed.

"Your partner, Silas Sweetlace, is a concern of some. What can you tell me about him?"

"I only met Silas in Livorno, the hub of Mediterranean trade for the English and the Dutch. The general tolerance of people of our kind by the Grand Duke of Tuscany, who did not want in any way to disrupt English trade through his city, was temporarily broken by a visit of the Roman Inquisition. It seemed urgent that we leave. I had had dealings with Sir Ambrose, who invited us both to Benbali."

"While you are popular and respected by the community, the same cannot be said for Silas."

"Some members of this community are insecure. They need the help of Silas to present their books to local authorities in a form that reduces their taxes, yet they are scared about the knowledge that this gives him of their affairs."

"Do they have reason to be worried?"

"Possibly. Silas remembers every piece of gossip he hears and is ready to believe the worst about everybody."

"Do you know anything about his past before he met you in Italy?"

"No. When we became partners, we agreed that our respective pasts would remain a closed book. It was the present and future that were important to us in those early days."

"Silas and you were angry with each other last night. Why was that?"

"A minor quarrel. Silas has been disappearing into the old town from time to time over the last week and refuses to tell me why."

"What do you suspect?" Rowland stared at the floor. Luke answered his own question. "He has found a lover among the local population?"

"Or was he meeting Jethro Chatwood?" countered an increasingly emotional Rowland.

"In either case, they risk the most horrendous of deaths if caught in such acts outside the English quarters. The North African Muslim has an extreme view on such behavior, punishing it with disemboweling, drawing, and quartering while still alive. Would they be so foolish? Where will I find Silas?"

"Today he started an inventory of the Goodrich warehouse—a mammoth task as the place has thousands of small items."

10

Luke and Strad made their way to the Goodrich warehouse. Lucy Goodrich and Silas Sweetlace were busy counting and recording items. Luke took advantage of the situation to question James, who was sitting alone at his desk. "Mr. Goodrich, you are aware of my mission and that, at the moment, I am informing myself of the workings and problems of this community. I would like to hear your views and where you think my probing should be directed."

"Simple, dismiss Denton, and send him home in irons. Everything he does is toward the enrichment of the Denton-Applegarth partnership. He does nothing for the rest of us or for England. He continues to act for Charles Stuart."

"He certainly appears to be a ruthless businessman who would use any means to increase his profits, but do you have any evidence of his corruption and his support for the exiled king?"

"Selling innocent English girls into slavery and a life of degradation somewhere in the interior is not the act of an English Christian. He could have bought these girls himself, freed them, and sent them home. He was appointed by the late king and has never hidden his royalist sympathies. That is why he has tried to have me removed on several occasions. I am a Puritan and strong supporter of the Lord Protector."

"Given Ambrose's influence with the dey and the former admiral of the corsairs, it is surprising that you have not been expelled."

"I would have been but for Commander Yusuf. He represents the interests of the local people to whom I provide many of the necessities of life at a price they can afford. The infidel Arabs have been my savior, and in return, I wish to take to them the message of the Gospel."

"A dangerous enterprise in this environment. It could lead to your imprisonment and death," pontificated Luke.

"If the Lord Jesus so decides, let it be," replied James.

A religious fanatic cannot be reasoned with, which forced Luke to change the focus of his questioning. "Have you had time to assess the Chatwoods?"

"An erudite young man who is certainly no merchant. She is a very attractive woman whose very appearance will tempt males within and outside our community."

"You probably have not heard, but they have been abducted."

"Arabs from the hinterland, no doubt. They will want Chantal as one of their many wives."

"Surely, with European abductions, we should receive a ransom note?"

"Not in this case—given Chantal's beauty."

Luke thought that James's concentration on the sexual attraction of Chantal Chatwood was surprising in such a moral and religious man. He changed the topic once again. "Why is Jethro Chatwood in Benbali?"

"One of my customers, an Arab seller from the bazaar, told me that his neighbors were talking about the young Englishman who seemed to be asking questions about old documents and European jewelry. They thought his demeanor was that of a scholar rather than a treasure hunter. Of course, Denton thought he was an agent of our current English government sent here to prepare the way for your visit. My wife had her first conversation with Chantal at last night's calamitous reception and received the impression that she was trying to find someone."

Goodrich's comments worried Luke. Someone was looking for treasure and a person—the same mission entrusted to Luke and Simon. It was John Thurloe's modus operandi to have two agents, unknown to each other, on the same assignment. Luke was annoyed. Were Jethro and Chantal English agents? If so, their abduction was of even greater concern.

Luke continued his probing. "James, I am surprised that you, as a deeply religious man, employ Silas Sweetlace, whose behavior must be abhorrent to you."

"Neither May nor Sweetlace has exhibited signs of their predilections in my presence. I have never seen them engage in any behavior you could be offended by. Labeling them as queans is part of Denton's smear campaign to keep them subservient. Their alleged sins *are* an abomination to the Lord, but he is a merciful God who will readily accept their repentance."

"Is there anything in Silas's past that might be useful to me?"

"He and May were part of the English community at Livorno who initially accepted employment here with Denton, although nowadays both of them, in varying degrees, work for all of us."

"Do you know anything about Silas before he went to Italy?"

"No, I have never had a conversation with him that strayed from business matters. But talk to my wife. Lucy is his mentor."

"I'll talk to both of them soon. If I were able to change the situation here, what would you suggest?"

"I repeat, sack Denton, and expel him from Benbali, and then dismantle the network of corruption and greed that pervades this city."

"How can an outsider change the local business and political network of which Denton is only part?"

"My contacts are with the Arab population who has little time for the current dey. There are rumors of what they call *the English connection*, plotting to overthrow him. Your visit is seen by the masses as part of this welcomed conspiracy."

"Why are these alleged plotters called the English connection when the most powerful Englishman in the city is the dey's strongest ally?"

"Unlike the other Barbary Coast states of Tripoli, Tunis, and Algiers, which are virtually independent of Turkish control, the sultan has retained stronger influence here, and his representative—the pasha—is not simply a figurehead. He exerts considerable power. His English concubine, Lady Elif, strongly influences his decisions."

"Elif hardly makes *an English connection.*"

"True, but the source of Benbali wealth is predominantly derived from the plunder of the corsairs, who recently elected an Englishman as their commander. Influence on the pasha, and control of this wealth creating fleet are powerful forces pitted against the dey."

"If such rumors are widely circulated, why has the dey not acted to prevent a coup?"

"Simple. Your presence, with the ability to call on a powerful English fleet, makes him nervous. My friend Yusuf, with his Arab police, is also an unknown factor. Above all, the janissaries who control the citadel, which with its cannons dominate the town, are not a united group. The sultan, learning from his mistakes elsewhere, recently replenished his troops here with intakes of fresh soldiers from Anatolia and reassigned many of the Benbali veterans elsewhere. It makes it difficult for the current dey to maintain a grip on his electorate."

Luke's mind was racing. The internal politics of Benbali created a great opportunity to exert English influence. If only he were still a cavalry commander. Several companies of Cromwellian cavalry could soon conquer the city. Such dreaming was unrealistic. He had no cavalry. And he had no remit to establish an English enclave on the North African coast, yet Benbali would be an ideal base for the English Mediterranean fleet.

He thanked James for his comments and asked if it was convenient to speak to his wife. James called across the warehouse, and Lucy, after a hurried discussion with Silas, answered the summons.

"Mistress Goodrich, I am asking all the English community for their views on the current state of the situation here and what changes I should introduce. This, in part, relates to the performance of individual members, their standing in the local community, and their loyalty to the current government."

"There is no loyalty to our government outside this room. James and I delight in the rule of the godly Lord Protector, but

Denton and his cronies are appointees of the late king and have now transferred their loyalty to his son."

"Have you evidence that Denton acts for Charles Stuart against the interests of the current government?"

"Only rumor—and indirectly. Denton had great influence with the former commander of the fleet, Nasim. Over the last few years, ships carrying goods for English merchants known to be Royalists were given safe passage. Those carrying goods for the strongly pro-Cromwell merchants of London and Bristol were attacked and their ships and cargo taken as prizes. Sir Ambrose Denton was in a position to give the local corsairs information on which English ships they should target."

"You want Ambrose and his supporters expelled?"

"That would be the first step. Make James consul in his stead, appoint a godly minister to the community as the Dutch have done, and use your naval power to effect a change in the government of Benbali by rooting out corruption. We would like to trade without having to pay a sweetener to every low-level official. The legal fees, dues, and taxes are high enough."

"Tell me about Rose Denton and Patience Applegarth."

"Lady Denton should be sent home for her health's sake, both physical and mental. Patience is a likable woman who is married to a man who hasn't an ounce of personality. He simply obeys Ambrose. He doesn't have a single thought of his own. No wonder Patience spends considerable time in the pasha's palace, where I believe she teaches the English slaves to read and write. She is too friendly with these women who have converted to Islam. She admits that she has found enlightening passages in their ungodly book. I pray that she will not slip into the jaws of the infidel. If she does, her boring husband is to blame."

"Patience Applegarth relieves her boredom by escaping to the pasha's palace. In other communities, women find solace in having affairs. Is there any such illicit activity within this community?"

Lucy Goodrich appeared amused at Luke's question. She eventually replied, "No. There are too few women, and all three of us have major impediments to fall into such evil actions. Rose is too ill, Patience has interests elsewhere, and I swore before the Lord to be ever faithful to James no matter what."

"What about the newcomer, Chantal Chatwood?"

"In time, she might become a problem. James did say she had a certain allure that men find attractive. She has been here for so little time that very few know her."

"I understand that you have had at least one long conversation with her. Why are the Chatwoods here?"

"They are not traders. Jethro's manner is that of the landed gentry with a distain for commerce, but according to his sister, he is an expert in precious stones. She asked if I had any jewelry which Jethro could value for me and said that if I wanted to sell, he could arrange it. I showed Chantal what I had, a family heirloom in which she showed great interest, and she gave me the impression that she was the expert, not Jethro. Later, she let slip that they were looking for something or someone."

"Do you know anything else about them?"

"Their method of arrival here was unusual. They did not disembark from any European vessel. They came on the sultan's personal warship that brought the last detachment of replacement janissaries from Constantinople."

"They came from the Turkish capital, perhaps even from the sultan's court?"

"Not necessarily. They could have boarded the ship elsewhere, but this possibility panicked the local authorities. An English general is bad enough, but a personal spy of the sultan could be their death knell. I do not believe the Chatwoods have been kidnapped by Arabs of the interior. The dey and his cronies, which include Sir Ambrose, are responsible."

"Do the Chatwoods speak Turkish or Arabic?"

"Jethro is fluent in Turkish, but his Arabic is poor. He found it difficult to make himself understood in the souk."

"Which suggests he is a scholar rather than a spy," concluded Luke.

11

"I notice Sweetlace has left the warehouse. Where does he fit into this community?" Luke asked.

"Don't believe the lies that Denton and Applegarth spread about him. He is a sweet man who has been led astray by that Denton pawn, Rowland May. That man is evil personified. He spends his whole time finding legal ways for Denton and his coterie to flout the laws of both Benbali and England. I am doing all I can to break Silas's infatuation with May, which I believe is starting to bear some fruit. I have sown doubt in his mind about how far he can trust his so-called friend, and I am helping him gather information that he can use to fend off any attacks on him by the Denton faction. He has revealed much to me of their devious financial practices and the outright corruption of local officials, and he has given me some evidence should anything untoward happen to him."

"Apart from yourself and May, is Silas close to anyone? Has he developed a new special friend since he came to Benbali?"

"Not that I know of, but he told me May had accused him of being too friendly with some of the local sailors."

"Does he speak any of the local tongues?"

"No, but he is fluent in Italian and spends some time in the Genoese community."

"Has he told you anything about his life before he arrived in Livorno?"

"Not directly, but his accent reveals a West Country upbringing, and once, he told me stories he had heard from people returning from the Americas. Putting those facts together, I guess he may have worked in Bristol, the center of our American trade." Luke thanked Lucy for her frank comments.

As he left, he ran into Silas returning to the Goodrich warehouse. On the spur of the moment, he invited the bookkeeper to dine with him that evening.

Present at the meal with Luke and his guest were Simon, Ninian, Miles, and Strad. Luke allowed his friends to follow their own agendas.

Simon asked, "Have you, in your time here, heard of the golden Madonna?"

"Not until his young lordship mentioned it at the Applegarth reception."

"So it is not an item of local knowledge?" asked Ninian.

"I wouldn't say that. I spoke to some of my local friends only this morning, and they mentioned that, among the corsairs, some of the old-timers had heard of it and many other precious Christian religious artifacts that had been stolen by the Benbalis over the past three decades."

Luke intervened. "How do you communicate with the locals? You, like me, have no Turkish or Arabic."

"No need. A considerable number of the sailors are English born. In fact, the flagship of the English-born admiral, Hasan, is almost totally manned by English, Scots, and Irish converts to Islam."

Simon's interest was aroused. "What exactly do your sources say about the golden Madonna?"

"Nothing except that it would have been deemed an idol by its Muslim captors, melted down almost immediately, and distributed among the whole crew as is the custom."

"So your expert advice would be that the Madonna, even if it ever reached Benbali, has long been destroyed," concluded a disappointed Simon.

"Not entirely" was Silas's surprising response.

"What do you mean?" asked Luke.

"Some of my friends in the Genoese community were very cagey when I raised the issue. One told me that wealthy Italian merchants had, over the years, tried to rescue Christian objects by buying them at excessive prices. They had not heard of the golden Madonna, but as these deals were done in extreme secrecy, it remains a possibility."

Before a more optimistic Simon could pursue this possibility. Ninian asked, "As bookkeeper to the English community, have you dealt with a local merchant named Wasim?"

"My lord, there are several merchants named Wasim. Can you give me more details?"

Luke intervened. "During the purchase and return of several female English slaves a year or so ago, this Wasim sold back an elderly nanny who, we understand, helped bring up his daughter."

"That Wasim. Yes, he does a lot of business with us."

Ninian had picked up on Silas's emphasis. "What do you mean *that Wasim?*"

"His daughter, Nour, is regarded as the most beautiful woman in the city, and many leading figures were negotiating with Wasim for her hand. Suddenly, all negotiations came to an end, and the girl was taken into the pasha's household."

"As a wife?" asked the now troubled Ninian.

"I am not sure. Ask Lady Elif," replied Silas. "Strange that you should mention Nour. I saw her as I came in. She is looking after you as one of Lady Elif's attendants."

Ninian slumped across the table. Luke thought, *Is this boy a weak link in our team, prone to faint whenever confronted with an unpalatable fact?*

The view was expressed more bluntly by Strad. "This royalist fop is a girl." Even Miles considered it was time for the Cromwellian officers to discard their royalist aristocratic partners. He helped the now conscious but distraught Ninian from the table.

Luke falsely but deliberately attributed the sudden loss of consciousness to something the young peer had eaten. Silas was not fooled. "Ambassador, forbid the young man from attempting any contact with Wasim's daughter. It is dangerous and will destroy your credibility and standing with the pasha."

Luke was well aware of the problem and refocused on questioning his guest. "Are you happy in Benbali?" he asked, hoping to catch Silas off guard.

"That is not a term I would use to define the level of satisfaction available to me in this life. I was content to come here from Italy but am now less content than when I arrived. This is a small community driven by political, religious, and personal divisions, and Denton's control is not necessarily benevolent."

"Would you welcome his removal?"

"Not necessarily. Denton has built up a network of business and political partners that gives the English community a lot of advantages over the Dutch and Genoese."

"What if these advantages are wiped out, not by any action of mine but by a local coup that overthrows Denton's friends?"

"He would establish similar relationships with the new power group that he has with the current authorities. He has invested a lot of his personal wealth into this town—and into the pockets of its leaders. He owns and finances at least two of the newest ships in the Benbali fleet."

Luke took a deep breath. "The English consul owns two of the Benbali corsair fleet that, in the past, have attacked English ships?"

"Yes, and he takes his share of the profits as owner."

"Denton and Applegarth are an unlikely couple for business partners. Do you have any comments on that arrangement?" asked Luke.

"Don't be misled. Gregory Applegarth is not the dithering fool and submissive underling that he pretends to be."

"What makes you think that?"

"On one hand, he *is* a complete incompetent and does not have any redeeming traits of personality that would make him likable. His mistakes have been costly to Denton. Yet he has been retained and is constantly praised to outsiders by Sir Ambrose."

"Any explanation?"

"There can be only one—Applegarth has something over Denton. He is blackmailing his partner to maintain his position."

"From my observation, Ambrose is not a man to take such a situation lying down. He would have dealt with Applegarth swiftly and decisively if that was the case."

"I agree. Applegarth therefore must have made sure that if anything happens to him, his evidence against Denton would become public."

"An interesting hypothesis. But I don't think Gregory has it in him to sustain such an activity. What of his wife, Patience?"

"Gregory *is* blackmailing Ambrose, and Patience *has a hold over* Gregory. She acts as a very independent woman who spends more time in the pasha's palace than in our community. She claims that she works with Lady Elif, teaching the many English slaves to read and write, but she has a love interest there."

"That sounds a little like malicious gossip, Silas. Any evidence?"

"Applegarth hasn't a single romantic, sensual, or sexual bone in his body. If only he gave Patience a tenth of the time he spends on his horses, the situation may not have occurred. The woman is starved of affection, let alone love and sexual fulfillment. Recently, when she returns from the palace, she just exudes sensuality. Teaching people to read and write is not an aphrodisiac."

"I did not see any horses around the Applegarth residence. I am a former cavalry officer and spent most of my life with horses. I would love to ride while I'm here."

"He leases stables on the edge of town, and when he is not in the warehouse, he is with his horses. He rides them daily before he starts work. The local Arabs claim he is a natural horseman."

"A very different view of Gregory from that which I have been given by others. How do you see the Goodrich couple? They seem to be friendly toward you despite your gender preference."

"I fled England several years ago when people holding similar views to the Goodriches took over Parliament and were intent on enforcing the death penalty on anyone with homosexual thoughts, let alone actions. James and Lucy are a caricature of an extreme Puritan couple down to their insistence on wearing black clothes in this North African heat. But they believe, through prayer, they will save me. Consequently, we get along quite well, to a point where Lucy confides in me and I in her."

"Any confidences that might help my investigation?" probed Luke.

"Only that, in his youth, James was a wild one and was punished by the ecclesiastical courts on numerous occasions for inappropriate relationships. During the war, a traveling Baptist preacher converted him."

"Did those relationships involve men and boys? That might explain the Goodriches' attitude to you."

"Perhaps, but Lucy's current worry is that James is too close to some of the women he is attempting to convert."

"Lucy is the more aggressive evangelist of the two?"

"Yes, she is convinced that the world will end in a year or two. To her, there is an urgency in her appeal to local Muslims. She readily accepts that she could face death if the local authorities decided to implement their law against the conversion of Muslims to another faith."

"Why hasn't the law been implemented or, at the least, the couple expelled from Benbali?"

"Two reasons. The authorities favor the more moderate Turkish interpretation of the law, and the predominantly Arab population who accepts a more fundamentalist view of the situation has not put pressure on the dey to act because James has become a vital part of the local economy and is very supportive of local Arab small-business holders."

"The Chatwoods—any comments?"

"Their arrival has frightened the local administration. They were warned about your visit and expected you to remove Royalists from the local English community and, given your naval power, extract a treaty guaranteeing exemption from corsair raids for English merchants. But the Chatwoods' arrival baffles them."

"What do they suspect?"

"They were undecided whether Jethro Chatwood was an agent of the sultan investigating the loyalty of the Benbali elite to the Ottoman Turk or an English agent preparing for your visit."

"Surely, the Sultan would not choose an Englishman for his purposes?"

"There are rumors that your ambassador in Constantinople, Sir Thomas Bendish, has the ear of the sultan. He has convinced the sultan that his natural allies against his Catholic enemies in the Mediterranean are the English and the Dutch and that the equally Protestant Sweden is his ally in the battle for eastern and central Europe. He seeks a Protestant alliance to counter the current pope, who is trying to unite the Catholic powers of Europe in an all-out attack on Islam. Chatwood may have been in Constantinople and proved an ideal choice for a combined English-Ottoman assertion of influence along the North African coast."

"He could be one of our agents. The head of my government's intelligence, John Thurloe, has a habit of sending more than one agent into a situation and keeping them unaware of the other's existence," Luke surprisingly confessed.

12

"Why have the Chatwoods been abducted?" asked Miles, who had just rejoined them after supervising Ninian's recovery.

"The gossip on the streets is that none of the stories coming from the authorities are to be believed. It is extremely rare that agents of the Arab sheikhs would enter the city and seize a foreign visitor whose potential value as a ransom victim is unknown. In addition, unless the dey has finally discovered the reason for the Chatwood visit, he would be reluctant to order their abduction. I would probe the details of this alleged event. How it could happen in the busy bazaar and how so few credible witnesses were there amaze me," Silas said.

"Your explanation?" continued Miles.

"The Chatwoods are English agents, and their disappearance has been organized from within our community. Maybe they came here to find a missing Englishman or woman who does not wish to be found."

"What are you suggesting?" asked Luke.

"None of us know anything about the past life of people who claim to be James and Lucy Goodrich or Gregory and Patience Applegarth or Ambrose and Rose Denton or even Rowland May and Silas Sweetlace. None of us may be whom we claim to be. New arrivals could recognize any one of our friends from a past life and reveal their true identity."

"You include your partner, Rowland, and yourself?" added Miles.

"Yes, I know absolutely nothing about Rowland's English past. Our paths first crossed in Livorno, and we both agreed that whatever had happened to us in the past was a closed book."

"Surely, over the time of your close relationship, he has let slip something about his past?" probed Luke.

"Only that he comes from a landed family who, during our civil wars, strongly supported the king but who, since he has been here, is a fervent believer in the current government's use of its naval power."

"Silas, I need to ask you about yourself. Your rational discussion of the situation suggests to me that you are well versed in politics, as well as finance."

"In England, I was the steward to a powerful political figure whose identity I will not reveal."

"Thank you. You have given me much to think about. Let us all enjoy the meal."

When dinner had concluded and Silas had left, Luke, Simon, and Miles considered the information they had gleaned from the unpopular bookkeeper. Luke summed up. "Silas has given us more information than the others put together. The search for the golden Madonna has reached a dead end, and any rescue of the Fyson girl is impossible. The local English community is dysfunctional and its links with a corrupt administration too close—and we are being drawn into a local coup. Our immediate task remains to discover who poisoned Ninian and prohibit any further pursuit of his sister, Nour. How is Ninian?"

Miles responded, "I took the precaution of placing one of my men at the door of his room. When he recovered, he was beside himself, threatening to storm the woman's quarters of the pasha's palace to find Nour as she is apparently no longer in this building."

"I will warn Elif immediately and find out from her what the latest information the authorities have on the Chatwoods. One of them must have been the intended victim of the poisoning, and the attacker, having failed, struck again the very next day. I will concentrate on this issue. Simon, as of tomorrow, you will take over the negotiations for a treaty. You know the extent of the concessions the government is willing to make."

After Simon and Miles left the room, Luke, using gestures, asked an attendant whether Elif was still in the house or had returned to the palace. He returned a few minutes later, followed by Elif, whose sylphlike body continued to intrigue the English soldier. "My lady, I have a problem that may affect you and the pasha. My companion Lord Fyson is determined to find his sister who was kidnapped by Benbali pirates over a decade ago. He has found her, but she is now part of the pasha's household and is actually one of your handmaidens within this house. I do not know how to advance the mission of my companion without disrupting the status quo."

"Who is this young woman?"

"Nour, the adopted daughter of the merchant Wasim."

"I know the girl very well. She does not know a word of English and believes herself to be a native-born Benbali. She is also a very devout Muslim. You could never convince her that she is English, and she would never contemplate leaving here for England. Lord Fyson's mission will end in tragedy for him. Even if the girl were willing to leave, protracted negotiations with the pasha would be necessary. The girl is not a slave. Wasim freed her when she was but a child. That complicates the matter even further."

"On another issue, I want to be involved in the search for the Chatwoods. Both Yusuf and members of the English community have raised doubts about the accuracy of reports concerning their abduction. Can the pasha give me a more accurate account of what happened?"

"Even better. Tomorrow the pasha receives Yusuf on routine matters of state. Yusuf controls internal policing and has spies throughout the city. I will alert him to your request, and if you could present yourself at the palace at noon, you can question him on the latest news of the abduction. If you give me details of Nour's abduction from England, I will ask Hasan to find crew members of the corsair ship responsible, if any are still alive." She then turned toward Luke with outstretched hands. "Come, your bath is ready, and I am ready to satisfy your every need."

When Luke's visit to the pasha and Yusuf was delayed for a day, he began his own investigation into the disappearance of the Chatwoods. Ismet's men who formed a cordon around the English quarters reported that they did not see the couple leave the enclave, despite the report that Yusuf's men had escorted them into the bazaar. "Does this mean that they are being held captive within the community?" asked Miles.

"Or worse, they were probably killed there and disposed of," commented Strad.

"Surveillance within the community is the responsibility of your men, Miles. Interrogate them thoroughly!"

Miles's intensive questioning of the English soldiers who were stationed within the premises of each of the English residents but not within their living quarters revealed only a few snippets of useful information. They confirmed the Turkish reports that the Chatwoods had not been seen.

One piece of information immediately aroused Luke's interest. A soldier patrolling the Denton warehouse, upon reaching the waterfront side of the building, saw a figure disappear into the shadows. He followed it, but the fleeing figure eluded him.

On his way back from his pursuit along the riverfront, he saw a barge heading toward the river's mouth and claimed he heard a loud splash emanating from the vicinity of the barge. Luke took the informant and some of his fellows to the area of the splash and began to drag the river with improvised hooks and ropes they had purloined from the warehouse. It was slow work.

As Luke sat on a bollard supervising, a familiar voice rang out from the Dutch enclave across the river. It was Pastor Claasen. "Luke, dragging is too slow. Get the keen-eyed local boys to dive for you. They will find whatever is there in minutes. There are a few of them swimming farther downstream."

"Thanks, Jan," said Luke as he sent Miles along the river to recruit some of the youngsters.

After two or three dives from five or six boys, one of them came to the surface and gestured to Miles. Miles and the boy engaged in a heated conversation, after which the latter led his fellow divers back to the mouth of the river. "What was all that about?" asked Luke.

"The boy was furious that we had not told him that they were diving for dead bodies."

"Bodies?"

"The lad said he found a large hessian bag that appeared to contain something the size of a human body, which was difficult to move as it was probably weighed down to prevent it from floating to the surface."

"Did he indicate exactly where the alleged body is?"

"Yes, I will direct our hooks and drag lines to its location," replied Miles. Eventually, a large soggy bag was dragged ashore. It was similar to those found in the warehouses that contained cereals or spices. It had a large "D&A" printed across its front. The top of the bag had been roughly wired together, and on the wires' removal, the top of a human head became visible.

"Who is it?" asked Ralph, who had just joined them.

Miles lifted the body gently as two of his men pulled away the bag. Ralph, Miles, and Luke gave an involuntary gasp of dismay. All three knew the victim. It was Jethro Chatwood.

Luke turned to Miles. "Get those boys back. Pay them double, and tell them that there could be another body, and whoever finds it will get a silver coin." The boys searched for over an hour but found nothing.

Luke's comment reflected the general sentiment. "Where is Chantal? Is she still alive?"

Ralph indicated to Luke that he was about to leave and take all of Miles's men with him. It was time to rotate the English troops still on board the *Cromwell* with those guarding the English quarters. Ralph would resume command of the *Cromwell*, and John Neville would have his week ashore.

Luke sent Jethro's body to the pasha's doctor to determine, if possible, the cause of death. Then he and Miles crisscrossed the

English quarters informing its residents of the gruesome news. According to protocol, the consul was the first informed. Ambrose, who had noticed the activity outside his premises, opened the discussion with a direct question. "Did you find what you were looking for?"

"Unfortunately, yes. We recovered the body of Jethro Chatwood."

"And his sister?" asked Ambrose.

"No, there was only one body in the area. The local boys made a thorough search. But if Chantal's body was not weighed down, it could have floated out into the bay and will take weeks to find," admitted Luke.

Ambrose then asked, "How did Chatwood die?"

"I don't know" was Luke's lame response.

"Whatever, we must bury the body immediately. In this heat, it will deteriorate quickly. I will take the body and organize a funeral," Ambrose offered.

"Not possible. I have sent the body to Dr. Sharif to see if he can determine the cause of death. And as the senior English officer here, I will organize the funeral. Jethro has not been a member of your community for very long. I will ask the Dutch chaplain to conduct a service. An Englishman dying in an Islamic country deserves a decent Christian burial. Is any part of the local cemetery designated for the use of Christians?" Ambrose indicated that there was a small Christian cemetery within a larger Jewish burial area— both clearly separated from that of local Islamic population.

Miles interrupted, "General, if I died in Benbali, I would not wish to be buried here. Surely, Jethro can be buried at sea with an English service conducted by Captain Croft." Luke warmed to the suggestion and nodded his approval.

Ambrose returned to the subject that clearly troubled him. "Where is Chantal? What are you doing about finding her?"

"When my replacement troops arrive from the *Cromwell*, we will begin a house-to-house search starting at the Chatwoods but expanding to every edifice within the English quarters. Tomorrow I will meet with Commander Yusuf to monitor how the wider search is progressing, assuming optimistically that we do not discover her body."

Luke and Miles informed the other residents of the English quarters and then returned home. They immediately sensed trouble as they entered the building. Elif and Ismet were waiting for him. Elif was visibly agitated. Almost shouting, she said, "The girl Nour has disappeared, and so has Lord Ninian."

"The young fool! Has he kidnapped her?" asked Luke.

"It is a logical assumption," replied the furious Elif.

13

"Where would the boy go? He has no money. He knows nobody other than our party," asked a frustrated Miles.

Ismet disagreed, "He has some money. He was seen at the market haggling for horses."

"He must have traded an item of personal jewelry to effect the purchase," suggested Luke.

"But to ride where?" asked a persistent Miles.

"Yusuf's men will find them in very short time—two innocents abroad," surmised an optimistic Luke.

"Why would Nour go with a complete stranger who, I hope, did not frighten her with professions of brotherly love and eventual return to England?" asked a now perplexed Miles.

"He must have used force," concluded Luke.

"Not necessarily. She may have made it easy for him. Nour is trained to obey a man to whom the pasha had offered hospitality, but she has not been here long enough to know that no woman leaves the pasha's household, except in the company of a Nubian guard," explained Elif.

"Will they even be able to communicate with each other?" asked Ismet.

"The boy speaks Arabic, but I do not know whether it would be easily understood here. He learned it in Syria," Miles replied.

Later that day, Miles received his newly disembarked men, and John Neville reported to Luke. "Did you get the silver Ninian collected for you?" he asked.

For a moment, Luke, Miles, and Strad were tongue-tied. It was John Neville's turn to wonder what he had said to create such a reaction. "That comment explains a lot," Luke finally replied and explained the situation.

"I thought it strange that you should send Ninian the very morning of the changeover when I could have brought whatever you required later that day."

"How did he get to the *Cromwell* without being seen?" asked Miles.

An Arab entered the room and spoke to Elif, who informed the others. "I can answer that question. Yusuf has just sent a message that one of his men, early this morning, was in the Dutch enclave. He observed a man across the river hiding behind a warehouse. While the English soldiers, readying for embarkation, were having breakfast inside the warehouse, the skulking man emerged, stole a small boat, and rowed down the river into the bay."

By next morning, Miles and his men had completed their detailed search of the English quarters without finding Chantal. Luke made his way to the pasha's palace. While Yusuf and Murat Pasha discussed matters of state, Luke talked to the doctor in an antechamber, with Elif acting as interpreter. "How did Chatwood die?" asked Luke.

"He was stabbed."

"By what type of implement?"

"An English-type commercial knife."

"What do you mean?"

"It is not a wound caused by any dagger or sword either local or European. It was caused by a knife found in commercial warehouses for the cutting of parcels, bags, and lengths of string or rope," explained the doctor.

"So Chatwood was probably killed in a warehouse within the English quarters perhaps by someone who grabbed a weapon on hand. It may not have been planned," Luke concluded.

In the afternoon, Miles directed his men to re-search every inch of the English quarters looking for any items that might bear on the murder of Jethro and the disappearance of Chantal. Strad, bored by his role as equerry to the ambassador, sought a change of environment and eagerly assisted the soldiers in their search for clues. His eagle eye immediately spied something glistening in the sand between Denton's warehouse and the river. He very carefully dug around with his dagger what appeared to be a small diamond and was amazed at what he unearthed.

It was a gigantic ring that would have covered most of the fingers of a hand—a ring designed to indicate the power and position of the wearer. Its plethora of jewels and design indicated that it not only had been worn by a person of great wealth but was very similar with what he has seen a day or two earlier. The ring was a miniature version of the pendant that Patience Applegarth had worn to the welcoming banquet—a multitude of emeralds, sapphires, and diamonds.

Luke and Elif entered the large reception room of the pasha's palace. The original reason for the meeting, the recovery of the Chatwoods—now reduced to Chantal—was completely overshadowed in the eyes of the pasha and Commander Yusuf by the abduction of Nour.

Murat Pasha, resplendent in a golden turban, sat on an elevated golden throne. His companion rose from an adjacent low cushioned bench to greet Luke. Yusuf was tall and, unlike the other local authorities Luke had met, dispensed with the turban in favor of a typical Arab headdress worn by the tribes of the interior. He also wore a flowing white robe that contrasted with the multicolored silks of the pasha. He welcomed Luke with simple Arab hand gestures instead of the elaborate Turkish ritual. Luke had no idea of Yusuf's ethnic origins, but he had clearly adopted Arab, rather than Turkish, customs.

Luke bowed in recognition of the greeting and immediately addressed the pasha, apologizing for Ninian's actions. He assured the pasha that no harm would come to Nour as Ninian believed the girl was his sister.

The stone-faced pasha did not reply. It was Yusuf who eventually responded. "His Excellency has ordered that anyone who hinders the rescue of Nour faces immediate execution. He offers generous rewards for information. Both the pasha and I have made clear that the young Englishman must be taken alive and returned to you to be dealt with."

Luke expressed his gratitude at this merciful response and asked, "Have the pair been sighted?"

"Not recently. My men have ascertained, after intensive questioning of several stallholders in the souk, that your man bought two horses and a range of Arab clothing to hide Lady Nour's features and high status and his own European origin. The young peer is not the naive innocent you led us to believe. The horse trader claimed that he had an excellent knowledge of horses and bargained successfully for two steeds that were renowned for their stamina. He has shown great skill in removing Lady Nour from the palace, and reaching wherever he had left the horses without being seen by anyone."

"Where will he head?" asked Luke. "His ultimate aim is to take Nour back to England, but what is his immediate plan?"

"Whatever it is, it is fraught with danger. Two young people traveling alone are perfect targets for enslavement or ransom. The easiest way for Lord Fyson to get out of Benbali would be by boat. If the money he stole from you is sufficient, he could bribe his way aboard a ship, but the very display of large sums for such a purpose would endanger him," warned Yusuf.

"The purchase of horses suggests his escape will be overland—but to where?" asked Luke.

"The safest route would be to reach the Spanish enclave of Oran, which is between here and the Moroccan border," answered Yusuf.

"As a Papist, he would certainly receive more favorable treatment there than most Englishmen," commented Luke.

Elif, with her eyes, sought permission from the pasha to speak. Receiving his approval, she commented, "Oran *is* their destination. Lady Nour accompanied her father, the merchant Wasim, there on many occasions. He traded our agricultural products for goods from the Americas. If Lord Fyson listens to his captive, that is where they will head."

Yusuf turned to Luke. "I will send a detachment of Arab cavalry in the direction of Oran. They have fast steeds that will rapidly overtake young Fyson and Lady Nour. I understand that you were a brilliant cavalry commander in the army of the Lord Protector Cromwell. Would you and your Arabic-speaking officer, Oxenbridge, like to accompany them?"

Luke readily accepted. He sensed that the pasha was about to conclude the interview and asked, "Your Excellencies, I still seek your help on another matter—Mistress Chantal Chatwood has gone missing. The body of her brother was found yesterday, and my men are searching the English enclave and its environs for her body. I hope they are not successful and that she has been abducted. I would appreciate any information and help that your men can provide me on this matter."

The pasha replied, "We will help in any way that we can."

Yusuf asked if there were any other matters Luke wished to raise. Upon receiving a negative response, he announced, "The pasha would like to raise a sensitive issue with you." He waived all the servants from the room, leaving only Luke, Elif, Yusuf, and the pasha in the large chamber.

Murat spoke very quietly, with Elif translating simultaneously. "Your visit is ill-timed. It comes in the middle of a design led by myself to replace the dey and his corrupt allies. He will undoubtedly use your visit to protect his position and thwart our plans. We hope that you will discuss our plans with Admiral Hasan and that you will not act against us in any steps we take to clean out corruption from our own administration and that of the merchant communities."

Luke replied diplomatically, "You can count on us to support any action to remove corruption. I hope to effect similar changes within the English quarters before I leave." Luke bowed to the two officials and, as instructed by Elif, began backing out of the room.

Conforming to this protocol, Luke accidentally backed into Ismet, who rushed into the room unannounced. He was highly agitated. He indicated to Elif that she and Luke should remain where they were. He approached the pasha and Yusuf and explained his otherwise unacceptable behavior.

After a considerable and heated discussion between the three men, the obviously furious pasha signaled for Luke and Elif to return to his throne and asked Ismet to explain. Elif translated his report. "I was present with Lord Stokey as he negotiated with the dey on your behalf. During the conversation, the English lord mentioned that his fellow peer had abducted one of the pasha's household and hoped it would not complicate their discussion. The dey seemed unusually buoyed by this information and immediately summoned the governor of the citadel, General Osman. After considerable discussion between the two and questions to Lord Stokey regarding the possible path taken by Lord Fyson, he instructed Osman to take a selection of his personal janissary bodyguard and search for the runaways. I interjected, suggesting that this was an internal policing matter and should be left to Commander Yusuf. Ahmed Dey declared it was a matter concerning the external affairs of Benbali and indirectly involved a foreign power. He then ordered me to inform Commander Yusuf of his decision and asked for any relevant information he had to be passed on to Osman. The dey has taken the matter out of the hands of the pasha and commander."

Luke turned to them. "Your Excellencies, it is apparent that you do not view this development kindly. What alarms you?"

It was an animated Yusuf who responded. "Ambassador, in terms of the internal politics of Benbali and your negotiating strength, this turn of events could be very disadvantageous. The dey may use his possession of Lord Fyson and Lady Nour as bargaining pawns against you and against the pasha and me."

"To what end?"

"To prevent us from taking steps against him and prevent you from gaining a more favorable treaty."

Luke turned to Yusuf. "How long would it take to have your men ready to ride?"

"Within the hour."

"Then we will be well ahead of the dey's janissaries. How will they travel? They have no cavalry."

Ismet replied, "They could still reach Lord Fyson before us. As I left the citadel, I saw the sloop that belongs to the garrison hoisting sail and Osman's men boarding. I suspect the ship will take them along the coast, and they will disembark just ahead of the fugitives and block their path. There are many places along the shoreline where the coastal road passes through narrow gaps between the mountains and the sea."

An agitated pasha, after a spirited discussion with Yusuf, announced, "General, I must withdraw my offer. The dey leads the executive government of Benbali, and we are not yet in a position to remove him. For Yusuf or me to deliberately disobey a direct order may lead him to take action against us and thereby set back our plans for months. We must abandon our pursuit and leave the matter in his hands."

14

Luke had a solution. "Your Excellencies, do not fret. The dey does not control me. I will follow the fugitives. Give me three horses— for myself, my equerry, and an interpreter."

"The horses are no trouble, but neither the pasha nor I have any English-speaking officers other than Ismet who must remain here," Yusuf said.

Again, Elif directed her large shining eyes at the pasha. "My lord, English is my native tongue, and I am now fluent in both Arabic and Turkish, and I ride as well as any man. In addition, I will be useful when we find Lady Nour. My presence will give her a sense of security after this very upsetting and disturbing interlude."

The pasha placed his head in his hands and eventually agreed, "I will send my best horses to your residence, Ambassador, two for each of the travelers and two to carry your provisions. Unless you catch them quickly, it could be a four-day journey. Order the *Cromwell* to sail slowly along the coast to pick you up at the appropriate time and to resupply you. Lady Elif will be your interpreter, but she will disguise her appearance. I want no one to recognize her other than Nour, and she must be accompanied by one of her Nubian bodyguards. You should leave within the hour and follow the coastal road west. Colonel Ismet will immediately return to the dey and inform him that the city commander and I have obeyed his orders but that we could not restrain General Tremayne, who believes that as an Englishman has created the problem, an Englishman must solve it."

Luke returned to his residence and sent orders to the *Cromwell* to make sail and hug the coast, tracking the pursuing party. They were not to interfere with the dey's ship. As an afterthought, he sent a message to the pasha requesting that he place as many horses as he could spare aboard the *Cromwell.*

The adrenaline was flowing. Tremayne, the old cavalry commander, was in his element. If only he had a troop behind him instead of an equerry, a woman, and an African slave.

It was just after noon when Luke and his party left Benbali and began their pursuit of Ninian and Nour along the Maghreb coast. Oran, the Spanish enclave for which it was assumed the couple was heading, was about ninety miles to the west, a journey of three days under normal conditions—but these were not normal conditions.

Speed on the first day was essential if the fleeing couple was to be overtaken. Yusuf assured Luke that the horses could cover sixty miles in a day but would need to be rested the next. Luke, with half a day of sunlight available, would push on as fast and as far as he could on day one and use completely new horses from the *Cromwell* the next.

Just as they left Benbali, the dey's ship was seen well out to sea, heading in the direction of Oran. As they progressed along the coastal road, Elif regularly asked travelers coming from the west whether they had seen a young couple. Worryingly, no one had seen anybody who vaguely resembled the quarry. Even more of a concern, dusk approached, and Luke could not see the *Cromwell* with its much-needed replacement steeds.

Luke's party spent the night on the beach, with the two soldiers taking a four-hour watch. It was around midnight when Luke heard the distant thunder of multiple hooves on the partly cobbled road. He was aware that the coastal road near their camp was an old Roman road that local authorities had maintained. If the dozen or so horsemen whom he estimated were approaching had been on the sand, he would not have been alerted to their arrival.

He extinguished the fire, woke his companions, and moved them to a depression among the dunes where they would not be seen from the road. Luke hoped the horsemen would simply gallop past, but unfortunately, they slowed, stopped, and camped behind a dune on the far side of the road.

He saw enough in the moonlight, which emerged intermittently from an otherwise overcast sky, to bemoan the situation. "We are too late. It's one of Osman's patrols, and they have two prisoners—a male and a female. Nour and Ninian are prisoners of the dey."

"Don't be too sure. I only got a quick glimpse, but I did not see any turbaned horsemen, and Osman does not have any cavalry. These are not the dey's men," said Strad.

"Even worse then for Ninian, captured by an unknown group of ruffians" was Elif's unhelpful comment.

"Let's get closer to make sure," said Luke.

"I will crawl through the dunes and find out all I can," said Strad.

"No, I will do it myself," Luke replied.

"You would both be useless. You would not know what you saw or understand a word you might hear. I will go," offered Elif.

"Absolutely not. It is not a woman's role, and I have an obligation to the pasha to protect you. This could be a bunch of marauding killers and rapists. Who else would be abroad in this place at such a time?"

"People like us," mused Strad, whose humor was not appreciated by a stressed Luke.

"This is a stalemate. We must do something, especially if the prisoners are Nour and Ninian," commented Luke.

"We can. My Nubian bodyguard was once a soldier in the Niger and speaks Arabic and a number of African tribal tongues. I will brief him."

Elif spoke at length to her bodyguard, who seemed delighted to be entrusted with such a mission. He was to observe all he could and listen to any conversations that might help identify the group and its prisoners.

An hour passed. The Nubian did not return. Luke grew increasingly agitated. Finally, the tension proved too much. "I am going to see what has happened to the African. Strad, if I do not return, await our ship, and return immediately with Elif to Benbali."

Luke did not cross the road in the vicinity of the horsemen's camp. After taking a circuitous route, he crawled to the top of a low dune from where, in the distance, he saw a number of tethered horses and a large fire, around which sat a number of people.

He moved around the edge of the dune to get a closer look— and stumbled over a body. It was not the Nubian. The victim wore the flowing traditional robes of the desert Arab with one major difference. The robe was black, not white, and the cord that held the headdress in place was red, not black.

As he rifled the corpse for any useful information, he sensed a presence behind him. He turned suddenly to catch the presence off guard. He withdrew his sword just in time. It was the Nubian.

The two men made their way back to Elif in silence. Elif listened as her bodyguard reported at length. She informed Luke and Strad, "This is a troop of Abbasids—a fundamentalist group of nomadic Arab and Berber extremists who want to recreate a caliphate in the image of the Abbasid dynasty of a thousand years ago. They are determined to remove all Turks and all Europeans from the Maghreb, and their sole weapon is assassination. If those prisoners are Nour and Ninian, they will not be prepared for ransom but for the most horrendous of executions where it will cause the most alarm."

"Your man could not tell whether the prisoners are our quarry?" asked Luke.

"No. He heard them speak, both in Arabic. It could have been Nour and Ninian."

"We have to assume that the prisoners are Nour and Ninian, and given what you have said, we must rescue them. These Abbasids are the same group that Ismet thinks tried to kill me on my first day in Benbali," said Luke.

"An impossible task, General. There are ten or twelve of them and three of us," replied Strad.

"Four," added a fired-up Elif. "They have only stopped here for a short while to rest their horses. They cannot dally because they are probably being pursued."

"That helps our cause," said Luke.

"What's your plan?" asked Strad.

"Many pronged. I will free the prisoners, with the Nubian as my assistant to remove anyone who gets in the way. I will effect this rescue during a diversion that you will create, Strad. Untether their horses, and send them off with as much noise as you can make in every direction. Elif, at the same time, you will lead our own ten horses silently along the beach and join the Roman road some distance to the west. And making as much noise as you can, ride in this direction. Hopefully, our opponents will think that it is the pursuing patrol almost on their heels. In the panic to regather their horses and escape, they will not waste time trying to recapture the escaped prisoners."

Luke and the Nubian were soon in position, awaiting Strad's diversion. The situation was promising. The gang was gathered around a blazing fire, aiming to modify the chill of the night air. The prisoners, excluded from this luxury, were huddled together against a large boulder some distance from the main group. The Nubian indicated to Luke by hand signals that they were shackled together at the feet.

Strad slowly untethered the horses, and when this was done, he fired his pistol and shouted loudly as he slapped as many horses as he could. The group around the fire quickly recovered from their surprise and made off after the retreating steeds, except for one man who had been directed to watch over the prisoners. This obstacle to Luke's plan was quickly disposed of as the Nubian efficiently and quietly broke the man's neck before he knew what had happened.

Luke's plan to rescue the prisoners appeared stymied as they were shackled together not only at the feet but also by the hands. They could barely walk and certainly not quickly enough to escape the attention of returning gang members. Before Luke could act, the Nubian picked up the male prisoner and indicated to Luke he should do the same with the woman. Together, they carried them to safety as they heard the clatter of approaching horses along the road. The gang also heard it, and one by one, as they recovered their own horses, they headed off into the night.

An hour later, Luke's group and the two prisoners gathered around a fire that Strad had relit from a branch of the Abbasid's blaze. The prisoners remained shackled as Luke had no means of removing the fetters. The rescued prisoners were not Nour and Ninian.

Elif recognized the male and, after some pertinent questioning, informed Luke, "This is Ibrahim, now sheikh of the Baji tribe, and his sister. They were with their father trading with the Spaniards in Oran when the Abbasids struck, rampaging through the market, decapitating every Arab they came across trading with a European. The Baji are allies of the Europeans and Turks and are therefore anathema to the Abbasids. Their father, the then sheikh, was killed, and they were captured. I have met Ibrahim before. He visited the pasha on a number of occasions with his father."

"Does he have any other relevant information?"

"He says that the Abbasids were not concerned that the Spaniards had sent a cavalry troop after them. They were confident that their horses were so much faster than the lumbering Spanish cavalry that their pursuers had, in frustration, returned to Oran."

"What do they wish to do?"

"To return to Oran with us to claim their father's body—and to be unshackled."

"It is a bit risky trying to smash the fetters with local rocks. When the *Cromwell* arrives, it will have implements that will make the task safer."

It was Strad who, at first light, saw the *Cromwell* anchored just offshore. Ralph Croft, having seen a fire on the beach and guessing that it was Luke's party, led his men ashore at dawn with supplies—and the much-needed fresh horses. Ibrahim and his sister were freed from their shackles, and the trek westward recommenced. The rest of the morning was uneventful with no sign of Ninian and Nour.

Around noon, a large group of horsemen approached them, both on the road and along the beach. Luke and Strad immediately recognized the newcomers by their helmets. It was a Spanish patrol. "We are in serious trouble. We are at war with Spain. We could soon find ourselves in a Spanish dungeon," concluded a pessimistic Strad.

15

"What can we do?" Strad continued.

"Let's hope it's the Spanish patrol sent after the Abbasids," said Luke.

"Osman may have reached Oran and alerted the authorities to a runaway Englishman and a female member of the pasha's household and sought Spanish help in apprehending them. That description of Ninian and Nour equally applies to us. The patrol may arrest us, mistakenly thinking we are the fugitives," suggested an alert Elif.

"It could be even worse. Osman may have deliberately misrepresented us as English spies attempting to infiltrate Spanish territory to assess the strength of its naval defenses," mused a growingly concerned Luke.

"Having rescued Ibrahim, we are on our way to return him to Oran. That should hold us in good stead," added the now optimistic Elif.

Luke relaxed. "Elif, tell the Spanish officer that I am the English ambassador to the North African Islamic states who is making an official visit to a Spanish neighbor and seeks their escort to the governor of Oran and that, in the course of our mission, we have rescued Ibrahim and his sister from the clutches of the Abbasids." The Spanish cavalry commander, who understood Arabic, accepted Elif's explanation and treated Luke's party with the respect due to a visiting envoy—despite the stark fact that England and Spain were at war.

That evening, Luke and Elif were received by the Spanish governor. Luke immediately recognized the man, who had risen to greet them. The governor hugged Luke and welcomed him in faultless English. Elif could not contain herself and whispered to Luke, "How does a Cromwellian general know a Spanish governor who speaks English with the same West Country accent as both of us?"

"The Count of Varga y Verganza, who sits in the governor's chair, was born Nicholas Noakes, heir to a Somerset squire. He was educated in Spain, became a Papist, and serves the king of Spain, who rewarded him with a title. Four years ago, he returned to England as a Spanish spy but also to uncover the murderer of his father. Cromwell sent me to investigate the same murder. For a time, we were allies," Luke explained.

Varga added, "You have certainly come up in the world since then. The last time we met, you were one of Cromwell's secret agents, although nominally a colonel of cavalry. Now I understand, from the captain of the patrol that encountered you, that you have been knighted, have been promoted to general, and actually command a ship of the line, which I am informed is lurking just offshore. Or are you still playing your old games as a Cromwellian agent, and this is all a front to conceal some nefarious activity?"

"There is some truth in your suspicions. I am in Benbali negotiating a treaty with the locals to protect our shipping and enhance our trade. Unfortunately, one from my mission abducted a member of the pasha's household and is believed to be heading toward Oran. That is why I am accompanied by Lady Elif, who is here to calm the abducted girl's fears. In addition, she was the only person available who spoke English and Arabic."

"You must be highly regarded by Murat Pasha. He is very protective of his household, and such behavior as that of your colleague by lesser mortals would have led to summary execution. I am amazed that he has allowed his favorite, Lady Elif, to be your assistant."

Elif spoke. "My presence indicates the importance that Murat Pasha assigns to this enterprise. He would be very grateful if you could assist us in this quest. I hope Your Excellency can help the English ambassador and the Benbali authorities in their joint search for the missing couple."

Varga replied, "No doubt this is very embarrassing for you, Luke, and could endanger your diplomatic mission. But as our countries are at war, how could you expect me to help you?"

"Your Excellency is not at war with Benbali. You could argue that, in this instance, Luke is acting as an agent of the Benbali government and not as the English ambassador," suggested the astute Elif.

"You are in luck, Luke. As I have received no information regarding your visit, I have no specific orders as how I should respond to your intrusion. I could justify my assistance to an enemy alien on the grounds that he assisted me on another matter. I did receive information that an old friend, Simon, Lord Stokey, was heading in this direction, driven by a desire to return the golden Madonna to a Spanish monastery where a religious order expelled from England is now located. I was to give him every assistance. Do you know anything of him?"

Luke smiled. "Yes, he is a senior member of my mission."

"How can that be? England's most important Catholic peer and active Royalist allied with you, a fanatical Protestant and fervent supporter of Oliver Cromwell?"

"My mission has several aims. One of them, in which Charles Stuart and Oliver Cromwell have combined, is to rescue an English aristocrat who was captured by the Benbali corsairs. In fact, the young woman who has been abducted by one of my group is that aristocrat. The young kidnapper thinks he is rescuing his sister and returning her to a beloved England. In reality, the girl has no memory of England, is a Muslim, and is a new member of the pasha's household."

"Are you also involved in Stokey's search for the Madonna?"

"To a point. I will help him find it, but I have orders to confiscate it on behalf of the English government, and I am sure Charles Stuart would expect it be handed over to him. Simon's only chance of getting it back to your Spanish monastery is if he could get it to you or the local Benbali Catholic priest. But it won't be an issue. Islam, as you know, deplores the depiction of the divine, and every Muslim would melt down such an offensive item at the first opportunity. It was probably destroyed decades ago."

"I agree," said the governor. "For over a decade, Oran has not recovered a single piece of religious Christian art intact."

The conversation was interrupted by an equerry, and after a brief discussion with him, the governor issued an order. Varga turned to Luke and Elif and explained, "The commander of an English man of war flying a white flag has sought permission to enter the Oran harbor to collect the English ambassador and Lady Elif for the return trip to Benbali. I have rejected the request—until dawn tomorrow. Tonight enjoy my hospitality."

"One last question—has a small Benbali vessel commanded by its leading general arrived here?" asked Luke.

"Yes, General Osman was most anxious that if any of two groups, each involving an Englishman and a member of the pasha's household, should arrive in Oran, I hand them over to him as both are suspected of plotting against the dey of Benbali. Is that what you are really in the region to achieve, the overthrow of the current Benbali government?" asked Varga.

"There are rumblings against the dey, and the local authorities whom I have had most to deal with *are* plotting a coup, but it would be undiplomatic of me to get involved."

"Yes, and not in England's interest. The one constant complaint I hear regarding Benbali is that it is run in the interests of the English merchants. The English consul is the dey's partner in every dubious transaction."

"True, Benbali is run in the interests of the English consul and the dey but possibly not in the interests of England or Benbali," Luke conceded. "Where is General Osman now?"

"His ship is in the harbor, ready to take you back to Benbali."

"Interesting," mused Luke.

"No, Luke, you will not abuse my hospitality by taking any steps against a Benbali ship. I remember how you think," exclaimed the suspicious Varga.

"Is there no way you can detain Osman here for a week or so? During that period, the coup may have occurred. Osman is a strong supporter of the current dey. It would be in Spain's interests to be rid of a dey who is in alliance with the English consul," suggested Elif.

"How could I justify helping an enemy agent effect a coup against a friendly neighbor?" was Varga's response.

Luke let the matter rest and asked, "May I speak to my equerry?" Varga nodded approval, and within minutes, Strad appeared. He whispered to Luke that the Spaniards were not such a bad lot and that he had been well entertained by the castle's garrison.

Luke spoke to him in earnest for several minutes and asked Varga, "Is it possible for my man to be transported to our ship anchored just outside your harbor?" Varga nodded in the affirmative, and Strad followed one of the governor's men out of the room.

Luke could not help smiling. Elif noticed the air of self-satisfaction and asked, "What are you up to, Luke?"

"Your master, the pasha, will be very pleased with me."

Luke and Elif were treated to a banquet, at which many of the leading officials and citizens of Oran were present. Luke was introduced as the English ambassador to the Islamic states of North Africa, currently negotiating a treaty to protect all European merchantmen from corsair attack, and on the personal level as the man who tracked down and brought to justice the murderer of the governor's father.

One of the guests whom Luke later discovered was Varga's deputy railed against the English government's betrayal of Spain. Spain was the first European power to recognize the Cromwellian regime and fully expected English help against France. Instead, the powerful English navy invaded parts of the Americas and had seriously affected Spanish activities in the Mediterranean long before formal war had been declared. The deputy wanted to know if Luke's visit to Oran foreshadowed a change of policy.

Luke, warming to the role of ambassador, replied diplomatically, "There are many English merchants who deplore the attack on Spain and many members of the council of state who see that the real danger to English power is France. Unfortunately, they are, at present, a minority. Continued assistance by Spain to Charles Stuart, who claims the English throne, does not help the cause of those Englishmen who want peace with Spain."

Varga intervened. "Luke, you should not forget that your current ally, the Royalist Lord Stokey, prevailed on our government not to send troops to England. An advance guard had already landed in Wales and was withdrawn at his request." Inwardly, Luke had to concede that England had been the aggressor in the current conflict with Spain; but outwardly, he continued to defend his country's actions, citing the activities of the Spanish Inquisition as justification for anti-Spanish activity.

A black-clad guest who was clearly a cleric spoke. "Ambassador, I am the local representative of the Inquisition, Fr. Diego Cisneros, but I have no intention of challenging a highly respected visitor. I wonder if you could convey to Lord Stokey my compliments and invite him to visit me here when he leaves Benbali."

When the banquet had concluded, Luke and Elif were led by a servant to another part of the governor's palace. Varga had assumed that the pasha had offered Elif's full services to the ambassador. Neither of the visitors objected to the arrangement. Elif, radiant in the afterglow of their activity, murmured, "It's a pity that Ambassador Tremayne has not kidnapped Lady Elif and forced her to return to her native England."

Before Luke could question her further on this comment, she was fast asleep—or pretended to be.

16

When Luke and Elif appeared the next morning on the balcony of the governor's residence, they were both drawn to an apparent catastrophe in the harbor. General Osman's ship was half submerged and its former occupants clamoring together on the foreshore. Luke smiled and commented, "Should we offer them our assistance?"

"What exactly happened?" asked Elif, well aware of Luke's involvement.

"Someone opened the sea cocks during the night, and the vessel has slowly sunk."

"Why would the Spaniards do such a thing to a vessel belonging to a friendly neighbor?" asked Elif with a mischievous look.

"We must ask the governor. Here he comes."

"One of your schemes, no doubt, Luke," observed a not-too-pleased count.

"Can the ship be raised? The dey of Benbali will not be a happy man. And I imagine General Osman, his janissaries, and his sailors will have to walk home," noted a pompous Luke.

"Not at all, Luke. You caused the Spanish government embarrassment. You solve the problem. Your warship will enter the harbor to collect the Benbali soldiers and sailors marooned by the mysterious sinking of their ship. Your generosity in this regard will no doubt be favorably received by the dey."

Strad joined the group and whispered to Luke, who appeared alarmed. He quickly turned to the governor. "I am sorry, Nicholas, but I cannot agree. The *Cromwell* left all its soldiers in Benbali. I cannot risk taking on board half a company of elite Turkish troops. Osman could take over control of my ship with ease. I will take him and his officers back to Benbali, but his troops will have to walk."

The annoyed count continued. "Ever the active agent. Ambassadors don't do that sort of thing, sinking a ship from the city with whom you are seeking to negotiate a favorable treaty. You amaze me."

"My generosity in assisting Osman can be turned to my advantage. I will put the *Cromwell* through its paces and demonstrate to the general the superior speed and firepower of the new English ships and suggest that if he does not use his influence on the dey to accept our conditions, Benbali may feel the full power of the English navy. Admiral Stokes, with the whole Mediterranean fleet, is ready to act and can be recalled to the North African coast within a few days."

"And I will also take advantage of your visit to Oran. On behalf of the Spanish government, I would like a tour of your ship. It will enable me to justify my benevolent treatment of a current enemy."

"And don't forget we rescued two important Arabs who were abducted from your marketplace," added Luke.

Luke, the governor, and his deputy were soon aboard the *Cromwell*. Elif diplomatically conveyed Luke's offer to General Osman to return him and his senior officers to Benbali. She invited him to join the Spanish governor on a guided tour of the *Cromwell*.

Strad was unhappy that Luke was showing the Spanish and Benbali military one of England's most modern frigates and did not hesitate to bombard Luke with his concerns. Ralph and John, who knew the exact capabilities of the ship, were not alarmed. The latter explained that the frigate's advantages over its rivals stemmed from the new textiles used for its sails and the new alloys from which its cannons and their projectiles were constructed. A simple inspection would not reveal these secrets.

The Spanish governor, quickly aware of this fact, soon disembarked and ordered his artillery to fire a salute as the *Cromwell* left the harbor.

When the ship was well out to sea, Luke invited Osman to his cabin, where Elif was ready to act as interpreter and Strad to take notes. This was a perfect opportunity to understand Benbali politics from the perspective of the dey and his allies.

Luke, at first, sought Osman's assistance in understanding the problems confronting the treaty he sought to negotiate. "You have been present at the negotiations between the dey and Lord Stokey. Progress seems to be slow. What are the obstacles to a quick settlement?"

"Essentially, the dey is hindered by the recalcitrant navy. Its new admiral, Hasan, is an aggressive, selfish man who refuses to give an inch. You want two simple things—that our ships do not attack yours and that we release all English slaves for you to repatriate to England. The dey is ready to agree, but as it will cost us, arguments have occurred about who should pay what."

"The repatriation of English slaves should cost the Benbali government and people nothing. I will buy the freedom of the slaves concerned at 5 percent above market rates," Luke replied.

"Money isn't the issue. The navy still depends on the galley slaves for its mobility. It is reluctant to free any slaves from its galleys."

"Any navy that wants success in the Mediterranean has largely replaced its oared galleys with sailing ships," commented Luke.

"Exactly Hasan's argument. If you take his galley slaves, you must replace them with up to three English men of war. The dey believes this is excessive and will only bring retaliation from your government. Hasan also believes that if you deprive the navy of rich English merchant prizes, you must replace these targets with other suitable quarry. You cannot expect the city to take a major cut in income. Hasan wants a commission from your government for him to attack all other ships, making him an English privateer, rather than a Barbary Coast pirate—a solution the dey strongly opposes."

"Lord Stokey would have made it clear that the English government would not approve of indiscriminate attacks on any Christian shipping," Luke replied hypocritically.

"A point on which the dey agrees. He wants to keep good relations with the Dutch and Genoese. At the last meeting, Hasan was demanding the right to attack all ships other than those of England and Holland. In particular, he wanted freedom to attack Portuguese merchantmen returning from the East Indies just beyond the Straits of Gibraltar, which would also upset our Islamic neighbor, the king of Morocco."

"And also the government of England. Portugal is our new ally. I must raise a very delicate point with you. I do not want to spend weeks in negotiation, and just after we sign, the government of Benbali is overthrown. I have picked up rumors of an impending coup. Is the dey aware of this, and what is he doing to counter it?"

"The dey is elected by a council dominated by the Turkish janissaries of the citadel but with some representation from the navy and local Arab interests advanced by Commander Yusuf. The nominee of this council then receives authority to govern in the name of the sultan from the pasha. It is a delicate balance. At the moment, Hasan wants a dey more in tune with the navy's demands. And because the Benbali navy has regularly provided an effective fleet for the sultan every season, I fear that His Highness has listened to unfounded complaints against the dey."

"How have the sultan's anti-dey views been manifest?"

"By replacing more than half my men, many who had been here for decades, with a new contingent of Turkish janissaries whose loyalty to Benbali is problematical. These newcomers are inclined to listen to the navy and to my new deputy, Colonel Ismet, who probably commanded most of them in Constantinople." Osman gave a slight nod in the direction of Elif. "I would like to discuss this matter further but not here and now. Visit me at the citadel with your army commander the day after we dock in Benbali." Osman would not discuss the matter in front of a member of the pasha's household, whose sympathies he knew lay elsewhere.

Luke obliged and changed the subject. "Your men found no trace of Lord Fyson or Lady Nour?"

"No. As you left shortly after we did and did not come across them, they must have fled in another direction—none of which would be in their best interests."

"What do you mean?"

"If they went inland, the Arab sheikhs are a law to themselves. They would see Lady Nour as a suitable additional wife, and your young lord would bring a good price as a slave destined to darkest Africa. If they went east, they would soon be in Algerian territory. Algiers is unhappy with England. Some of their leaders want a treaty such as you are negotiating with us and are furious that you came here first. They consider themselves the dominant of the Maghreb states. Others there are fearful that your fleet is ready to bombard the city as Blake did to Tunis. The young couple would make a good bargaining chip for them in dealing with you and with us. They also resent our closeness to the sultan and the favored treatment they think we receive."

The discussion was interrupted by the sound of thunder, and within minutes, Ralph entered the cabin. "Luke, there is a major storm approaching. We must shelter until it passes."

Osman intervened. "These storms are unpredictable and can be very dangerous. The safest approach is to protect the ship from the wind. The next bay is well protected from the prevailing wind by its high and extensive headland. Seek shelter there." Luke agreed.

The *Cromwell* laboriously made its way through cyclonic winds and the heaviest of rain to the relative calm of the protected inlet. It spent the night in this safe location, but as dawn broke, Luke was faced with another problem. The storm had gone, but so had the wind. For the whole morning, the *Cromwell* lay becalmed. Just after midday, a gentle zephyr developed that was just enough to give the ship some movement. The *Cromwell* slowly headed out into the open sea, where the wind was barely sufficient to raise more sail.

An hour later, with a strong breeze blowing, Captain Croft reported a merchantman on the horizon. He sought permission to pursue it, reminding Luke that all English ships in the Mediterranean were ordered to stop and seize any vessels delivering goods to Spain or its allies. As the *Cromwell* approached the vessel, it was identified as a Roman ship bearing the colors of the pope, probably out of Algiers, carrying wheat, olives, and livestock to Italy.

"Damnation!" muttered John. "I would have loved to have tested our guns, but this looks like a neutral ship on a normal commercial voyage."

"Not necessarily," remarked Luke. "These goods could be intended for Naples, a Spanish territory, and therefore a legitimate target and prize of war. Fire across its bow, and we will talk to its captain and, if necessary, search the ship."

Ralph suggested caution. "Luke, we do not have any men for a boarding party. We are unarmed sailors. Your one weapon is their fear that you will blast them out of the water. I suggest you and Strad use the longboat while John and I maintain the *Cromwell* at a distance and in a position to fire, if necessary."

As they were rowed to the Italian ship, Strad asked, "How are you going to make yourself understood? Neither of us speaks a word of Italian."

"There is an even greater worry than our lack of Italian. The ship is low in the water but not because it is overloaded with valuable prizes. Scarcely concealed are two decks of heavy cannons. This is a well-armed merchantman. I will need to adopt a much gentler approach than I intended," admitted Luke.

17

Luke and Strad were led to the captain's cabin. Standing beside the seated officer was a young man who spoke in perfect English and a small older man holding a large volume. "Welcome aboard the *Principe di Roma*. I am an English merchant based in Rome who owns the cargo aboard this ship, which is destined for His Holiness, the pope. What can we do for you?"

Luke explained who he was and that he was carrying out orders to prevent any goods being transported to Spain and its allies. Could he prove that the ship's cargo was not intended for Naples, Milan, or to Spain itself? The merchant nodded, and his clerk led Strad to an adjacent cabin to check the relevant documents contained in the large volume he clutched to his breast. "I would take you through the documentation myself, but I may be needed here to translate for the captain," commented the merchant.

A purser entered the room and, under the captain's instructions, provided wine and cheese for his guests. The merchant then asked, "General Tremayne, the captain is keenly interested in your ship. We have heard that these new English frigates are very powerful. Could it blast us out of water from where it is?"

"Yes, it is one of the newest frigates, which is faster and better gunned than the earlier models. In particular, it has a new type of cannon made from a special alloy that enables it to fire much further and more frequently than anyone would expect. It could bombard every citadel, infidel, or Christian along the North African coast and remain out of range of the enemy guns."

Strad returned, verifying the ship's cargo and destination. Luke thanked the captain and the merchant for their assistance. Just before he left, he asked, "Another requirement of commanders of English ships in the area is to seek out English slaves and free them. Are there any English aboard?"

The captain looked imploringly at the merchant. The merchant addressed Luke. "We have no English slaves, but we do have an English passenger who came aboard just as we sailed, offering a high price for passage to Rome. If we had not cast off, we would have returned him to the Algerian authorities who were demanding his surrender. They claimed he had kidnapped a high-ranking local woman."

"Had he? Did he bring her on board?" asked a highly excited Luke.

"We thought not. He claimed he was an English peer of papist persuasion and that he was accompanied by his male servant. However, it soon became obvious that this servant is, in fact, female—and an infidel to boot. I trade constantly with Algiers and do not want to be compromised. Could you transfer them to your vessel?"

Luke was amazed. He was lost for words for over a minute. It had to be Nour and Ninian. The merchant expressed concern. "Are you feeling ill?"

Luke explained, "No, this is a miracle. For the last few days, we have been trying to track down this couple who has seriously embarrassed me in negotiations with the Benbali authorities. I have on board a senior female member of the pasha's household, from where the girl was abducted. She will immediately look after the young woman. Will they come with us of their own accord?"

"No, when the young man saw your ship approaching, he asked the captain not to reveal that they were aboard and to hide them until you had departed. This ship, as you have probably noticed, is not a simple merchantman. It is well furnished with guns and has a small company of soldiers to resist boarding. Some of these soldiers will accompany you and take our two passengers forcibly back to your ship." Luke thanked the merchant and the captain and, with Strad, descended the ladder into the longboat.

A few minutes later, two young people descended the ladder, followed by four armed Italian soldiers. Luke was very courteous. "Welcome back, Ninian. Lady Nour, Lady Elif awaits to welcome you aboard the *Cromwell*."

Ninian remained silent. Nour glared.

Luke faced several problems on his return to Benbali— determining his position on the expected coup, finding Chantal Chatwood, solving the murder of her brother, controlling the wayward Ninian, reforming the English community, deciding the fate of the English consul, and completing the treaty with local authorities, which seemed to rest on the extent of sweeteners that the English could offer. The morning after their return, Luke assembled his men to discuss the situation and determine which of the above should take priority. Present were Miles, John, Simon, and Strad. Ralph was aboard the *Cromwell*, and Ninian refused to leave his room.

Simon reported, "The treaty regarding both the protection of English shipping and the freeing of English slaves is ready to be signed, but the dey is opposed by the navy. Hasan insists that the annual grant from the English be substantially increased, well above the figure for which you have approval to offer. Also, he wants the exemption of his galley slaves from any freedom and the gift, or at least a chance to purchase, a Cromwell-class frigate."

"Osman told me as much during our voyage home from Oran," commented Luke.

Simon continued. "We must force the dey's hand. Insist that he sign today. Any successor will probably demand much more. I will explain that our current offer is the best they can expect and that any delay could result in an English naval attack designed to wipe out the Benbali fleet. That should bring Hasan into line."

"If you force the dey's hand, you may provoke a coup leading to a much more demanding successor," cautioned Miles. "After all,

Hasan is a leading conspirator, as well as the man taking the hard line against us in the negotiations."

"I agree. We must reconsider our position in regard to any coup. My sympathy up until now has to be with the plotters, especially with their emphasis on removing corruption, in which our own consul seems to be enmeshed, but Hasan's demands are excessive. It may be better to support the status quo than assist change that may lead who knows where. For the moment, we stay neutral. Perhaps we can remove Ambrose without upsetting Ahmed Dey. I will accompany you and Simon to the citadel today and continue my discussion with Osman," said Luke.

The meeting was suddenly interrupted by Ismet and Elif entering the room, followed by two large Nubian slaves dragging a young man—Ninian. Elif was angry and blunt. "Not good enough, Luke. If you cannot control your party, the pasha offers his dungeon to contain the malcontent. Lord Fyson tried to break into the women's quarters of the pasha's palace. If he were a Benbali, the Nubian protectors of the women would have decapitated him on the spot. He seems totally unaware of the seriousness of his crime. And there is worse to come."

"In what regard?" asked an apprehensive Luke.

"The boy did not tell Nour that they were siblings. She so enjoyed his company on their adventure together that she has fallen in love with him."

"Have you put an end to that nonsense by clarifying the real situation?" asked Luke.

"No, that must come from Lord Fyson when he puts an end to his relationship with Nour and promises never to see her again. Both Islam and Christianity agree on the depravity of incest."

"Good god, he has not taken the girl's maidenhead?" asked the practical Strad.

"No!"

"What shall we do about the situation?" asked Luke.

"Nour has temporarily been removed from the palace and this residence. She will be safe from Fyson's endeavors for the near future. Confine him to his rooms here, and in a week, I will arrange a meeting between him and Nour where he will explain the situation—and end their relationship. Then you must send him home."

"That's a bit unfair," commented Simon. "You cannot prevent him from ever seeing his long-lost sister again."

"My lord, you must. This is a woman whom I expect will be horrified to discover she is English born and the sister of the man she now loves romantically. The pasha has asked me to remind you all that if this matter cannot be solved to the benefit of Lady Nour, then the English mission will no longer be welcome in Benbali. If it wasn't for me, the pasha would have already taken action against you."

"And what action would that have been?" asked Strad either naively or provocatively.

"Your expulsion from Benbali without any treaty—a departure that could involve aggressive action from the citadel and the fleet. Let's be blunt. Fyson's behavior is jeopardizing your mission. Why a Cromwellian general accepts this behavior, typical of a spoiled aristocrat with royalist affiliations, I cannot fathom." Elif, Ismet, and the Nubians stamped out of the room.

Luke turned to Ninian. "You heard all of that. I have to agree that your personal aspect of this mission has placed the more important matters of state at risk. I am confining you to your apartment within his house and will place guards outside your doors and windows. Miles, have your men watch him day and night.

"I also need a report on your investigation of Jethro's murderer and Chantal's disappearance, but let's leave it until after our visit to Osman. He was quite forthcoming but did not want to talk in front of Elif, whom he correctly saw as very much the eyes and ears of his potential enemy, the pasha."

"Don't give any ground to either party in this developing conflict. Let both sides desperately seek your support, and in the process, you can strike a deal and support the party that offers us the most," advised Miles.

"Can we change the internal power balance in Benbali?" mused Luke.

"Yes, by simply using the firepower of the *Cromwell*. If we side with the pasha, Commander Yusuf, and Admiral Hasan, we bombard the citadel. If we support the dey, you could destroy the whole corsair fleet as they lie locked in the harbor. You could also use your influence to persuade certain key figures to change sides. If they hesitate to comply, you can always threaten them with the might of the complete English Mediterranean fleet," answered John, spoiling to use his naval artillery.

Luke and Miles met Osman on the roof of one of the towers of the citadel that had been converted in part to a garden filled with citrus trees. The officers sat on large cushions, a position from which Luke had a good view of the *Cromwell* and the *Wildfire* riding at anchor in the next bay. Osman placed guards at the door leading onto the roof and had cleared it of everybody else. The commander of the Benbali army and the two English soldiers were alone.

Osman thanked Luke for coming so soon after his arrival back in Benbali and commented, "I could not speak freely in front of Lady Elif. She is close to the pasha, but more importantly, she is a powerful figure in her own right. She seems to be an ally of Hasan, which may or may not be in line with the pasha's wishes."

"Maybe this apparent closeness reflects their English ethnic origin rather than any current alliance," suggested Luke.

"That is a question that you are better placed to answer than myself."

"You control the large contingent of Turkish janissaries that provide the army for Benbali. Are you responsible to the dey or the pasha?"

"I was appointed to command the Benbali forces by the sultan personally, who can—through his representative, the pasha—suspend that authority at any time. However, once appointed, I obey the dey and his council."

18

"If the pasha joins a conspiracy against the dey, he could suspend you from your position and temporarily replace you with a new commander?" Luke asked.

"Yes, but it would be risky. The pasha would have to justify his decisions to Constantinople, and if the sultan was not satisfied, the pasha would lose his life. Murat Pasha is timid. He would not risk that. I control the army and can crush any uprising against the dey. Previous sultans were no fools. They foresaw the possibility of civil war in the North African territories and made sure that other centers of authority did not have coercive power. The pasha does not have a single soldier under his command. All his bodyguards are seconded from the citadel and remain under my control," Osman explained.

"What about Commander Yusuf? He seems to have an effective armed unit."

"He has a large number of lightly armed men capable of enforcing taxation and law and order against the unarmed populace. His men are barely trained and have no access to a range of weapons such as those stored here in the citadel. The talk of armed force is misleading. Any coup against the current dey will not dare use force. They will try to manipulate the laws of the country to achieve their end. The conspirators will coerce council members to vote down the current dey and replace him with another more favorable to their interests."

"And this council is dominated by janissaries who invariably elect one from their number to the position of dey?"

"Yes, and consequently, any change of government depends on the officers of my army."

"Which you claim you can control?"

"Yes, but not as well as I did. As I explained on the ship, half my current contingent of troops has been replaced by new recruits from Anatolia who may be led astray of other figures such as Colonel Ismet."

"In what way do these new troops differ from your veterans?"

"Many of those who have been here some time have married local girls and live in the town. They are part of the local society. They report to duty here as rostered, but many have time to develop lucrative sidelines of their own. They have become more Benbali than Turkish."

Miles interrupted by pointing out to sea. In the distance, at least eight ships appeared on the horizon and were heading toward them. Osman asked, "Is that Admiral Stokes returning to assist you in your negotiations?"

"I have had no notification of such," replied Luke.

"Your sailors are not taking any chances. Both your ships are raising sail. They will not be caught at anchor should the visitors prove hostile," remarked Osman as he sent one of the guards to get a message to Hasan that a potential enemy fleet was approaching.

The Benbalis must have had a secret signal from the citadel to the navy to alert them to such an emergency. Within minutes, the Benbali fleet was also raising sail, and the oared galleys were already exiting the harbor. As the approaching fleet neared, Luke, Miles, and Osman watched through telescopes as it changed formation into two lines of four ships each. "This is trouble. The lead ship has just raised its colors—a white Maltese cross on a bright red background. This is the war fleet of the Christian privateers, the Knights of Malta," announced Osman.

"Surely, they won't attack my ships?" said an alarmed Luke.

Osman disagreed. "I suspect they are after your ship more than ours. The knights see a polarized world—Catholics and the rest. Heretics, such as yourself, are as bad as we infidels and the hated Jew."

"The Benbali fleet and the two English ships are dispersing. They will not provide easy targets. The Maltese must realize they are outnumbered, and if they keep on their present course, they will be encircled. Both the *Cromwell* and Hasan's flagship have circled around their flank and will attack the last ship in each of the enemy's columns," summarized Miles, admiring Ralph Croft's tactics.

The citadel's batteries opened up as did the lead Maltese warship as it turned so that its gun ports confronted the Benbali fortress. Luke noted that the Maltese adopted the traditional but waning approach to naval battles—disable the enemy and get close enough to board. Their decks were cluttered with troops ready for purpose. The Benbalis and the *Cromwell* made this old-fashioned approach impossible. The English blasted the enemy rear guard out of the water, and it and the rest of the Maltese fleet did not have the range to retaliate.

Six hours later, at the discussion involving Ahmed, Osman, Hasan, Luke, Miles, Ralph, and John, it was agreed that the Maltese attack was suicidal once the Benbali fleet and the *Cromwell* and the *Wildfire* were in the open sea and ready to combat it. The Benbali officials heaped great praise on Ralph and John for the systematic way they used their ship's mobility and superior range to mercilessly disable or sink several Maltese ships before their commanders called off the attack.

The Benbali authorities were elated. The dey hoped that this would be the first of many joint naval enterprises between Benbali and England. Luke brought the meeting back to the main issue. He suggested this was the perfect occasion to sign the treaty.

The Benbalis celebrated their victory the next day with the pasha inviting local authorities, citizens, foreign diplomats, and merchants to his palace to eat, drink, and listen to self-congratulatory speeches. The pasha singled out John Neville for his masterly display of naval gunnery and Ralph Croft for his superb tactical maneuvering of the *Cromwell* in the ship's major contribution to the Benbali victory. John was modest in reply, suggesting that it did not require much skill to blast your enemy out of the water if they, through lack of range, could not retaliate.

As the day progressed, Luke was surprised that there was an unlimited supply of wine that the Benbali authorities consumed at a rate equal to the Europeans. Luke asked Elif how this clear breach of Islamic practice that banned the consumption of alcohol could be not only tolerated but aggressively pursued by professing Muslims, especially those in authority.

She replied, "The Turks have always had a tolerant attitude to alcohol. One sultan was nicknamed the Sot because of his overindulgence. The excuse is that the prophet Muhammad banned alcohol for the common people because they would drink to excess. The social elite knew how to drink sensibly and therefore need not comply. It is one of many Turkish customs that alienate the local Arabs, who often see this foreign governing class as second-rate Muslims. Notice who is not drinking wine, and you will uncover the core of a potentially anti-Turkish group among the locals."

Luke was intrigued by Elif's remark and quickly isolated seven or eight guests who stuck to cold mint tea—only two of whom he recognized, Yusuf and the merchant Wasim. The consumption of food and drink escalated after midday.

Midafternoon, Miles drew Luke aside. "Something is amiss. All the senior officials, except the pasha, have disappeared. The dey, General Osman, Admiral Hasan, and Commander Yusuf are no longer here."

Luke's consumption of wine after a fairly long abstention led to a mellow, if not uninterested, response. "Don't stress, Miles, they have a country to run. They were probably only given half a day to celebrate."

Matters appeared more serious when a group of local merchants tried to leave. They returned to the reception room highly agitated. Miles reported to Luke that they had been turned back at the door and told to remain in the palace until further notice.

The situation escalated further a few minutes later when a cohort of janissaries entered the reception room and placed themselves at all exits. A Nubian attendant struck a large gong.

The pasha rose and spoke to the group in Turkish and then Arabic, followed by Elif, who announced in English, "The pasha regrets that you will have to stay here for your own safety. There has been some unrest, but it is being contained."

"Rubbish," whispered Miles. "It's the coup."

Luke nodded in agreement and sought out Elif. He asked, "What is really going on?"

She replied, "There has been an attempted coup. The pasha has only been told by Yusuf that the garrison in the citadel has been mobilized and is on the move and that he was activating his own men to prevent any disorder spreading to the populace. We don't know whether the dey has been replaced or has arrested those who plotted against him."

Luke was irritated. "Elif, don't lie to me. You and Hasan are as thick as thieves in plotting against Ahmed Dey. Has Hasan made his move?" Elif smiled seductively and moved away.

Progressively through the late afternoon, soldiers escorted individual guests from the room. Luke once again approached Elif. "Are the men I have just seen being escorted out of the room going to their execution?"

"We are not barbarians, Luke. The last three men who left are members of the dey's council. I guess they are needed to elect a new dey or confirm the existing one. The victors will need their actions legalized by the pasha. Be patient. You will soon know what has happened."

Then the unexpected occurred. Three well-armed janissaries approached Luke and Miles, indicating that they should accompany them. When Miles tried to remonstrate, he was forcibly restrained by a large Nubian attendant. Luke was intrigued more than worried. "No one will harm the English ambassador," he whispered to Miles.

Miles was not quite sure. "We are completely at their mercy. They could cut our throats and blame it on their opponents." Upon hearing this, Luke was now less confident of their safety.

They were escorted toward the citadel from whence the sound of musket fire and the occasional cannon blast could be heard.

The Englishmen were shown into one of the antechambers of the citadel, where they were greeted by Hasan, who was direct. "General, help us."

"To achieve what? As an ambassador of a foreign power, I cannot get involved in internal politics or, as it appears at the moment, in a coup that is going badly. To put it bluntly, I am obliged to side with the victor—the legitimate government of Benbali."

"We are, or soon will be, that legitimate government," announced Osman, whose presence with Hasan surprised Luke.

"In that case, you do not have a problem. If you have a new dey whose election is validated by the pasha, we will automatically support your new regime."

Hasan explained, "Several hours ago, a group of janissaries led by Colonel Ismet arrested Ahmed Dey and called a meeting of the executive council to elect his replacement. The action was premature, and other elements in the coup were not ready to act. Later, janissaries loyal to Ahmed rescued him from the Ismet clique and have barricaded themselves into the northern wing of the citadel with command of the cannons on the north tower."

"Surely, you can break into the wing controlled by Ahmed as I imagine you have superior forces at your disposal?" commented Miles.

"No. The citadel was built as four separate wings, with each wing controlling the cannons on their tower. To move into another wing once the adjoining doors are closed is almost impossible. We hope to move ships' cannons into the room adjacent to the door and blast it away."

"Why the delay? It seems an obvious approach," agreed Luke.

"The guns on Ahmed's tower can blow my fleet out of the water. They won't do that given that the fleet provides most of their income, but they have already sent a cannonade along the wharf, ensuring that I cannot move anything off my ships. That is where your help is desperately needed."

19

"You want me to bombard the north tower from the safety of the *Cromwell* while you transport cannon to the citadel?"

"That would be perfect, but I know the English envoy would not openly take sides in that manner. Ahmed may eventually win, so you must preserve your neutrality," replied Hasan with a hint of sarcasm. "I simply want to borrow two of your ships' cannons that can be unloaded in the next bay, well beyond the range of the north tower guns, and brought here along an inland road toward which Ahmed's guns cannot be directed."

"Why can't you elect a new dey and have the pasha confirm it, and I could then openly support your activity?" asked Luke.

"The requisite number of council electors is not available. A third of them either willingly joined Ahmed or were captured and taken into the north wing as hostages."

The conversation was interrupted as a cohort of highly armed troops entered the room. Its leader spoke at length to Osman.

Luke was apprehensive. He had always believed that the general was a supporter of Ahmed Dey. Was this a double cross? Were the troops there to arrest Hasan and maybe himself and declare for Ahmed? Was Osman about to pledge his loyalty to Ahmed and bring the coup to a sudden end?

Luke was wrong. After a brief questioning of Hasan by Osman, the admiral addressed Luke. "The general suggests that you allow one or more of your cannons to be stolen. This will protect your neutrality if Ahmed wins."

"No, I cannot involve the English government in your activities, whatever my personal views may be. Can I speak to Ismet?"

Osman replied, "He is a prisoner."

"Ahmed captured him!"

"No, he is *our* prisoner."

"But he began the coup on your behalf. He is your candidate to be the next dey."

"Quite true," responded Hasan.

"Then why imprison him?"

"This coup is led by Ismet. From the moment its outcome swung into the balance, both Osman and I decided to reduce our involvement. The troops attacking the door into the north wing have orders to refer to the officer in charge as Ismet. Should Ahmed prevail, we can assure him that we took steps to rescue him and had immediately incarcerated Ismet. Like you, Luke, we must not be seen taking sides—until the winner is clear."

"Without the ship's cannon, what are you going to do regarding the defensive door to the north wing?" asked Miles.

"We will lay down explosives that should shatter it. Unfortunately, on the other side is a narrow corridor that is easy to defend. We will lose many men advancing along it. That is where the cannon would have been excellent. A constant cannonade along the passage would have seriously disrupted the defenders. The corridor is too long to hurl grenades. Mortars may help, but the walls are solid stone feet thick," answered Osman.

Another soldier entered the room and spoke to Osman, who briefed Hasan. Hasan, with an evil smile, informed Luke, "England is getting involved after all. The English consul wishes to talk to us." Luke immediately made it clear that he would veto any action of the consul implicating England in the overthrow of Ahmed Dey.

Ambrose entered the room, and before he could speak, Luke directed his anger toward him. "Consul, you will, in no way, involve England in this conspiracy. You are part of Ahmed Dey's profitable network and have worked with him for years to your mutual advantage. Frankly, I do not trust you. Why betray your partner of a decade now?"

Ambrose was not troubled by this verbal onslaught. Full of his own importance, he responded, "Gentlemen, you are military men. You do not understand the merchant's mind. Trade and moneymaking have no loyalties. My current assessment is that with the army under General Osman and the navy headed by Admiral Hasan, united against Ahmed, he cannot retain power. It is in my interests to protect my investments and the financial interests of Benbali. Ambassador, do not panic. My assistance only involves providing information that might improve the coup's chances of success." He continued. "Before I help, I want an undertaking that all my agreements with the current dey will be maintained, if he is replaced."

"How can information help us dislodge Ahmed from the north wing?" asked a skeptical Hasan.

"It will not only enable you to dislodge Ahmed. It can be done with little damage to the citadel or loss of life. Both are detrimental to trade. Ahmed, in desperation, could still turn his cannons on the city and the fleet. He must not be pushed into a corner. Offer him safe conduct to Algiers if he surrenders."

"What's your information?" asked an impatient Hasan.

"Not before you and General Osman sign this document guaranteeing my privileges. It is in English and Turkish."

Osman showed his displeasure and clearly wanted Ambrose to reveal the information before he placed his incriminating signature on the document. A compromise was reached. Both Benbalis signed the document but gave it to Luke for safekeeping until they could assess the value of Ambrose's information.

Luke was delighted. He now had in his possession a document he could use against Ambrose whichever way the coup went. Luke turned to him and asked, "So what is the vital information you have that will ensure victory over your longtime partner?"

"This citadel is built over both an original Roman fort and a medieval Norman castle. Parts of the older buildings remain. Some are in use. Others have been sealed off for centuries. You can enter the north wing without going through the thick obstructive door and then being forced into a narrow corridor where the defenders could cut you down."

"How?" asked Hasan, who had translated Ambrose's remarks for Osman.

"You come up from a floor beneath where the Norman dungeons are located. Few know that this level even exists."

"And how do we enter this subterranean level?" queried Luke.

"Through the old Roman drain that empties into the sea. In recent times, it has been used by persons secretly visiting the dey and bringing him goods that he concealed from the public."

"Such as yourself?" remarked Luke unnecessarily. His disdain for Ambrose continued with his abrupt dismissal of the informant. "Thanks for your assistance. Wait in the antechamber as we assess your information."

Ambrose hesitated, incandescent with rage at Luke's attitude. He finally succumbed to Luke's stare and left the room.

Hasan, surprised at Luke's attitude, asked, "Why banish your own consul?"

"I don't trust him. Given your training and culture, you and the general will personally lead the assault through the sewers. It's a perfect ambush. Both of you will be caught in this subterranean chamber and massacred. I can see your heads displayed on the north tower to show your supporters that the conspiracy had failed. They would instantly surrender."

Hasan admitted that Luke could be right and asked what they should do.

"Keep your powder dry and your bodies safe. Release Ismet from his confinement. Allow him to lead your men into the sewers. If it is a trap, Ismet and a few of his men are collateral damage—and you live to continue the assault or begin negotiations with Ahmed. And Ambrose's double-dealing is revealed."

"What do we do with Ambrose during this critical period?" asked Hasan.

"Leave that to me," replied Luke. "Plan your attack while Miles and I interrogate Ambrose in the next room." Luke was determined to put pressure on Ambrose through a series of lies and half-truths.

Seated across a small table from his consul, the English ambassador feigned anger. "Ambrose, you have seriously embarrassed England and myself by openly supporting this coup and to no advantage for yourself. Osman and Hasan doubt your loyalty to them, believing you remain Ahmed Dey's strongest ally. They suspect that what you suggested is a trap and were on the point of arresting you until I intervened on your behalf."

"It is no trap. I will prove it. I will accompany Osman and Hasan into the drain. That should confirm my loyalty. They must move as soon as low tide is reached. The entrance is underwater at other times."

Luke and Miles headed for the door, and out of hearing of the consul, Luke said, "Let Ambrose think Osman and Hasan will lead the assault. Upon reaching the entrance to the sewers, Osman and Hasan will withdraw and leave a surprised Ambrose with Colonel Ismet and his men."

Miles commented, "Luke, you can turn this situation to your advantage. You can prove your neutrality and play a major role in determining the outcome of the coup."

"How?"

"You and I could join Ismet's group, and when the time is right, announce yourself as a mediator between the factions."

Luke pondered Miles's suggestion for some time and eventually replied, "Yes, you and Strad will accompany me. At this point, I will not inform Osman and Hasan that I will try to negotiate a compromise. They will see us joining Ismet as a commitment to their side. Let them think that for the time being."

That evening as the sun set and the tide was at its lowest, Ambrose led Colonel Ismet and a cohort of janissaries, accompanied by three Arabs who remained in the shadows, to the sewer outlet. Ambrose was surprised that Hasan and Osman were nowhere to be seen.

Once through the seaward grate, the sewer was large enough for the men to progress without having to bend or crouch. A little way along the sewer, Ambrose began to moan and groan and eventually called out in Turkish to Ismet, "I have to go back. I cannot stand the darkness and the confined space."

Ismet consulted with two of the Arabs and ordered one of his men to escort the trembling Ambrose back to the entrance. The taller Arab, Luke in disguise, commented to his similarly dressed companion, Miles, "We will soon know whether that was an act to get out of here before Ahmed springs his trap or the man has a genuine fear of confinement."

Eventually, the group reached a grille that opened easily into a large, cavernous chamber. It was a room that had recently been used as the walls contained tapers, which Ismet's men lit with their own. Given the markings on the floor, boxes and bags of goods had been stored there until very recently. Spillage of various cereals and vegetables suggested that the dey had plenty of food to withstand a siege.

A surprisingly wide staircase led upward to a solid-looking trapdoor. Attempts to open it failed. Ambrose had not told them that exiting the cavernous cellar depended on someone above either opening or at least unlocking the door. "What's the point? Why did Ambrose lead us here if nothing could be achieved?" asked Miles.

Luke muttered, "It's a trap."

"Rubbish, we can retreat back down the sewer at any time," answered Miles. Ismet suggested that they wait while he sent a man back down the sewer and return with more men and enough explosives to blast open the trapdoor.

One of the janissaries lifted the grate and reentered the exit sewers. This action, or some remote control, triggered a sudden and devastating development. A massive stone block rolled out from the wall, completely covering the grate. Retreat was impossible. They were trapped.

20

Miles was optimistic. "What can Ahmed hope to achieve? Killing a few janissaries doesn't help his cause. Osman and Hasan will be able to blast their way into here before we die of starvation."

"Remember, Ahmed probably thinks Hasan and Osman are here, and he has no inkling that there are three Englishmen present. I will go to the top of the stairs and shout this out, demanding an opportunity to negotiate," suggested Luke.

"Don't waste any time. Look up!" shouted Strad. Part of the roof had been rolled back, and through the gap, ceramic containers were thrown into the cellar. They immediately shattered bursting into flames.

"My god!" exclaimed Miles. "It is Greek fire—a mixture of resin, pitch, sulfur, and naphtha and, by the smell, other ingredients to create a toxic gas. We will either be burned alive or suffocate with the gas. Do not let any of the fiery liquid touch you!"

"If the men climb the pediments at the base of the columns, they will be safe for a time," advised the pragmatic Strad.

"Not for long," replied Miles. "The heat will become overwhelming. Luke, get up those stairs and start talking."

Luke and Miles climbed the stairs, and Miles shouted in Turkish a simple message. "Osman and Hasan are not here. The English ambassador is and wishes to talk with Ahmed Dey."

In response, the Greek fire was thrown in the direction of the speaker. It missed. The burning mixture increased the temperature tremendously and produced a choking gas that already had a few soldiers fighting for breath. Ismet instructed his men to cover their faces. Most unwound their turbans to achieve this.

After ten minutes, which seemed a lot longer to the imprisoned Englishmen, a voice in Turkish echoed from above the chamber saying that the trapdoor would be opened to allow the English ambassador and his interpreter to talk to the dey. Should any others attempt to climb the stairs, the chamber would be instantly ignited. In addition, a representative of the dey would enter the cellar to inspect the group to validate Miles's claim that the suspected leaders of the attempted coup were not present.

Luke and Miles followed the dey's officer until they entered a room that was familiar to them. It was the room in which the treaty between England and Benbali had been signed. The dey received the Englishmen with typical hospitality in terms of food and drink and then remarked, "I am surprised to find the ambassador in the company of rebels."

Luke was quick to explain. "Your Excellency, I am not taking sides in this internal dispute. I have come, against Osman and Hasan's wishes, to seek to mediate. It is not in England's interest to have our new ally torn apart by internal insurrection. You can only win by blasting Hasan's fleet out of the water, which would destroy your main source of income and our major partner at sea. Hasan and Osman can only win by dislodging you from this citadel, which will largely be destroyed in the process, rendering the city defenseless against a seaborne attack, which the Christian corsairs from Malta have just attempted and who no doubt will try again."

"What is your real purpose in coming here?" asked the skeptical dey.

"There is no hidden agenda. I have completed my mission by signing the treaty with you, and as soon as I have reformed the English community and settled on my country's representation here, I will depart. It is in England's interests to keep you in power as your opponents, especially Hasan, want further concessions from us in the form of advanced naval developments in ship design and cannon manufacture."

"Since your arrival here, I was reliably informed that you supported Hasan against me," commented a suspicious dey.

"Not incorrect, Your Excellency. I was certainly opposed to what your opponents pointed out as the exorbitant costs of trade here because of what they claimed was a corrupt network of officials headed by yourself and some foreign merchants. That picture of the situation has not been proved and, if true, may be due to the merchants involved, rather than the local officials—and there is no guarantee that your replacements would be any more honest."

"Why did you suspect the opportunity presented to you by Sir Ambrose to attack me through the sewers was a trick?"

"Ambrose and you are part of a well-established network and the closest of allies. I just did not believe him," replied Luke.

"Ambrose is your problem, and part of any mediation will be my insistence that Ambrose leaves Benbali. He told you the truth. He betrayed me, but fortunately, his plan to tell Hasan and Osman of the sewer entrance was revealed to me before we retreated into the north wing."

"Why has Ambrose turned against you?"

"As an unscrupulous merchant, he believed he could gain more concessions from Osman and Hasan than he had from me."

"Even for a man obsessed with money, he is taking a major risk. As it has played out, neither side has a clear advantage. A more cautious man would have waited until a result was known," Luke commented.

"For the moment, I remain the dey. A majority of the executive council who elect the dey are with me in this wing."

"Kidnapped?"

"No, they stand willingly with me as the duly elected executive officer of Benbali. If the forces of Hasan and Osman entered this wing, they would kill several of the council to make way for their nominees. At present, I cannot legally be replaced."

Luke and Miles eventually completed their negotiations with Ahmed Dey, who meticulously outlined his requirements for an immediate end of hostilities. As the Englishmen were about to leave to take his proposals to Osman and Hasan, Ahmed said, "Gentlemen, I have a surprise for you. Follow me."

They entered an adjoining room and were indeed astonished. Sitting at a window bench was Chantal Chatwood. Luke finally found his voice and asked, "Mistress Chatwood, what are you doing here?"

"With the murder of Jethro, I sought the protection of my old friend Ahmed."

"Protection from whom?"

"Lord Peregrine Morton."

"I recall the name, the monster of Scarfe Abbey, a royalist psychopath who, having taken the surrender of Sir Everton Scarfe, massacred the whole household—men, women, and children— and then burned the abbey to the ground. I thought he had been executed in the Tower of London a decade or more ago."

"If only that were true. Let me explain. I am not Chantal Chatwood. I am Lady Elizabeth Scarfe, the youngest and only surviving child of Sir Everton. At the time of Morton's assault, I had been taken, as a six-year-old, by my governess to visit her relatives. As a result of the arson, it was assumed, given that the bodies were burned beyond recognition, that the whole family had been killed. On a recent visit to England, I saw my own memorial stone."

"What happened to you?"

"My governess took me to a distant cousin of hers, William Chatwood, a merchant who was about to leave for Constantinople as an associate of the English ambassador Sir William Bendish. I was later brought up by the Chatwoods in that city and became fluent in both Turkish and Arabic."

"Is that where you met Ahmed?"

"Yes, about sixteen years ago as a newly graduated janissary. He was assigned to the bodyguard of the English ambassador. He became very close to my governess over a period of several years."

Luke then asked, "Why seek Morton in Benbali?"

"Morton committed further atrocities and was disowned by the king and handed over to the London authorities. He was found guilty of mass murder and condemned to be hanged, drawn, and quartered as if he were a commoner. On the eve of his execution, he escaped from the tower, apparently aided by his brother, and disappeared. For some years, with the aid of the son of my adoptive parents, Jethro Chatwood, we sought news of the killer. Eventually, pieces of evidence came together to suggest that he had escaped to Livorno and was posing as an English merchant. More recently, an agent in Livorno was convinced that one of three or four merchants who moved to the North African coast was Morton."

"So you and your friend Jethro came here to look for him? Have you had any success?"

"Not until a couple of days before Jethro's murder. He returned from the souk highly excited. He had discovered a ring that he said was typical of that worn by English aristocrats and gentry to indicate their position as the current holder of the family estates and titles. It was usually handed down from father to son."

"Was it a missing Scarfe ring that might prove Morton had been in Benbali?"

"Unfortunately, I did not recognize it. But I was only a child when the family jewels were looted. It could easily have been part of the collection, but it did not depict Scarfe heraldry. Jethro thought if we could identify the family to which it belonged, it might lead us to Morton. He was going to ask your aristocratic companions, the lords Fyson and Stokey, if they recognized the design. He had already asked around the English quarters without success. That was his mistake. Then on the night of your welcoming banquet, he became quite obsessed, almost unhinged. Patience Applegarth was wearing a pendant that depicted the same design as the ring. He could hardly contain his interest, which probably alerted Morton. That is why Jethro was killed. He was getting too close. I immediately put myself under the protection of Ahmed."

"You should have come to me."

"Forgive me, but I was not sure where you stood. You could have been a knowing accomplice of Morton and implicated in the murder of Jethro."

"If you have such doubts, why are you speaking to me now?"

"The Benbali authorities, on your appointment as English ambassador, have sought information about your past. In recent days, Ahmed received a detailed summary of your past activities—a longtime confidant of Cromwell and his head of military intelligence who has spent a lifetime combating Royalists."

"Once, that was easy. If you were a Royalist, you were an enemy of Cromwell and the army. Now Cromwell is welcoming many Royalists into his administration. It makes my role much harder. Can you tell me anything about the night Jethro was murdered?"

"An Arab from the souk brought a message that if Jethro met a third party at the rear of the Goodrich warehouse, he would discover the identity of Morton. We agreed that I was to stay at home and, if anything happened to Jethro, to come straight to Ahmed for protection, until your credentials could be verified."

"Why did you and Jethro spend so much time in the souk dealing with Arab traders?"

"Two reasons, one I have already alluded to. First, Scarfe Abbey was looted by Morton before he murdered the inhabitants and burned down the house. If Jethro and I could find any of my family possessions in Benbali, it would prove that he was probably here. The ring may yet do this. Second, decades-old rumors indicated that Peregrine, Lord Morton, had a physical scar, abnormality, or disability that his friends thought may have contributed to his vicious personality. The English merchants, in their dealings with the Arabs, are more relaxed, and we hoped that Morton may have revealed some peculiarity to these men."

"Which of the English community do you suspect?"

"There is not much of a choice—Ambrose Denton, Gregory Applegarth, James Goodrich, Rowland May, and Silas Sweetlace. At the moment, I do not have a prime suspect."

"What do you intend to do now?" asked Luke.

"If you are successful in bringing an end to this attempted coup and Ahmed is restored to power, I will stay here. If Ahmed is removed, I will seek your protection until Morton is uncovered, although Ahmed suggests that I place myself under the direct protection of the pasha, given my strong links with Constantinople."

When Luke and Miles emerged from the north tower unharmed, followed by Strad, Ismet, and his men, Hasan and Osman momentarily believed they had won. They were furious when Luke announced that he had negotiated an agreement with Ahmed, which they were to consider. They were incandescent when they realized that, by its terms, Ahmed would remain as dey. Hasan moved to arrest Luke.

21

Cooler heads prevailed, and over the next few days, Luke successfully negotiated with a reluctant Osman and a decidedly unhappy Hasan. His trump card was that, as both sides were evenly matched, any prolonged conflict would destroy much of the infrastructure and economy of Benbali, with a resultant drop in all their incomes. His supporting argument was the *Cromwell*.

As Ahmed continued to have the support of the majority of the council, he was the legitimate ruler, which any foreign ambassador would be obliged to support. "In that support, I could blow most of the Benbali fleet out of the water, destroying your major source of income in prizes and slaves," Luke threatened as a recalcitrant Hasan continued to argue.

Luke lied, claiming that Admiral Stokes was due back at any time and that the English Mediterranean fleet had the capacity to raze Benbali to the ground.

The agreement required the pasha to validate the reelection of Ahmed as dey and the reappointment of Osman to control the army and Hasan the navy. The navy was to leave the Benbali harbor as soon as possible in search of prizes. The rebellious janissaries were redistributed among their loyalist comrades, and the most outspoken were sent to man frontier posts on the Moroccan and Algerian borders.

Colonel Ismet would be held entirely responsible for the uprising and be sent to Constantinople and face the justice of the sultan himself.

Miles protested about this treatment of Ismet. "He was Osman and Hasan's candidate. They go on as usual, and he is sent to certain death. Even you, at one stage, were happy to see him as the new dey, and he has been a very friendly and efficient commander of your bodyguard."

"He does not go to certain death. He is the sultan's man. He will probably be promoted."

"There is no mention of Ambrose in the proposed agreement," noted Miles.

"Ahmed wants me to expel him immediately. I let Osman and Hasan believe Ambrose had deliberately led Ismet into a trap so they will not trust him. Neither side will now support Ambrose. His actual punishment has been left to me with the clear stipulation that he would not, in any circumstances, be acceptable any longer as the English consul."

"So what are you going to do with him?" asked Miles, feeling some sympathy for the embattled consul.

"Come with me, and you shall see," Luke replied.

Luke and Miles were received by a nervous Ambrose, who was immediately on the defensive. "Ambassador, I did not lead you into the ambush. I am delighted that you survived, but I am surprised that you threw your weight behind Ahmed Dey and supported his reelection."

"I supported neither side as is the custom when confronted by internal conflict. When the matter is resolved and there is legitimate government, I am bound to support it. I mediated a successful compromise that will enable Benbali to continue to prosper."

"What happens to me? Do you have the agreement I made with Osman and Hasan?"

"No. At their request, I destroyed it. They are in no position to carry out its terms. Ambrose, you have cut your own throat as a merchant in this city. Ahmed has revoked all your privileges, special agreements, and concessions. He has asked me to expel you immediately and declares you any longer acceptable as English consul."

"Are you about to expel me?"

"Not yet. Your dealings as a private person in Benbali are up to you. You are astute enough to rebuild bridges, which may eventually regain the dey's trust—if that is what you desire. You must act quickly in that regard because, with my departure, he will expel you—or worse. As you are no longer acceptable to the government of Benbali as English consul, I must replace you in that position immediately."

"Given the situation, I prefer to return to Italy now, until everything calms down."

"No, I can't allow that until we have solved the murder of Jethro Chatwood."

"And finding his sister, the delightful Chantal."

"Chantal has been found and is safe." Ambrose seemed surprised but did not pursue the issue.

Luke finally returned to his residence, where Elif welcomed him. "The pasha extends his congratulations on your diplomacy. He was surprised by your actions but amazed that you managed to get Ahmed, Hasan, and Osman to agree. I am surprised because, when we last talked, you seemed decidedly to favor Hasan's move on the dey and the elevation of my friend Ismet in his place."

"Simple politics. Don't interfere unless the victory of one side is clearly in England's interests. Originally, the rebels were in this category and certain of victory. Then Ahmed signed a treaty that is very favorable to England, and the rebels lacked the power to overthrow him. A prolonged conflict was in no one's interests."

"You have certainly passed your first test as ambassador with flying colors," purred Elif.

"Now I must revert to my previous life and solve Jethro Chatwood's murder," Luke announced.

"The pasha tells me that Ahmed Dey has been protecting his sister, who is an English gentlewoman with close connections to the sultan's court."

"Until I reform the English community and solve the murder, she is safer in the citadel than in the English commercial quarters."

"During your absence, the Dutch chaplain came to see you twice. He told me that he had information that might assist you in the murder investigation. I said you would visit him as soon as you returned—but not before I remove all that tension that recent events have had on your body. Come to bed."

Eventually, after a massage that both calmed and excited, Luke fell into a deep sleep. Elif rose from the bed and moved to a low table where she had left some of her belongings when she disrobed. She picked up her ornamental bejeweled dagger. She ran her finger gently along the blade and returned to the bedside.

She hovered above the sleeping Luke, dagger in hand, and pondered the suggestion of a friend that this man was too dangerous and should be eliminated. After all, he had betrayed her friends Hasan and Ismet. The English ambassador was a traitor to the cause of reform.

Elif smiled to herself, replaced the dagger on the table, and climbed back into bed, nestling up to the sleeping Luke and showering him in kisses.

When Luke awoke, Elif had long gone. The pasha had sent for her just after dawn.

It was midmorning when Luke made his way to the Dutch chaplain, his friend and former comrade, Jan Claasen. As they ate heavily spiced Dutch cakes and drank sugared black coffee, to which Luke was becoming addicted, Jan explained, "We are directly across the river from the Denton warehouse. From this rooftop garden, I have an uninterrupted view along the opposite bank of the river of the English commercial waterfront."

"From where your Dutch merchants can spy on their English rivals," teased Luke. "So what did you see on the night of the murder?" Luke continued, anticipating Jan's information.

"Unusual activity."

"What do you mean?"

"The English on the whole are a lazy race. I have never seen any activity after dark anywhere along the English side of the river other than at the Goodrich factory—except for the night of the murder. Just after dark, a couple of barges came upriver heavily loaded with goods, which were unloaded and carried into Denton's warehouse, which was exceedingly well lit."

"Nothing so far that helps," complained an overeager Luke.

"You were always impatient. When the unloading had been completed, one of the barges with most of the men involved moved back downriver. All the lights in the warehouse except one were extinguished. Half an hour later, the door of the warehouse opened, and two persons carried a heavy bundle to the remaining barge and, without showing any lights, immediately poled downriver. A few minutes later, I heard a loud splash."

"Why didn't you tell me sooner?"

"I thought you knew where the body was when you began dragging the river close to where the body was thrown."

"Who in Benbali has barges of the type you saw?"

"Almost everybody involved in local transport. Most goods from the ships are loaded into the barges and moved around the harbor and upriver. It is cheaper and quicker than unloading onto the wharf and then finding costly land transport to move them to a destination."

"Do the English merchants own their own barges?"

"No, there is a fraternity of competing Arab barge owners who are former or current sailors or fishermen."

"Thanks, Jan. That does give me a point to restart my investigation. Whoever was manning the second barge disposed of Chatwood's body. I will work back from there."

"Luke, there is no hurry. Settle back and enjoy the cinnamon cakes. I have even more pertinent information."

"What is it?" uttered an exasperated Luke.

"An hour earlier to the events I have just described, I saw a man stagger out of the Goodrich warehouse, walk unsteadily along the waterfront, and then enter Denton's establishment."

"Did you recognize him?"

"No, but by his attire, he was European."

"The staggering—was he drunk?"

"Drunk or injured, I could not tell."

Ambrose was not happy to see Luke return. "How can I help now?" he asked coldly.

"The night of Jethro Chatwood's murder—did you receive an unexpected delivery of goods?"

"Not unexpected, but the delivery was inexplicably late."

"Why inexplicably?"

"The delivery was of long-promised nonperishable goods from one of our ships that its captain had failed to sell directly. He had all day to send them to me yet left it until after dusk, much to the annoyance of the bargemen, who did not stop complaining."

"Apart from the lateness of the delivery, was there anything else unusual about that delivery?"

Ambrose thought for a while and commented, "I was surprised that the goods were spread over two barges. They would have fitted easily onto one. I made it clear I would not be paying double and that they would have to share the return for one barge load of goods. They were not happy. I suggested they take it up with the corsair captain, who had recklessly ordered two barges when one would have sufficed."

"Did the barges return downriver together?"

"No, I was just closing my warehouse doors when I noticed one barge well down the river and surprisingly containing most of the crew of both barges."

"Did you see the second barge depart?"

"No, why do you ask?"

"I have a witness who saw the two men on this second barge throw over what was probably Chatwood's body. Can you get me the names of any of the bargemen involved in the deliveries to you that night?"

"Yes, the head bargeman on one of the vessels is named Ali. He has been in that role ever since I have been in Benbali."

Luke, accompanied by Miles as interpreter, made his way around the harbor foreshore to where several barges were unloading goods. Ali seemed delighted by whatever Miles said to him but became a little unhappier as the discussion progressed. Miles explained to Luke the bargeman's darkening mood. "He remembers the night in question quite well. He claimed he was cheated of half his fee. He thought that we, being English, had come to pay what he believed he was owed."

22

"Ask him to explain further," said Luke.

The bargeman was very happy to oblige. "The night in question, we took the goods from the *Star of Benbali* to the warehouse of the English consul. I was surprised that only part of the anticipated cargo was loaded on my barge, and I was further astonished when a second barge followed us upriver with the rest of the cargo. A man leading that barge, Kareem, said we had only collected half the load. The English consul refused to pay for two barges when he had only ordered one and advised me to seek redress from the master of the *Star of Benbali*. When I approached the captain the next day, he was completely nonplussed. He had not authorized a second barge and had thought that we had taken all the goods. One of his men claimed that the second barge had been loaded with some of the goods at the same time as mine from the other side of the ship."

"What do you know about this second barge after you had unloaded the goods at the English warehouse?"

"The unloading was done from both barges by men I knew. Kareem, the head bargeman on the second boat, and one companion never left their barge to help with the unloading. When the task was finished, he ordered his men to return to the harbor aboard our barge. As we drifted with the tide back downriver, the second barge remained moored to the Englishman's dock. The next morning, it was back at its rightful moorings, but its owner was furious. He blamed me for illegally using it after dark. He had not given Kareem permission to use it."

Luke was delighted with Ali's evidence and indicated that if the bargeman came with him now, he would be recompensed for his losses. He would be a useful source of information and a potential ally.

Luke had no sooner ushered Ali out of his house when a distraught Elif sought his immediate attention. "What is wrong, my lady?" asked a concerned Luke.

"Nour has disappeared again," she explained as tears ran down her face.

"I thought she had been taken to a safe place until her obsession with young Ninian had moderated," commented Luke.

"She was taken to the residence of a former member of the pasha's household located in the mountains to the south of the city. She was accompanied by two of His Excellency's janissaries. Some time yesterday, she disappeared from the grounds of that residence. An extensive search has failed to find her."

"Was she ever told that her desires were misplaced and that the object of her affection was her brother?"

"No, I thought that to suddenly confront her with such news might lead her into some act of folly—maybe self-harm."

"Has she tried to reach Ninian here?" asked Luke.

"I don't know, but she has not succeeded. Ninian remains confined to his apartment, and your guard says he has had no visitors. A thorough search of this area has failed to find any trace of her."

"I will talk to Ninian. He may have an inkling of where she might have gone."

"Keep him confined. The pasha does not want him complicating the situation any further."

After a difficult confrontation with Ninian, who initially refused to speak, Luke retired for the evening without the comfort of Elif, who continued to monitor the search for Nour from the pasha's palace. He was awakened early the next morning by Miles.

"We have an unexpected visitor who wishes to see Lord Fyson urgently."

"Nour?" asked Luke hopefully.

"No, it is her adoptive father, the merchant Wasim."

"Show him into the reception room. We will talk to him—before he sees Ninian."

Wasim was surprised that he was confronting the English ambassador. He explained, "I have come to see the infidel who has ruined the life of my daughter and humiliated me in the eyes of the pasha. Why has he not come to see me and attempted to put right the situation?"

Luke apologized for Ninian's behavior, explaining that his pursuit of Nour was not a romantic frenzy or obsessive lust but stemming from brotherly love. Miles summarized the attack on Fyson Abbey and the kidnapping of Nanny Squibbs and the toddler Anne, and he explained that the presence of Ninian on this mission was simply to find his sister and negotiate her return to England.

Wasim listened intently and gave Luke and Miles a detailed and convincing reply. Both men were astonished yet pleased with what they heard. It solved several problems. Luke thanked Wasim and asked him to repeat what he had just said in the presence of Ninian.

Ninian entered the room. Luke informed him that Wasim had come to talk to him about Nour. "What he is about to tell you will both sadden and please you."

Wasim began quietly but pertinently, "Nour is not your sister, my lord."

"How can that be?" interrupted Ninian, whose distress was immediately evident. Luke hoped he would not pass out.

Wasim continued gently. "I went to the Benbali market one morning after three of our ships had returned with prizes and captives. I bought two separate lots of slaves from two different ships at different times of the day. The first was a young Italian girl whose parents had been killed by the corsairs during their boarding raid. I bought this orphan as my wife had had difficulties becoming pregnant. It was my intention from the start that should she prove a loving child, I would free her from slavery and adopt her as our legal daughter. Later that day, an English nanny was auctioned. Given my wife's ill health, I purchased her to look after the girl we called Nour."

"What happened to the toddler who was captured with Nanny Squibbs?" asked a partly relieved Ninian.

"Years later, when Nanny Squibbs learned enough Arabic to communicate with us, she explained that the toddler did not survive a day after her capture and had been tossed overboard. I am sorry to give you such sad news." Simon, who had joined the group, placed his arms around Ninian, who now sobbed openly at the news of his sister's demise.

Luke thanked Wasim for his information and then ordered Miles to offer the services of the English troops to Yusuf and the pasha in their search for Nour. Wasim shook his head in opposition to such a move. "There is no need. Nour is safe. She is at home under my protection. I would like the young lord to accompany me, and with Nour, the three of us will seek the pasha's forgiveness. You may not realize it, but Nour and I could face death for what she has done."

"The pasha is already aware that Ninian's motives were that of a brother trying to rescue one whom he thought was his sister. I will let Elif know that the three of you wish to see the pasha and explain the situation in full."

Simon, still obsessed with finding the golden Madonna, could not resist a final question. "Did Nanny Squibbs ever mention a golden Madonna?"

"No, but it may have been the treasure she mentioned that would make her last days in England very comfortable."

"What exactly did she say?" probed an excited Simon.

"When I suggested that she not return to England as most of her family and friends were dead and she may be left in poverty, she laughed. She replied that I need not fear for her future because she alone knew the resting place of a great treasure."

"The cunning old woman," muttered Ninian. "Father often hid things in the nursery. As it was only visited by the nanny, there was little chance of something being found. He probably hid the Madonna in the crib before the corsairs attacked. Squibbs found it there and threw it overboard."

"She must have done so before the corsair ship left the Tamar estuary. If it were tossed out into the open sea, she would have no way of knowing where it was," said Miles.

"The Tamar is navigable right up to the jetty of Fyson Abbey. Simon, you should return to England at once and start the search of the river from its mouth to the abbey," suggested Ninian.

Luke threw up his arms in mock distress. "My first mission as ambassador has brought mixed blessings. There is no sister to be rescued, and the Madonna probably never left English waters. At least I have negotiated a favorable treaty but still have unfinished business—solving the murder of Jethro, uncovering the identity of Lord Peregrine Morton, and leaving the English community in better shape than when I arrived. Ninian, go with Wasim. Simon, you may wish to consider the suggestion of an immediate return to England, although it may be too late. Nanny Squibbs has probably already alerted an array of treasure hunters to scour the river."

Five days later, Simon left Benbali on a Genoese merchantman bound for Livorno. It was escorted part of the way, much to the amazement of its Italian captain, by a corsair fleet of five.

Hasan was complying reluctantly with one of the conditions of the ceasefire that brought the attempted coup to an end—set to sea immediately and capture prizes and slaves. Everybody knew that this was not only to bolster the faltering Benbali economy but also to remove Hasan from the scene while the political situation stabilized.

Simon, emphasizing that there was no sister in Benbali for Ninian to rescue, pleaded with the young peer to return to England with him. Ninian's decision to stay was undoubtedly influenced by the very lenient decision of the pasha regarding his exploits with Nour. Nour was expelled from the pasha's household and returned to her father. Wasim was not punished and not required to return the pasha's gift to him on the original transfer of Nour to the pasha's household. The pasha surprisingly thanked Ninian for the way he had looked after Nour during their adventures and hinted that now that she was no longer his property and not Ninian's sister, the two youngsters would probably see a lot more of each other.

Simon had almost finished his negotiations with Father Battista regarding the freeing of English slaves, and Luke assigned Ninian to complete the necessary paperwork. Luke also gave the departing Simon a long list of requests. He was to ask Cromwell to send Luke's former military intelligence unit to Cornwall to assist him in the search for the Madonna and, most urgently, that Thurloe's agents be directed to uncovering all that they could on the background of the members of the English community in Benbali and on Peregrine Morton.

The treaty signed by Luke with the dey of Benbali was entrusted to Simon to deliver to the Lord Protector personally, as well as a very intimate letter to Lady Matilda Lynne, the woman Luke planned to marry after the completion of this assignment. A draft of his proposals for the reform of the Benbali English community with possible options were listed for the benefit of Cromwell's leading minister, John Thurloe, although Luke had no intention of waiting for approval before he implemented them. As the *Santa Magdalena* left the Benbali harbor, the guns of the *Cromwell* and of the citadel gave Simon, Lord Stokey, a deafening salute.

Later that day, Luke was delighted to receive an invitation from Ahmed Dey to attend dinner that evening in the citadel with Elizabeth Scarfe and himself. As the sun set, Luke and Strad, as his bodyguard, began their walk across town.

23

❦

As they passed the area of the shoreline where the barges were docked, the bargeman Ali, whom Luke had compensated for his losses, ran along the harbor front and spoke quickly and excitedly to the Englishmen. Both parties realized that, without interpreters, neither could understand each other. With gestures, Luke established that he would return in the morning with Miles to discover what the bargeman had wanted to report.

Before they parted, Ali placed a sizable metal object into Luke's hand. "What is it?" asked Strad.

"It looks like a seal with an extra long handle. He will no doubt explain its importance in the morning."

Luke, Ahmed Dey, and Lady Elizabeth dined together at one table well separated from several others, which seated Ahmed's senior staff and Strad. Ahmed Dey was not hesitant in front of Elizabeth to resurrect the smattering of English he had picked up years ago in Constantinople. This relieved her of the onerous task of translating what each of the men said.

Ahmed probed Luke about his immediate intentions. The dey was pleased that the matter involving Lord Fyson and the pasha's lady Nour had been settled amicably, that Lord Stokey was returning to England to pursue his search for the golden Madonna, and that the first flotilla of Benbali ships had left port to cruise the Tyrrhenian Sea to harass Italian, Spanish, and French shipping. A second flotilla would sail for the Straits of Gibraltar in a few days to prey on Spanish treasure ships from the Caribbean. Portuguese merchantmen from the East Indies, by dint of Luke's intervention, were not to be attacked.

Luke emphasized that keeping to that provision would be a test of the Benbali resolve to implement the treaty. He continued. "How many Benbali ships will remain to defend the city?"

"Two of ours and two of yours, but the citadel alone can keep most enemy vessels well offshore.

"Are you hinting that I stay here until one of your fleets return?"

Ahmed smiled. "Are you not committed to stay until you solve Jethro's murder?"

"Yes, and until I reform the English community and appoint a consul. While coming here, I was approached by a bargeman who thrust this metal object into my hands. Do either of you know what it is?"

Elizabeth sighed, and a tear ran down her face. She sobbed quietly for a minute or so and then announced, "I do not know what it is, but Jethro showed it to me the day he died. He said it might lead us to Morton and that he would take it and the ring with him to the planned meeting."

"Jethro had this with him the night of his murder?" reiterated Luke.

"Yes."

"It was found in the barge that carried Jethro's body away from Denton's warehouse. A bargeman will explain further in the morning. Do either of you know what it is?"

"Yes," Ahmed replied. "It is a branding iron used on slaves. I have seen several slaves in the Benbali marketplace with such a brand."

"Could it have belonged to the Scarfes?" asked Luke of Elizabeth.

"My family had no slaves. I was too young to know anything about branding irons, even for our cattle, but I later learned that the family symbol used on the coat of arms, shields, pennants, seals, and presumably branding irons was an eagle with outstretched wings and a scarf around its neck."

"Then this three-pointed star enclosed within a circle could belong to the Morton family," suggested Luke.

"Or it could have belonged to the maternal side of Elizabeth's family," countered the logical Ahmed.

"There was a giant shield on the wall of the great hall in Scarfe Abbey, but I do not recall its details," commented Elizabeth mournfully.

The three enjoyed the variety of courses brought to their table—and one another's company. Luke was pleased that he had used his influence to have Ahmed remain as dey. He felt he could now trust this experienced Turkish administrator.

At the appropriate time, Luke made moves to leave. This prompted Ahmed, unexpectedly, to raise a new issue. "Luke, we both know that Osman and Hasan were behind the plot to remove me. Part of the agreement between us was a requirement that I exile the previous commander of the fleet, Nasim, whom Hasan replaced. Before I do that, you should talk to him. He will give you an insight into Hasan that might change your views about him. Hasan still remains a danger to me—and to the treaty."

"And Osman?"

"No, with the vast majority of the janissaries supporting me, he clearly now depends on my support for survival. He fears the sultan. One more mistake on his part, and he will be sailing to Constantinople to an unpleasant fate."

Luke and Strad were eventually escorted home by a cohort of Ahmed's janissaries.

The next morning, Luke, Strad, and Miles went to see the bargeman Ali. As they approached the tethered barges, they sensed tension; and on their arrival, people scattered. Eventually, one bargeman, slower than the rest, was apprehended by Miles, who asked where they would find Ali. He gesticulated wildly and disappeared.

Miles reported, "Last night, there was a serious altercation during which Ali was killed. His family blames us. It would be wise to leave now."

As they turned to head back to their residence, a young child approached Miles and whispered something in Arabic. "The child says to follow him. He has a friend who can tell us what Ali had wanted to say."

Strad protested, "No, this is a trap. Grab the child, gather together our troops, and then let the child lead us wherever."

The child tugged on Miles. "Come now before my friend suffers the same fate as Ali."

"Ask the child our destination," said Luke.

"The bazaar" was the answer.

"There are usually plenty of Yusuf's men patrolling the bazaar. We will seek their protection," said Miles.

The boy led them deep into the Arab trading quarters and reached a shop that displayed a range of brightly colored spices. The combined aromas cleared the head. The boy indicated that they should enter through a curtained door.

They found themselves in a small warehouse full of barrels and bags of dried vegetables, herbs, and spices. Seated in the center of the room was an elderly Arab who rose to greet them. Miles immediately asked, "What was it that Ali wanted to tell us?"

"I do not know. I am not Ali's friend but have simply made my shop available so that his friend can talk to you without being seen by the other bargemen. Unfortunately, you have arrived before him. Let me serve you with the latest coffee from Brazil to which I have added the most delicious spices."

Luke, who had taken to coffee with relish, readily accepted the offer. Their host suggested that the drink was not to be sipped but taken in one or two gulps to obtain maximum enjoyment. They consumed several cups.

All three lost consciousness.

Luke came to, with Miles and Strad looking down on him with obvious relief. "Thank god. We thought you might never come round. You drank more of the drugged coffee than both us combined," remarked Miles.

"Or you were given double the dose of whatever was added to it," added Strad.

"Where are we?" asked a still groggy Luke.

"It is an old Roman fort built around a small oasis somewhere in the middle of the desert. The outer walls have fallen away, and the larger amount of rubble in the corners was probably watchtowers. We found a broken tablet commemorating the victory of a Patricius against the Nubians, and over in the far corner, the floor mosaic of a now demolished room can be seen," Strad related.

It suddenly dawned on Luke that his companions were wearing Arab clothing—as was he. "Our kidnappers have stolen our weapons and our clothes," Luke remarked, adding, "Why are they not guarding us?"

"There is no need. Where can we go? While you were still out to it, Strad and I climbed the sand hills to both the north and south. There is nothing but dunes as far as the eye can see. And we have no footwear. We could not walk on the sand during the day."

"We must be many, many miles inland. The coastal mountains to the north are not visible," said Strad.

"This old fort is probably on a north–south route across the Sahara to Tombouctou. Our kidnappers are probably waiting for the next caravan heading south to sell us into slavery," suggested Miles.

"If I am really a danger to someone in Benbali, why wasn't I killed?" asked Luke.

"Two possibilities. It's a question of time. You are an immediate problem but will not be by a date in the future. Therefore, the abductors will probably want to make money out of you. You will be ransomed. When you are ransomed and returned to Benbali, you will no longer pose a threat. Miles and I may not be so lucky," lamented Strad.

"And the other interpretation?"

"That the kidnappers ignored the order to kill you, and you will join us as potential slaves in darkest Africa," concluded Strad almost gleefully.

"Long term, it is simply a question of whether all three of us or only you two finish up as white eunuchs in the court of an African king," mumbled Luke, attempting to inject some ham-fisted humor into the dire situation.

"We will starve to death first," announced Miles.

Strad was more positive. "There is plenty of water, and our captors have left us with a smallish bag of raisins. Some of the trees around us are date palms."

"But this oasis is too small to sustain wildlife that we could kill, even if we had the weapons to achieve it," added Miles.

"Don't be such a pessimist, Captain. Even on the sands, I saw a snake, and there are tiny wrenlike birds in the trees," responded Strad.

"Does any civilized person eat snake?" asked Luke, genuinely revolted at the thought.

"We all eat eels," concluded Strad, delighting in his officers' discomfiture.

Luke was slowly coming to terms with the situation. "What information could Ali have had that forced our unknown opponent to kill the bargeman and abduct us? It must relate to Jethro's murder," he concluded.

"And most likely related to the identity of Morton. Jethro was getting close, and then with Ali's help, we were also closing in. Or so Morton thought," suggested Strad.

"No, I disagree," said Miles. "It is more basic. You are seen by some of the supporters of Hasan, Ismet, and Osman as a traitor who at the last minute, despite your earlier sympathy with the rebels, engineered Ahmed's reinstatement as dey. That failed coup against the dey was supported by many important and influential people."

The last comment disturbed Luke. The pasha, Commander Yusuf, and Elif did not hide their sympathy with the dey's opponents. He half remembered an incident several nights earlier when, half-asleep, he sensed Elif standing above him with a bejeweled dagger in her hand. It must have been a dream.

24

In Benbali, the English mission was paralyzed. Both the ambassador and the commander of the English troops had been kidnapped, and Lord Stokey had already returned to England. The senior English officers were the sailors, Ralph Croft and John Neville, who came ashore to discuss the situation with Ninian, the only remaining civilian member of the mission.

Captain Croft assumed the leadership of the group and, with Lady Elif as interpreter, discussed the situation with Commander Yusuf. He had already begun the search for the missing Englishmen, being informed of the situation hours before the naval officers. His men shadowed all Europeans entering the bazaar.

They had followed Luke, Miles, and Strad to the spice shop. When they did not reappear, they informed Yusuf, who acted immediately. The shop owner was tortured until he revealed that the three drugged Englishmen had been smuggled out of his shop in large barrels onto a wagon that headed south. His failure to reveal who had provided the drug and who had paid him to act in the way he did proved fatal. His tongueless but still living body was placed in a cage and hoisted above the entrance to the souk to slowly expire in the relentless North African sun.

Yusuf's men eventually reported that a wagon loaded with barrels had been seen heading south on the only track that led to the mountain pass that, in turn, opened up a crossing of the Sahara in the direction of Tombouctou. Yusuf considered three possibilities—the men had been murdered, they were prisoners somewhere in the mountains held to be ransomed, or they were being taken further south into slavery. He mobilized the friendly sheikhs of the interior to search their areas for the wagon or any sight of the Englishmen. He readied his personal troop to immediately head south along the track.

There was no one in his group who could speak English. None of the other Benbali authorities could help in this regard. Hasan and numerous Arabic-speaking English sailors were sailing the Mediterranean. The pasha refused to allow Elif, who appeared distressed about Luke's fate, to accompany Yusuf. Elizabeth's offer was rejected as she spoke perfect Turkish but poor Arabic. Ninian offered his services and discussed the rescue operation with Yusuf, who explained, "Let's assume they are still alive and headed for slavery. No one embarks on crossing the desert on a whim. Transit depends on well-supplied and organized caravans that make the trip at regular intervals. The next caravan is not due to depart the last Benbali depot, an old Roman fort, for a couple of days. We should reach that destination before the next caravan leaves."

"What if they are not there?" asked Ninian.

"If they are not there, they are dead. But cheer up, young man. Most slave traders are too greedy to pass up such a prize as three white men. Slavers have a vested interest in keeping people alive. Let us hope they have not fallen into the hands of the Abbasid cult, whose sole item of faith is the murder of all nonbelievers, especially Europeans."

"Have they been active lately?"

"Unfortunately, yes. They recently killed a powerful sheikh in Oran. It was Luke who rescued his son and successor. Only yesterday, they murdered the bargeman Ali because they believed he was too close to the European infidels. They tried to kill Luke on the day of his arrival. They regularly kill travelers along the very road that leads to the old Roman fort." Such comments did little to lessen Ninian's depression.

Yusuf pushed his men hard. Ninian was alarmed that the horses could not keep going at the pace the commander dictated. His assessment was correct, but the logical outcome of distressed or dead horses was averted. Upon reaching a camp of Arab nomads, just beyond the mountains, Yusuf exchanged his horses for fresh ones.

The local sheikh was Ibrahim, the young man whom Luke had rescued from the Abbasids. He was determined to help save the man who had rescued him. He offered to lead four or more of his cameleers ahead of Yusuf's party to reach the Roman fort more quickly. The offer was readily accepted.

It was late in the afternoon when Yusuf's party saw the fort. Yusuf was troubled. There was no sign of life around it. Where were Ibrahim and his cameleers? Where was the slave caravan? Where were the Englishmen?

After surveying the grounds of the fort, Yusuf ordered his men to continue south. He told Ninian, "A caravan has just gone through here. The wind has not had time to remove the tracks. They must be just over the next dune. They travel at night because of the heat."

Yusuf was right. By the light of a pale moon, Ninian saw a caravan of twelve or more heavily loaded camels strung out in a long line, disappearing into the darkness. Yusuf overtook the caravan and examined its personnel and prisoners. None were English.

The caravan leader told Yusuf that he was to collect three English slaves at the fort. As he had already been paid to transport them to a slave market at Tombouctou, he had not sustained a total loss, but the sale of three Englishmen would have made him an immense profit. He had assumed, much to Ninian's distress, that they had probably died of mistreatment or from a fatal attempt to find safety across the desert.

Yusuf's attempt to trace the money trail faltered at the first step. The caravan leader was paid by a third party—a Moroccan moneylender. The original source would be difficult to trace.

Back at the fort, Yusuf and his men settled down for what was left of the night. Early the next morning, the watch whom Yusuf had set alerted the camp to an approaching single cameleer. It was one of Ibrahim's missing men.

After a fairly lengthy discussion with the man, Yusuf spoke gently to Ninian. "My lord, I have good and bad news. The good news is that Ibrahim arrived here ahead of the caravan and, when he saw it approaching, moved the Englishmen to a group of rocky outcrops to the west to await its departure or our arrival. In the dark, they did not see or hear us arrive and spent the early part of the night safely hidden in the outcrop but had to return to their home in the early hours of the morning because of an emergency."

"What was the emergency, and what's the bad news?" asked an anxious Ninian.

"Your comrade Stradling is dead and the ambassador seriously ill."

"What happened?" asked a shocked Ninian.

"The outcrop is infested with snakes. The Englishmen were barefooted. Sheikh Ibrahim suspects that Stradling stood on a snake and was fatally bitten."

"What about the ambassador?" asked Ninian.

Yusuf fired a series of further questions at the cameleer and eventually summarized the situation for Ninian. "Ibrahim's man thinks that Luke was bitten also but by the desert horned viper, whose venom is not usually fatal, whereas Stradling had the misfortune of being bitten by the aggressive and more venomous saw-scaled viper. The cameleer claims he heard the hissing sound of the saw-scaled just before Stradling complained of a bite. The ambassador could have been bitten by a scorpion, which can be deadly. The ambassador needed help as a matter of urgency. He was paralyzed and his tongue swollen and he in danger of choking. The sheikh took him immediately back to his camp, where he will be treated by one of his elders who deal with snakebites all the time. Captain Oxenbridge went with him. This cameleer has the body of Stradling secured across his beast."

An examination of Luke by an elderly Arab nomad experienced in treating many a snakebite confirmed the diagnosis of Yusuf's cameleer. Luke had been bitten by a desert horned viper. The venom was not fatal but, in some people, caused a range of allergic reactions. He believed the muscle paralysis would gradually disappear and that the swelling of the tongue would subside.

Luke's eventual return to Benbali was welcomed by the dey and the pasha, who were saved from serious embarrassment. Yusuf's successful mission was well received by the English community, and Elif and Elizabeth tried to outdo each other in assisting Luke's full recovery.

Luke officially appointed a committee of the two captains, Ralph Croft and Miles Oxenbridge, to act in his place. Their first task was to arrange the funeral of Bevan Stradling. Strad had been a loyal and effective sergeant and personal friend. Captain Croft would conduct the service aboard the *Cromwell*, which would sail out to sea. Everybody knew that Strad would prefer to be buried at sea than in a cemetery on Islamic soil.

Unknown to Luke, Yusuf continued to pursue the elusive money trail. If he could discover who paid the caravan leader to collect the three Englishmen at the Roman fort, he would discover who in Benbali organized the kidnapping. He was lucky. One of the sheikhs of the tributary tribes near the Moroccan border who had been alerted to Yusuf's search for a Moroccan moneylender active in the area reported that such a man was still in the region. The sheikh reported that this man had recently been to Oran and Benbali.

With a cohort of six horsemen, Yusuf apprehended the moneylender in a small village south of Oran. The discussion was not completely satisfactory, but it did push the inquiry along a step. The moneylender was quite open in disclosing that he received the funds to pay the caravan leader from a waterfront official in Spanish Oran.

Yusuf was now perplexed. He had assumed that the agent out to destroy the English ambassador was a member of the English community or a Benbali official upset by the role Luke had played in the abortive coup. Could it be that the international conflict within Christianity, between Catholicism and Protestantism, was being played out in his small city?

Then he remembered that the Spanish governor of Oran was reported to be a friend of Ambassador Tremayne. He would raise his thoughts with Luke. Two days later, he did. In the absence of Miles, Ninian acted as interpreter.

Luke listened intently to Yusuf's interpretation of events and replied, "I doubt that I am important enough for the Spaniards to want me dead. My hunch is that the source of the money and the need to remove me stem from here in Benbali. My only doubt is, like you, whether it comes from within the English community or from within your administration. Members of both groups may have recently visited Oran. I will check out the movements of the English community. Clearly, the bargemen know something. At the moment, that is our only clue."

Yusuf agreed and indicated that his first thought was to arrest all of them and subject them to the joys of his city dungeon and see if anything pertinent to the murder of Ali or Jethro Chatwood surfaced. On second thought, he realized they had already told him that the Abbasids had murdered Ali and did not know whether the assassins acted on their own account or as paid agents of an unknown enemy.

Not long after Yusuf left, Luke received a most welcome visitor, Elizabeth Scarfe. As they sipped mint tea on the roof garden of his residence, Luke was distracted by his companion's allure. She seemed to enjoy the attention and flirted with the vulnerable ambassador. "And why are you here, Elizabeth?" asked Luke teasingly.

"I have come to see that you have recovered from your abduction and snakebite. Ahmed was distraught when he heard of your disappearance. I bring his greetings as well."

"Is that all?"

"No, I have received information that might help you in your investigations. It concerns the three-pointed-star brand that convinced Jethro he was on the track of Morton and that the bargeman who was killed had returned to you."

Luke's interest in the conversation suddenly increased. "What have you learned?"

"That someone in Benbali has a tattoo of such a star."

"Tattoo or brand?"

"I don't know."

"Who has such a mark?"

"No idea."

"Who told you?"

"Admiral Hasan's predecessor as commander of the fleet, who remains under house arrest in the citadel."

"If it is a tattoo, the wearer is probably a sailor. If it is a brand, a slave?"

The conversation ceased. Luke and Elizabeth embraced with considerable passion.

Elif witnessed the scene. She was not impressed—and stroked her dagger.

25

The next morning, Luke was informed that an English warship identified as the *Greenham* approached the citadel and then diverted to anchor next to the *Cromwell* and the *Wildfire* in the adjacent bay. Luke rode to the shoreline to greet the *Greenham's* commander, who wasted no time in being rowed ashore and presenting Luke with a number of sealed documents. He recognized their origin by the ornate seals. They were from the Lord Protector, Admiral Stokes, and his old unit of military intelligence.

The young officer suggested that the letter from Admiral Stokes required immediate attention. It was a veiled order that the *Cromwell* and the *Wildfire,* instead of sitting idly at anchor, could join the *Greenham* to patrol the North African coast from Algiers to Oran to gather intelligence regarding Spanish merchantmen. There were detailed instructions for Captain Croft, who would command the small flotilla. The ships would return to Benbali every fortnight to resupply and receive further orders. Luke was free to withdraw the *Cromwell* from this arrangement whenever necessary to fulfill the objectives of his mission.

Upon returning to his residence, he read the letter from his former deputy and now successor, Sir Evan Williams.

Dear Luke,

It looks as if, although hundreds of miles apart, we are working on the same case. Sometime after you departed with Lord Stokey to look for the golden Madonna and young Lord Fyson for his sister, the Lord Protector recalled us from Yorkshire and sent the whole unit and a militia company to the area of the Fyson estate. Apparently, the old nanny had told locals that the missing Madonna was in the river between Fyson Abbey and its mouth. Locals gathered in hundreds and began trawling the riverbed. Lord Fyson was furious and used his servants to remove local fossickers from the river. A series of riots broke out, and we were sent with the militia to restore order and uncover what exactly was going on.

Just before we arrived, Lord Fyson reprimanded the nanny for the trouble she had caused, and she, in turn, claimed that she had lied and that his missing sister had died before the corsair ship had left English waters. Fyson was so incensed that he struck the nanny down. She never recovered and died the next day. Local feelings were such that, on that day of the nanny's funeral, the locals marched on Fyson Abbey, struck the marquess dead to imitate what he had done to the old woman, and set everything on fire.

I know how much you like working with Royalists. You can now send both your aristocratic companions home. There is no role for them to play.

A few personal observations and even more reminiscences followed.

The letter from the Lord Protector indeed contained an order to send Lord Stokey home and to inform young Ninian of the death of his elder brother and his succession to the title. Luke sent for Ninian to give him the bittersweet news. Elif informed Luke that

Ninian was absent, visiting the merchant Wasim to restructure his relationship with Nour.

Luke was immediately struck by Elif, who was even more enticing than ever. She smelled of rose water and was wearing even less than usual. There was no mistaking her intentions. Luke did not resist.

After hours of mutual pleasure, Elif smiled inwardly. That naive young English gentlewoman, Elizabeth, was no match for the wiles and experience of the older woman.

Luke was completely unaware that Elif had gone through a sleepless night deciding whether to punish him for his dalliance with Elizabeth or make an overt effort to dominate his affections. Her potential jealousy was a time bomb that might explode unexpectedly—a situation of which Luke was totally unaware.

Luke found Ninian first thing the next morning. He informed the young peer of the death of his brother and that he was now the Marquess of Fyson. As Luke outlined the details of his brother's murder, Ninian's initial distress changed into resentment against his brother and not the murdering peasants. "If he struck Nanny down in the way you outlined, he deserved his fate. He was always the brutal lord of the manor."

"If you wish to return immediately to England, I can delay our small flotilla that is about to patrol the coast. The *Cromwell* could take you to Oran, where your papist connections could get you passage to the Netherlands."

"No, Luke. I have no intention of returning home at the moment. The family's steward is very capable, and I will await his report on the estates before I do anything."

"That could take years."

"So be it. I may never return to England."

Luke noted that the doting brother had been transformed into a transfixed lover. Ninian was obsessed with Nour—or so Luke thought.

Later that day, as darkness fell, Luke's evening meal was disrupted by Miles with five of his men. "You must come immediately to the English quarters. Another body has washed up on the river's edge."

"Do you know who it is?"

"By his clothes and body markings verified by Silas, it is Rowland May. His face has been blown away."

"How did he die?"

"A musket blast to the chest and several to the face, all from very close range."

After examining the body, Luke and Miles went to see Ambrose, who was quick to divert suspicion away from the community and onto local officials. "Rowland was ambitious. He may have hitched his rising star to the success of the coup. I imagine, with its failure, that several deals negotiated by him would have gone sour. The other party probably killed him."

"Or his partners in the anticipated coup may have removed him so that their misplaced allegiance to change should not be known by the ever increasingly powerful Ahmed Dey," suggested Miles.

"Or yet again, he could have been murdered on orders of the dey as retribution for his treachery," added Ambrose smugly.

"Or you could have ordered it yourself to cover traces of your initial support for the insurrection," said Luke.

"Why would I need to? Ahmed knows that, at one stage, I supported Hasan and Osman. May could not have told him any more than he already knows." Luke reluctantly had to agree.

The next morning, Luke gathered the whole English community into his smaller reception hall. He expected eight people to be present, having sent a message to the citadel requesting Elizabeth's attendance. He waited ten minutes past the designated time of the meeting and was alarmed to find only seven people present. James Goodrich was missing.

Luke announced that he and Miles would question them at length over the day and invited them to accept his hospitality while this was taking place. Lucy Goodrich approached him. She was clearly anxious. "Where is James?" asked Luke.

"Gone, I do not know where."

"When did you last see him?"

"Yesterday afternoon, just after an Arab boy from out of town visited him."

"How do you know he was from out of town?"

"He was dressed in the flowing robes of the nomadic Arabs, which is not the normal dress of the urban Arabs from the souk."

"Did he tell you what the boy wanted?"

"Only that he must leave immediately."

"Any hint about his destination?"

"No."

"Have you heard from him since?"

"No, but I did find this on the warehouse floor not far from where he talked to the Arab boy."

Lucy handed Luke a crumpled piece of paper and commented, "Given the poor spelling, it must have come from an uneducated source."

Luke read the garbled note.

James Godich, Plese sed now, Frend

Miles asked, "Did James know of Rowland's murder before he left?"

"Yes, he was particularly upset by it and indicated he would see Ambrose straight away and hinted that the ambassador would be interested in what he might have to say."

"But these plans were put on hold by the visit of the Arab boy?" said Luke.

"Yes."

Luke indicated that Lucy should return to the others and enjoy some refreshment. She lingered and then turned imploringly to Luke. "Has James also been murdered?"

"I don't know," replied an honest but insensitive Luke.

After Lucy rejoined the others, Miles asked Luke, "That meaningless note—what do you make of it?"

"It meant something to James to send him off in such a hurry."

"Is it in code?"

"No, too short. It's a pity I don't have Thurloe's team of decoding experts here. They could determine what it really says."

"Young Ninian studied mathematics as well as languages. Maybe he could have a look at it," suggested Miles.

"What role is James playing?" mused Luke.

"Simple. He is the murderer, another victim, or neither," replied Miles in an attempt to be humorous."

"Take that note to Ninian. I will talk to Silas," responded Luke.

Silas was apprehensive when he realized that he was chosen first to be questioned by Luke. "I hope I am not a suspect," he bleated as he sat opposite his interrogator.

"You are all suspects—and potential victims" was Luke's enigmatic reply.

"I am getting worried. First, Jethro and now Rowland. Do you think I am next? Two of the three bachelors in the community have been murdered."

"To be murdered, you need to annoy someone to a great degree. Is there anybody whom you have alienated to that level?"

"Let us stop this banter, Ambassador. I know why Rowland was killed and who caused his demise."

"If you really have solved this problem for me, I would be very grateful. Who is responsible for Rowland's death?"

"Patience Applegarth."

Luke was not amused. "This is not the time and place for ridiculous claims. Evidence?"

"You hinted, when we last spoke, that my relationship with Rowland was not as close as it had been. You were correct. Rowland had a new love."

"Patience Applegarth?"

"Yes."

"Was this love requited?"

"I don't think so, but they were getting closer and closer and seeing each other more frequently. Rowland visited her whenever Gregory was out, and in the last week or so, he has been going to the pasha's palace at the same time as Patience was there."

"If Rowland and Patience were that close, why would she cause his death?"

"Patience has, over time, attracted the obsessive attention of someone in the pasha's household. This new love witnessed the growing affection between Patience and Rowland and misinterpreted its nature. A jealous Muslim rival murdered Rowland."

"Did Gregory know about either of these potential affairs?"

"I don't know."

"If he did, he had an even stronger motive to kill Rowland," concluded Luke, who thanked Silas for his contribution and greeted a returning Miles with a jubilant announcement. "I have found May's killer already."

Luke repeated Sweetlace's evidence and concluded, "Methinks he convicts himself in trying to divert blame elsewhere. Silas is the rejected lover and, in the fit of jealousy or revenge, killed his straying partner."

"And I have further good news. Ninian took one look at the note and decoded it. Apparently, it is the simplest of schoolboy codes in which the key message is in the letters that are missing.

James Good*r*ich, Ple*a*se se*n*d now, Fr*i*end.

"He believes it reads Oran, signed by someone with an initial *I*."

"The new marquess is not just a pretty face," replied Luke. "I will question our femme fatale next."

"Which one?" commented a smirking Miles.

26

As Patience sat across the small table from Luke, he sensed a radiance and sparkle that he had not previously noticed. Perhaps Silas was correct. Yet if Rowland had provoked such emotions in Patience, his death should surely have had a devastating effect.

Luke was direct, if not brutal. "Patience, if you and Rowland were lovers, why do you display no emotions on his death?"

Patience seemed genuinely shocked by the statement. "Rowland and I, lovers! He was a quean. Wherever did you get such a ridiculous idea?"

"From a common acquaintance."

"Elif?"

It was Luke's turn to be surprised. "Why would Elif make up such a story?"

"Luke, for a man of your experience and reputation, you are very naive."

Luke blushed. "I cannot imagine why Elif would be interested in your relationship with Rowland."

"She's not. She is interested in my relationship with Ismet, which is currently suspended because of his incarceration. Until your arrival, she and Ismet were very close."

"Lovers as well as plotters?"

"Yes."

"So she tried to convince Ismet that you were double-timing him with Rowland?"

"I assume so."

"Who killed Rowland?"

"If Ismet was not incarcerated in the citadel, I would have suspected him. These Turkish officers are very jealous. However, there is someone distraught by Rowland's growing lack of interest in him after a long-term partnership, Silas Sweetlace."

Luke was unhappy with Patience's gossip involving Elif. "If Elif was your rival for Ismet's affections, why are you and she so friendly?"

"Because whoever succeeds in that relationship, it can only be a fleeting affair. Elif is a critical part of the pasha's household, and I am the wife of an English merchant. Neither of us can risk what we have for any permanent involvement with the volatile Turk. My interests lie elsewhere."

Luke was taken aback by this unromantic description of their current affairs by two women he considered alluring. Luke's prejudices came to the fore. Women should not behave in this way.

Patience's husband, Gregory Applegarth, was the next to be questioned. His attitude was confrontational. He could contribute nothing. He was a busy man and needed to be back at his warehouse—now. Luke was surprised that the normally pliant and submissive Gregory was, on this occasion, presenting an entirely different persona. Was this contrived to deflect attention from his complicity in the murder of Rowland?

Luke thought that Gregory had the strongest motive—the infidelity, suspected or actual, of his wife—but being diplomatic, he suggested a less emotional motive. "I would have thought that you would be everybody's first suspect in May's murder."

"And why would that be?" replied a surprised Gregory.

"Ambrose is sending you back to England and elevating May as his new partner here. One simple way to stop this happening was to kill May."

Gregory relaxed considerably upon hearing Luke's comment and replied, "Your interpretation is only valid if I wanted to stay in this hellhole. I cannot wait to return to England. Killing Rowland would delay, if not prevent, that desired event occurring. I am the very last person to want Rowland dead."

"You may be happy to return to England, but does your wife have a similar view?" asked Luke, quickly changing the topic, hoping to catch his suspect off guard.

"That is a strange question. My wife follows my wishes. Married women do not make decisions that contradict those of their husbands. She will return with me, whatever her own preferences."

Luke lied, "That is not what I hear. Within the last hour, I was told that your wife was having an affair with Rowland and would stay here with him when you returned to England. That gives you a powerful motive to murder him."

"You are being ridiculous, Ambassador. Everybody knows that Rowland only had affairs with men."

"Have you not heard the rumors of your wife's infidelity?"

"How dare you! That is enough. You should not use this investigation to blacken the name of my innocent wife. I will not sit here and listen to rubbish. Now may I return to work?"

Luke, having failed to trick Gregory into any admission, nodded his approval.

Elizabeth Scarfe was the next to be interrogated. Luke asked, "Is Rowland's murder connected to that of Jethro?"

"I don't know."

"Did Jethro have any contact with Rowland before he died, or have you associated with him in recent weeks?"

"Yes to both questions, and they were concerning the same object. Jethro thought a lawyer might know something about the history and significance of the three-pointed star."

"And did he?"

"He told Jethro it was a brand used on slaves by specific masters but otherwise of no significance, but Jethro did not believe him. Rowland seemed more interested in whether Jethro had noticed the pendant that Patience Applegarth was wearing at your welcoming banquet and whether he recognized it in any way. That is why I went to see Rowland myself, on the day he was killed, to question him further on the matter."

"Did you get the same response as Jethro?"

"Yes. Concerning the brand, he reiterated that it would prove nothing. I asked him why he was interested in Patience's pendant, to which he replied he had seen something similar in England worn by a distant acquaintance and that he was trying to trace its origins."

"Had he questioned Patience about it?"

"No. He said he was currently not on speaking terms with Gregory, who had accused him of ogling his wife's breasts when, in fact, he was admiring and intrigued by the pendant. He thought it wise to avoid both Applegarths for the time being."

"Our only clue regarding the brand is Ahmed Dey's comment that he has seen it on many galley and general slaves over the years."

"Owners in the Mediterranean did brand their chattels, including slaves, with such individual markings," mused Elizabeth. "By the brand, you should be able to trace the owner who applied it. Does this mean that Jethro and Rowland's murderer, if it be the same man, was once a galley slave?"

"Or a slave in general. When I finish here, I will visit Wasim, who has frequented slave markets for decades. He may recognize the mark immediately from the description," said Luke.

Luke finished his interviews, which produced little of interest. Before he left the room, he spoke gently to Lucy Goodrich. "I have good news. Your husband has gone to Oran. Do you know anyone there who has the initial *I*?"

She was delighted with Luke's positive news and ignored his question. She cried with relief. "Why would he go to Oran?" asked Luke more aggressively.

"He is a merchant, and undoubtedly, he has a client with the initial *I*."

"Why should such a client send a coded message?"

"Oran is a Spanish territory, where the Inquisition exercises power. It does not like Protestants or Jews. Such people need to do a lot in secret. In Spanish eyes, James may be trading illegally with a Jew or a clandestine Protestant, someone who needs to keep their faith a secret," Lucy reiterated.

"The initial *I* suggests that his client is Jewish—an Isaac, Isaiah, Israel, or Ishmael," suggested Luke. He then assured Lucy that he was convinced that James's departure was not related to his murder inquiries.

Luke and Miles arrived at Wasim's residence just as Nour and Ninian were leaving. Luke could only hope that their continued relationship would cause no further controversy.

Wasim was intrigued by Luke's questioning regarding the three-pointed star. He was surprised that Ahmed was unaware of its significance. He confirmed that it was a slave brand used by Christian slave owners from the central Mediterranean. As a tattoo, there were several colored varieties emanating from different owners. All originated in Sicily or Malta.

Luke explained why he was interested in the star. Wasim agreed with the hypothesis that the bearer of such a tattoo may have murdered two people to keep his or her secret. He actually had a slave girl in his household with such a brand.

Luke was astonished. He had never entertained the thought that the murderer might be a woman. *At least that frees Elif from suspicion*, he thought. He smiled as he retraced in his mind every inch of Elif's body. It was completely bereft of any skin blemish— natural or man-made.

Wasim gave Luke more useful advice. "The keeper of the slave market keeps very detailed records. These records list the known origins of the slaves up for sale, their current owners, and any distinguishing marks. You should discuss this matter with Commander Yusuf, who is the government official ultimately responsible."

As Luke and Miles walked back from Wasim's, it dawned on both that the other person who knew the slave trade in detail was Ambrose. He seemed to have a monopoly of putting those persons enslaved by the corsair ships onto the market.

Upon reaching the Ambrose residence, they were met by a very agitated Rose. "Come quickly. Ambrose is dying."

Both men ran to Ambrose's bedchamber, where they found the pasha's doctor already present. "What happened?" asked Miles of the doctor.

"Sir Ambrose has been poisoned."

"Will he survive?"

"Of course, I will survive. Rose, in one of her moments, simply added a green to our salad that was toxic. I must seriously consider sending her home for her own good—and mine," he uttered half-jokingly.

The doctor raised his hand in disagreement. "Sir Ambrose vomited up his last meal. From what I have seen, I doubt that Lady Rose's culinary misadventures are responsible. This may not have been an accident. I will know more when I examine the contents of his stomach in detail. For the moment, he is not in danger. Whatever the substance was, it reacted too quickly and forced him to vomit before it could really take effect."

The doctor left, and Luke asked Ambrose about the slave market and particular brands, including the three-pointed star. "That brand is used by several slavers who work with the Christian privateers, the Knights of Malta. The brand comes in various designs and colors reflecting the ownership by different merchants. The only firm fact about anyone displaying that tattoo is that they are not Papists. The Maltese will not enslave their fellow Catholics. Anyone carrying a three-pointed-star tattoo is Islamic, Orthodox Christian, or Protestant. Dozens of Benbali galley slaves display such a marking."

"If this was an attempt to murder you, do you have any ideas about the culprit?"

"I have nothing in common with Jethro Chatwood and Rowland May, so if someone is trying to kill me, it is not for the same reason that they were murdered. Why risk such an enterprise if, as everyone expects, the Benbali authorities will exile me for my part in the failed coup as soon as you depart or if you will expel me from the English community before you leave. In a month or two, unless I can reverse my fortunes, I will be gone."

"If I assume you do have something in common with the earlier murders, then it must be something that the common murderer does not want you to impart either to the Benbali authorities or to me. If only I could discover what the three of you knew in common, I would have my murderer. Until I find an answer, I am giving you a twenty-four-hour guard. You may be the next target."

Luke left Ambrose in the care of a woman whom the doctor had left behind to administer him further purges and three of Miles's men who stationed themselves at all points of possible entry. He went in search of Rose.

27

Luke traced the sound of her wailing to an upstairs room. Its door was wide open, and Rose was kneeling on the floor, crying profusely, and wailing intermittently. Luke took her hands and lifted her to her feet. "Do not cry, my lady. Ambrose is fine."

"I am not fit to be his wife. I fail him at every turn, and now I nearly kill him through my incompetence. I should die and free him of this burden."

Suddenly, Luke became aware that, in her distress, Rose had developed an accent. Either she had a speech impediment that came on because of her distress or English was not her native language.

Luke was brutal. Totally ignoring her fragile condition, he commented, "I did not realize, Lady Rose, that you were not English."

"I am English," protested Rose limply.

"But during your comments earlier, you had a slight foreign accent."

"Oh, that. I spent many of my early years at the court of the Grand Duke of Tuscany. I used to speak fluent Italian. I met Ambrose in Livorno, a major port in the Grand Duke's territory."

"I deeply apologize for impugning your English heritage," replied a contrite Luke.

This proved too much for Rose, who broke into uncontrollable weeping and concerted self-deprecation, which was now openly in Italian. Luke called for a female servant to come and comfort her mistress. The servant entered the room and immediately administered a potion to the weeping woman. Luke asked its nature.

"It's valerian, sir. It will help the mistress calm down and eventually sleep. She needs this potion at least twice a day."

"Is Her Ladyship often distressed?"

"Almost continuously."

"Do you know what is worrying her? Is it recent events in Benbali?"

"No, it stems from her distant past. Whenever she is very upset, she rattles on in a foreign tongue."

"Yes, I have just heard her. It is Italian. She spent some time at the Medici court in Florence," replied Luke, noting to himself that this should be checked.

Luke and the maid chatted for some time as Rose was put to bed. She was soon asleep. Just as the two of them left the room, there was a sudden shout from the bed. They ran back into the room to find Rose sitting upright. She shouted, "Il dio la perdona! Il dio la perdona!" She fell back.

Luke raced to the bedside, fearing the worst. Fortunately, Rose had lapsed into a deep sleep. Luke was highly intrigued. What had Rose done that required God's forgiveness—il dio la perdona?

The next day, the reduced English mission of Luke, Miles, and Ninian gathered at Luke's residence. "Until the *Cromwell* returns, we are short of people for us to function as I would like. For the immediate future, Miles and I will concentrate on solving the two murders and maybe a third, the attempt on Ambrose. Consequently, Miles, you will need to hand over your military command temporarily to your deputy. Strad would have been very useful in these circumstances."

A tear ran down Luke's face. He continued. "I will have no time to carry out the day-to-day functions of an acting consul, especially as a number of merchant ships have docked overnight. I appoint you, Ninian, Marquess of Fyson, as acting consul. Go immediately to Sweetlace, and take him with you to Ambrose for a quick lesson on the duties of the office. Sweetlace will assist you on the routine and protocol of the office until you become accustomed to the role." Ninian seemed quite excited about his new position and left as ordered.

Luke and Miles settled down to review the state of their murder investigation and the possibly related issue of Peregrine, Lord Morton. Luke summarized his thoughts. "I accept Yusuf's conclusion that the bargeman Ali was murdered by the Abbasids. I will assume, until proved wrong, that the murderer of Jethro and Rowland and possibly the poisoner of Ambrose are one and the same person. This gives us a focus. What did these three persons have in common, or what did they know that the murderer did not want to be revealed? And is this murderer, whatever his current reincarnation, Morton?"

"I think Ambrose is the guilty party. He has had everything to lose since our arrival. Yesterday's so-called poisoning was a pretty crude attempt to put us off the track. We, like Jethro and Rowland, are getting very close to discovering that he is Morton," countered Miles.

"I disagree. Originally, everything pointed to Ambrose as a corrupt, ruthless, scheming, predatory, greedy, and totally untrustworthy person. All that is known. We know he acted corruptly and in his own interest as consul, and the local authorities are aware of his exact role in the abortive coup. What else could he have to hide? He knows that his days in Benbali are numbered. He knows that if I do not remove him, Ahmed will."

"If you remove Ambrose from the list of suspects, given the deaths of Jethro and Rowland, you are only left with James, Silas, and Gregory. All we can do is to put pressure on these three and see what eventuates," said Miles.

"If only the suspects could be limited in this way. We cannot exclude from our suspects as murderer the women associated with the English quarters—Lady Rose, Patience Applegarth, Lucy Goodrich, and Lady Elizabeth. Nor can we ignore the wider community. The interrelationship of the authorities—Commander Yusuf, Ahmed Dey, Murat Pasha, General Osman, Admiral Hasan, and Colonel Ismet—and people such as Lady Elif with the English community may be relevant to our inquiries."

"Are you suggesting that these murders may not be about the English residents but result from the victims knowing some secret regarding local authorities?"

"It's a possibility, which we cannot ignore," replied Luke.

"If that is the case, we might as well go home and leave the murder inquiries up to the local authorities. You have, after all, completed your designated mission."

"Not just yet. I owe it to my friend and comrade Bevan Stradling to find the culprit whose activities led to Strad's death. Miles, go back to the bargemen and see if you can find out any more details regarding the night of Jethro's murder and what the feelings are concerning the death of Ali." Miles departed.

Luke was about to revisit Ambrose and further question Rose when Elif and the doctor entered the room. "Dr. Sharif has completed his examination of Ambrose's stomach. I will translate his report, but he is here in case you have further questions."

"Was Sir Ambrose poisoned?" Luke asked.

"No doubt—in the salad were the leaves of a rhubarb-type plant that are toxic."

"Deliberately included?"

"No way of knowing. Lady Rose could have easily mistaken the poisonous plant for an edible green."

The doctor seemed a little agitated and interrupted Elif. She listened carefully and informed Luke, "The doctor says even if it were done deliberately, it could only make the victim sick with an early onset of vomiting and stomach pains. You would need to eat ten or eleven pounds of leaves for it to prove fatal. He concludes that it was most likely an accidental poisoning or, if deliberate, aimed at frightening or punishing, not killing, the victim."

"Or a pretend self-poisoning to put us off the track," replied Luke, recalling Miles's suggestion. The doctor conceded it was a possibility and left.

Elif had no intention of doing likewise. "You are neglecting me, Luke. The pasha will be cross that I am not extending the full range of his hospitality to such an important guest." She led him by the hand to his spacious bedroom.

An hour later, after a more subdued interlude than usual, Elif remarked, "I have failed. You are still tense, and even my most sensual acts have failed to divert your focus from some hidden problem."

"The problem is not hidden—the murders and the identity of Lord Morton dominate my thinking. Perhaps you can best ease my tension by answering a range of questions."

"Anything you wish, Luke," remarked Elif as she ran her hands gently over his body.

"Since you have been a part of the pasha's household over many years, details or at least rumors of events in the English enclave must have reached your ears. Let me start with Rose Denton."

"The least visible of all the English. Keeps to herself. Some claim Ambrose keeps her imprisoned. An unhappy soul but considered harmless."

"Have there been any surprising reports about her?"

"No, she's a nobody."

Elif rolled herself gently on top of Luke and kissed him passionately. After some time, she suddenly rolled off Luke, sat up, and said, "The comments of a visiting English merchant many years ago surprised me. He was astonished that Ambrose had remarried after the problems he had in England. Rose was not the Lady Denton he knew in England."

"How did Ambrose explain this?"

"It was never raised, being such a personal matter."

"She speaks English with a slight accent and is fluent in Italian."

"If she is Italian, it would explain another fact that is well-known but rarely discussed. She is a Papist."

"Does Ambrose know?"

"Yes. He is also a Catholic. It explains the very favorable deals he seems to strike with Catholic countries and the failure of Spanish ships to attack his merchantmen when other English and Benbali vessels are boarded."

"How do you know that Rose is a Catholic?"

"She regularly attends Mass conducted by Father Battista within the Genoese enclave."

"Does she spend much time in the Genoese community?"

"Yes, she has a guilty conscience over a number of issues, including her husband enslaving Christians. She works with the priest in arranging the freeing of English, Dutch, and Italian female slaves."

"Have there been any rumors regarding her precise relationship with her husband?"

"What relationship? Ambrose's only interest is money. Rose and he lead separate lives, and Rose only leaves her separate part of their residence to visit the Genoese."

"Let's move on to Gregory Applegarth. Most describe him as a not-too-bright puppet, being completely submissive to and manipulated by Ambrose."

"What you see is not quite what you get. I know more about Gregory than most as I am very close to Patience, his wife."

"I know, and I will question you about that later. How does the real Gregory differ from his public image?"

"Sometime in his life, he has been bewitched."

"Bewitched—in what sense? Much of so-called witchcraft is human ignorance."

"According to Patience, it is as if Gregory were two different personalities. At times, in the privacy of his home, he becomes an extrovert show-off, boasting of what he will do to Ambrose. He even speaks with a different voice and calls himself Peter. Peter and Gregory sometimes have a conversation with each other."

"Does this Peter threaten or harm Patience?"

"Quite the opposite. He is very loving and kind. She wishes that Peter would dominate."

"I once went to a trial of a witch who seemed to be two different people and who spoke with quite different voices. The court assumed that the devil had created a rival person within the poor woman. I will try to see Applegarth when Peter is dominant. Peter may be guilty of things that Gregory is unaware of or the reverse. Has Patience ever called in the church to exorcise this possible satanic situation?"

"No, she would prefer to get rid of Gregory totally."

"And she would prefer even more to seduce Colonel Ismet, much to your chagrin."

"We both were interested in how that ambitious young man would respond to the attentions of two mature, experienced women. My reasons were political—keep Ismet on the side of the attempted coup and encourage him to head it. What a failure!" bemoaned Elif.

28

"James Goodrich, is he the hardworking, saintly man he professes to be?" Luke asked.

"Since he has been in Benbali, he has not hidden his extreme Puritanism, yet is the most popular English merchant in the city with both Commander Yusuf and the people. He is honest and keeps his prices low, and his word can be trusted," said Elif.

"So no negatives?"

"Not in Benbali, but his past may be very different. From his own mouth, he describes his wayward youth. There may be things in that unreformed past that are coming to the surface now."

"Could the middle-class merchant Goodrich, in his former life, be the vicious murdering young aristocrat Lord Morton?"

"He certainly appears to carry some guilt, which clearly does not stem from his years here. Maybe his sudden departure for Oran has something to do with this deep-seated guilt."

"No, I am convinced that he has gone to Oran to assist a customer who may be Jewish and suffering pressure from the Spanish authorities," answered Luke. "And Lucy, his wife?"

"A strange one, but I can't help. Her deeds or misdeeds have not reached the pasha's palace because she spends a lot of time within the Arab quarters of the city, apparently bringing comfort to the poor and unfortunate while trying to convert them to Christianity. You must speak to Yusuf, who keeps an eye on her and also protects her. She should be arrested and condemned to death for trying to persuade Muslims to change their faith."

"Why is she protected?"

"This may say as much about Yusuf as about Lucy Goodrich. Whereas the dey, the pasha, and the general always speak Turkish, Yusuf uses Arabic in his everyday conversation."

"I have been told he is local born and married into a leading Arab family," commented Luke.

"He did marry into a local family, but he is not a local. Yusuf came through the same Turkish school for the elite administrators and soldiers as did the dey, the pasha, the general, and Ismet. He graduated at a higher level than the others, and after a few years in the difficult role of collecting taxes and policing internal security in the potentially rebellious North African province of Benbali, he was expected to return to the sultan's court as a potential grand vizier or chief minister."

"What went wrong? He has been here for years."

"As a newly appointed official, at great risk to his own safety, he rescued two kidnapped Arab sheikhs, fell in love with the daughter of one, and married her. He has retained the respect of both the urban and nomadic Arabs ever since. He has several times had to plead with the sultan not to move him to a new appointment, which is the Ottoman custom."

"And the sultan has agreed?

"Yes because the sultan recognizes that only Yusuf can gather taxes without insurrection. He, more so than the pasha, has the sultan's ear. In the balance of power between the local authorities, Yusuf has virtually built himself a small army to maintain law and order and the ability to call on hundreds of Arab militia that far outnumber the Turkish troops in the citadel, troops that many independent-minded locals see as an occupying army."

"What is Yusuf's ethnic origin?"

"Unlike the other officials who were Christian boys captured as slaves or sold by their parents and who underwent a heavy indoctrination into the Islamic faith, Yusuf was born a Muslim in the Egyptian city of Alexandria. People brought up in the faith are more tolerant of outsiders than are converts, such as myself."

Luke's interlude with Elif was both pleasant and informative. The following morning, he planned to follow up questions that had arisen in his mind concerning Rose, Lucy, and Gregory, but he received a note that Elizabeth wanted to see him immediately. He walked briskly to the citadel and was immediately taken to Elizabeth's quarters.

"Luke, forgive my demanding note, but I heard some interesting information that you should be party to before my source is expelled from Benbali—a source that is very anxious to speak to you."

"Ismet has been talking?"

"No, I have never spoken to Colonel Ismet. He is a determined enemy of Ahmed's. I am talking about Nasim, the former admiral who, as part of your agreement with his successor and Ahmed, was to be expelled as soon as possible." Elizabeth asked a servant to bring Nasim to her chamber.

Luke turned to her. "Will you act as my interpreter?"

"No need."

"Not another English-born renegade like Hasan?" asked Luke.

"No, Nasim was born in Holland, and you speak Dutch."

Despite his absence from the sea for months, Nasim still dressed as a corsair, with a bright sash, small turban, and gigantic scimitar. Luke asked him in Dutch, "You have information that Lady Elizabeth thinks might be useful to me in my attempt to find Peregrine, Lord Morton."

"When I was commander of the fleet, I had very good relations with the bargemen. One of their leaders, the recently murdered Ali, was a close friend and kept me informed of the machinations against me by Hasan and his minion, the relative newcomer to the bargemen fraternity, a devious character named Kareem."

"Did Ali tell you anything about the night of the murder of Mr. Chatwood several weeks ago?"

"Yes, Ali came to see me the day before he was murdered. He said you had spoken to him and wondered how much more he should tell you about the situation."

"The situation?"

"Under Hasan's protection, Kareem obtained almost a monopoly of business from my old fleet and left Ali and the older families struggling to make a living from the occasional merchantman that visited the port. Kareem used his religious links with the fanatical Abbasids to build up an army of thugs to do his and Hasan's bidding. I have already alerted Yusuf to the rise of this secretive private army. If they are not stopped, they will soon take over the waterfront and disrupt our trade."

"So what happened on the night of the murder?"

"Kareem usurped Ali's contract to unload a ship and take the goods to the Denton-Applegarth warehouse. Kareem later took a body from the warehouse and, a hundred yards downriver, dumped it overboard."

"This suggests that your successor as naval commander may have been behind the murder of Jethro Chatwood," probed Luke.

"And of old Ali as well," added Nasim.

"So Hasan is linked with Kareem and Kareem with the Abbasids. What else do you know about Hasan? He presented himself to me as of English birth and a reformer determined to rid Benbali of corruption. Your removal was the first step, and with Colonel Ismet as the nominated leader, he would then overthrow both Ahmed and Osman and elect Ismet as the new dey."

"Hasan is a smart operator and remains very popular with the non-Turkish, non-Arab citizens of the city who are dominantly sailors and bargemen. If he had won over Yusuf in the recent attempted coup, the result would have been very different. You are interested in the three-star tattoo or brand, a representation of which Ali gave you. Both Kareem and Hasan have such a mark."

"So it is reasonable to assume that Hasan and Kareem knew each other when they were slaves of the same master?"

"Yes."

"Can you refute Hasan's claim that he was taken from an English village three decades ago and slowly worked his way up the corsair hierarchy?"

"A pack of lies. I was on those raiding expeditions against the Devon and Cornish villages in the thirties. I lived on your island of Lundy for over a year. Hasan was not one of the people we captured in that period. His three-pointed-star tattoo indicates a very different origin."

"Which is?"

"He is a relative newcomer who, at one stage, was enslaved by the Catholic pirates of Malta. One of our ships cruising the Adriatic came across a Maltese galley that, upon being challenged, ran up a white flag of surrender. Upon boarding the galley, our men found that the slaves had taken over the ship, and their leader—an Englishman—had ruthlessly slaughtered the original officers and passengers. Some of the galley slaves later told our men that their leader, now our noble Hasan, was an amazing swordsman who relished the slaughter."

Luke outlined to Elizabeth what Nasim had said as she had no understanding of Dutch. Luke felt a little uneasy. Nasim's demeanor changed. The calm matter-of-fact narrator became increasingly stressed. His hatred of Hasan was obvious. Could Luke trust anything that he said?

Elizabeth was aware of the change of mood and expressed what Luke assumed to be calming words in Turkish—but to no avail. Suddenly, Nasim threw his arms in the air and shouted at Elizabeth. She turned to Luke. "He wishes me to leave so that he can tell you things not fit for a woman to hear."

"Do as he asks. It may calm him down."

"Be careful, Luke. This whole confession may be a ruse to get you alone."

"Why would he want that?" he asked. Elizabeth left the room.

Luke became apprehensive. He had reason to be. As soon as Elizabeth left, Nasim approached the standing Luke and drew his scimitar. With an exaggerated circling movement, he tried to decapitate the Englishman.

Luke's awareness of something amiss saved him from the initial blow, but he was well aware that his English sword was no match for Nasim's heavy and powerful weapon. Luke, as he parried the blows, asked, "Why this? I am not your enemy."

Nasim laughed. "Hasan began my downfall, but I was protected by Ahmed until you, until *you* forced him to send me away. What I have told you about Hasan, I have already told Ahmed, who will undoubtedly tell Lady Elizabeth. And between them, they will destroy him. This chat was my last chance to get at close quarters with you and exact my revenge. Now you die!"

Luke held off Nasim for some time, given his advantage of reach, but finally, a fierce blow of the scimitar connected with Luke's sword just below the hilt and sent it bouncing across the cobbled floor. Nasim moved in for the kill.

Suddenly, there was a shot. Nasim fell to the ground, injured but still alive. Luke turned around. Emerging from a wall panel that concealed a hidden door was Ahmed, flanked by two janissaries. Ahmed's pistol was still smoking. He signaled to his men, who moved quickly across the room, and one of them cut Nasim's throat as he struggled to rise.

Luke thanked Ahmed for saving his life, just as Elizabeth reentered the room, appalled by the spreading pool of blood emanating from the corpse and astonished at the presence of Ahmed and his servants. Ahmed quickly explained to Elizabeth in Turkish.

She turned toward Luke. "I am sorry I nearly got you killed. I had no idea that Nasim hated you as much as Hasan. Ahmed apologizes for deliberately eavesdropping on the conversation between us and Nasim. As an elected official, he needs to know everything that is happening. And as you were at one stage the focus of the last attempted coup, he thought it wise that he knew whatever Nasim was revealing to you. Unlike me, he had heard Nasim express threatening ideas regarding the English ambassador. In the end, his eavesdropping prevented your assassination."

A suspicious Luke was furious. "Ask Ahmed why his men killed Nasim when he was about to be exiled."

29

"Nasim tried to raise a crew from his former supporters and had taken steps to obtain a ship. He had a promise from Algeria to captain one of their vessels, which he could use against us. His knowledge of our navy and our defenses would have been invaluable to Algeria" was Elizabeth's answer.

Ahmed whispered something to her, which she immediately relayed to Luke. "Stay within your residence or in the English quarters for the next two days. Do not get involved in any actions that take place within Benbali during this period. Ahmed is taking steps to wipe out clandestine supporters of the recent attempted coup who are still active."

Luke and Elizabeth then moved to her reception room to discuss the situation. Luke was buoyant. "We have found Lord Morton, thanks to Nasim. It is Hasan."

"The evidence does point in that direction," replied a subdued Elizabeth.

"And the timing fits. Morton escaped from the Tower of London, and three months later, he has taken over a Maltese galley. Morton was a brilliant swordsman, and as you know more than most, he enjoyed slaughtering his opponents—combatants and innocents alike."

Elizabeth was more guarded. "If what Nasim said were true, I would agree wholeheartedly, but he was filled with such venom. He may have made up the whole story so that Ahmed and I would pursue Hasan within Benbali while he used the Algerian fleet to exact revenge at sea."

"Can you tell me anything else about Morton that might help me identify him? I asked Lord Stokey to find out all he could on his return to England, but his reply could take months."

"While we were in Constantinople, Jethro and others made inquiries. The only snippet of information that we obtained was that Morton, as a swordsman, was left-handed. Apparently, that is what gave him an advantage over many."

"Useful, but many swordsmen train to use both hands. The left-handed Morton may have retrained himself and now uses his right hand." Luke led Elizabeth to the middle of the room, put his finger to his lips, and whispered, "Can you trust Ahmed? If he was listening when we talked to Nasim, he may be listening now."

"Once, I trusted Ahmed with my life. He is the nearest to a father that I have ever known. But since I have been in Benbali, he has revealed a much more complex personality—aspects of which I do not like."

"So he sees you as a daughter, not as a potential lover?"

"Luke, that is beneath contempt. How dare you!" Elizabeth threw her hands up in disgust and made clear, as she stamped out of the room, that Luke should go. His attempts to apologize fell on deaf ears as Elizabeth disappeared into the depths of the citadel, and two guards appeared to guide a reluctant Luke toward the entrance.

Ahmed met him again at the main gate. "Luke, in following up on Kareem seek Yusuf's help." Luke thanked the dey once more for saving his life.

Elif quickly informed his household and the English community that Luke had survived an assassination attempt while in the citadel. Ever ready to provide comfort for the stressed ambassador, she could not hold back her initial observation. "You must not trust Lady Elizabeth. She led you into a trap. She was slow to return to the room when you were attacked. Surely, she would be waiting just beyond the door to return? She must have heard the noise of combat—and she did nothing."

Although Luke realized that Elif was jealous of Elizabeth, the comment struck a chord. Perhaps he was naive, being manipulated by a woman who had spent her life in the byzantine labyrinth that was the Ottoman court. Did she know that Ahmed was listening and would save him? If she did not, why did she not reenter the room earlier or, alternatively, seek help from any of the large number of janissaries in the area? Was her petulant response to his questioning of her relationship with Ahmed overdone?

On the other hand, discretion was important in dealing with Elif. He would not reveal all the information that Nasim had given him. Hasan and Elif were close. He must proceed carefully with his questions, if he were to successfully prove that Admiral Hasan was Lord Morton.

The next morning, on the roof of his residence, Luke sipped cold mint tea and ate nuts, raisins, dates, and cold camel meat so heavily spiced that he remained ignorant about its real nature— much to Elif's amusement. He was soon joined by Miles and Ninian, who alerted him to troop movements around the harbor. Luke explained that Ahmed had forewarned him of such activity and had advised strongly that the English should not get involved.

Suddenly, the cannons on the citadel opened fire. The Englishmen looked anxiously for the target of this cannonade. They were alarmed. The first shot had landed in the river, not far from the Denton warehouse.

"They are attacking us!" observed Ninian.

"Relax, my lord," said Miles as the second shot hit the barges further around the harbor. "That first shot was to find their range. The barges and ships in the harbor are their target."

"You are right, Miles. Look, a company of janissaries has just surrounded the bargemen. No doubt they are being forced to follow the dey's instruction under the threat of continued bombardment," commented Luke.

The men were interrupted by a weeping Elif. "Luke, send your troops to the pasha's palace. His janissary bodyguard has been withdrawn by order of the dey. He may shell the palace next."

"Elif, I cannot interfere in the internal politics of Benbali. Ahmed told me not to get involved in what might occur today. Bring the pasha here. The dey will not attack me. Force him to break the rules, not me."

Before Elif could reply, one of her Nubian servants entered the rooftop and spoke to her. She was visibly calmed. "The crisis is over. Yusuf has sent a whole company of his Arab militia and a troop of his elite cavalry to protect the pasha."

"Commander Yusuf is not supporting Ahmed Dey in his crackdown on opposition groups?" asked Luke.

"Yusuf and the pasha represent the link with the Ottoman court. There have been rumors that the dey wants Benbali to follow Algiers and Tunis toward more autonomy, if not independence. The force that could give the dey victory or defeat him completely is the absent fleet. I must warn Hasan."

Luke asked, "Is that wise? If you are caught helping Hasan, you may bring down the pasha and put both your lives in jeopardy."

"If I don't act, the dey will destroy Hasan and the fleet. He is flooding the harbor side with troops ready to board our ships as soon as they enter port and has his cannon directed into the harbor to keep them under his control. Hasan must not return to port."

"The dey will not destroy the ships. The navy, when it returns, will have many prizes—the economic lifeblood of the city. Ahmed simply wants direct access to the prizes and cut out the middleman role of the sailors and merchants."

"And then arrest Hasan on trumped-up charges of treason," added Elif.

"Come, Elif. Hardly trumped up. Hasan is not innocent. He and you plotted against the legitimate government of Benbali."

Suddenly, the citadel's cannons fired two more shots out to sea. "The dey is a devil. Those shots tell us all that our ships are about to return. He must have known this much earlier, which has provoked his planned ambush of his own fleet. I now have no time to warn Hasan," bemoaned Elif.

Within half an hour, the group on Luke's rooftop saw a large fleet of ten or eleven vessels approaching the harbor entrance.

The corsairs had captured three or four prizes. The fleet reached a position offshore where the prevailing winds would push them through the harbor entrance. The fleet failed to turn. It continued on an easterly course.

Elif was overjoyed. "Allah is great. Hasan has been warned."

Luke wondered how. The dey would be furious. Someone had betrayed him. "And he blames us," said Miles as he pointed to the dey approaching Luke's residence.

Luke met him in the courtyard. "What do you want? As advised, I have not left here since I returned from the citadel yesterday."

"Why did Hasan not enter the harbor?" asked a furious Ahmed.

"Because he had word that your men might confiscate his ships and booty."

"How could he? My men only took up their positions this morning. There would have been no time to get a message into the city, let alone to a fleet miles offshore."

"Then you need to look at your inner circle. How long have you been planning this exercise, and who knew about it? The warning must have been sent days ago."

"I have been betrayed. I must leave at once to root out this coterie of traitors."

Luke returned upstairs to Miles, Ninian, and Elif. "What did you say to the dey? He galloped away without waiting for his men," explained Ninian.

"And look, his men have not followed him. There are units of janissaries emerging from everywhere, and they are marching in this direction," said Miles.

"Is this another coup? We are not important enough to be attacked. Are they marching on the pasha?" replied Luke.

"No, they are coming to protect the pasha. Look who is leading them—Ismet," announced an excited Elif. "I must return to the palace and welcome him—and discover what has happened."

"I would join you, but in these volatile circumstances, we foreigners must not take sides," announced Luke.

Ninian, in his role as acting consul, headed for the English warehouses to assess if the initial cannonade had done any damage. Miles went to the English quarters to muster his troops and obtain any intelligence that they may have picked up.

Luke suddenly felt concerned for Elizabeth. She was a longtime friend of the dey, but what if she had been persuaded to betray him? She was close enough to have been aware of his plans to destroy Hasan and take over the fleet. He decided to go to the citadel to offer her protection.

As he passed through a group of bargemen on the harbor front, one of them whom he recognized as a friend of Ali called out, "If you are following the dey, he headed for the souk."

Another man shouted, "When you do catch up with the dey, thank him!"

"For what?"

"His troops arrested and decapitated the men who murdered Ali. Their heads are in this basket. Do you wish to display them?"

This alarmed Luke. Decapitation was apparently a fact of life in Benbali. He looked at the heads. The horror was tinged with disappointment. Kareem's head was not there. Luke asked the basket holder why. The man replied that Kareem had disappeared a several days earlier. Ali's friends assumed the dey's men had dealt with him then.

Luke wondered why Ahmed had killed Kareem and his associates. Ahmed knew that Luke wanted to interrogate Kareem regarding the murder of two Englishmen. Was Kareem the dey's man and not Hasan's minion? Did Kareem know too much about Ahmed's involvement in the murders and had to be removed?

30

When Luke reached the citadel, it was in lockdown. The gates were closed and the towers manned with archers and musketeers. The guards who normally stood outside every entrance were now behind the locked gates.

"Ambassador Tremayne wishes to visit Lady Elizabeth Scarfe!" he shouted at the shadowy figures behind the nearest gate.

Eventually, the gate was opened, and Luke was led into the citadel and found himself in a reception room. A soldier whom Luke recognized as one of Osman's deputies entered the room. "This is not a good time for a social visit, Ambassador," announced the soldier.

"This is not a social visit. Given the developing situation, I wish to take Lady Elizabeth to the safety of the English quarters."

"She may not wish to go. She is very close to Ahmed Dey," he replied.

"May I see her?"

Elizabeth was relieved to see Luke. He quickly explained, "It appears that a civil war is commencing. I have come to take you to the English quarters. Both sides will respect our neutrality."

"It will take me a while to gather my things. Could you return later tonight?"

Osman's man spoke in Turkish to Elizabeth in an abrupt, directive tone. "The soldier has told me I must leave immediately for my own safety. He will send my things when the situation is calmer."

Luke led Elizabeth to his residence. Lady Elif was not happy. She was furious.

As soon as Elizabeth had settled in, Luke questioned her, "Ahmed has been betrayed. Was it you? Did you warn Hasan of Ahmed's plot against the navy?"

"How could I? I was a prisoner of my own choosing in the citadel. I had a guard with me every time I left my bedchamber. Ahmed kept a tight watch on everybody. I am surprised that he did not discover any traitor within his close circle."

"Who else knew the dey's plans? Commander Yusuf or the pasha?"

"Not likely. Ahmed saw both of them as enemies."

"Then who?"

"Since the failed coup, Ahmed's right-hand man and adviser has been General Osman."

"Osman is certainly a twister. Before the last coup, he was with Ahmed and then, at the last minute, sided with the rebels. And after that, he appeared reconciled with Ahmed. He may have changed sides again. But why?"

"Osman depends on the court at Constantinople for his position. The pasha and Yusuf are Benbali's links with the sultan, whereas the dey's power base was local."

"But both Murat Pasha and Yusuf seemed to have observed strict neutrality in this current unrest. The division seems to be within the janissary contingent based in the citadel. Many seem to be resisting Ahmed's orders."

Luke's questioning of Elizabeth was interrupted by Elif, who entered the room unannounced. She suggested that the hour was late and that Elizabeth should be allowed to retire. Luke was being summoned to bed by the less than tactful Elif.

It was well after midnight when Luke was awakened by Elif rising from the bed. She had been disturbed by a gentle knocking on the bedchamber door. Luke found his sword and followed Elif to the door. She opened it cautiously and then burst into a tirade in Turkish.

Standing before her was one of her giant African bodyguards. He flinched at her tirade and gradually explained his nocturnal knocking. Elif turned to Luke. "Your noble Elizabeth is not the woman of virtue you proclaim. My man says there is an intruder hidden in her chamber."

"Who is it?"

"Let us see for ourselves?" An eager Elif gloated. She did not wait on protocol. She burst into Elizabeth's bedchamber. Disappointment was written all over her face.

Elizabeth was in bed alone. A male figure lay on a mattress of several pillows placed on the floor beneath an open window. Both were surprised by the intrusion.

Luke, who had not entered the room, heard Elif apologize. "I am sorry. My men told me there was an intruder hiding in this room."

The male rose to his feet and asked to speak with Ambassador Tremayne. Luke, hearing his name mentioned, entered the room and confronted the intruder—Ahmed Dey, ruler of Benbali. Ahmed spoke rapidly to Elizabeth, who translated. "The dey seeks temporary sanctuary in the English quarters."

Luke was blunt. "I doubt whether the local insurgents would give much weight to the concept that somehow the English quarters are English territory."

Ahmed replied, "You are quite right. My enemies will not respect any such argument. However, with the return of your English ships expected at any time, no one will risk offending you for fear of retaliation by your invincible navy."

"You can't stay here. This is not part of the English enclave but a residence belonging to the pasha, who may or may not be one of your enemies. I will take you to the English quarters. The house once occupied by Lady Elizabeth when she masqueraded as Chantal Chatwood remains empty. Stay there, and I will have Miles post a guard."

Within half an hour, Luke and an awakened Miles had seen Ahmed relocated safely in the old Chatwood residence. Luke asked him, with Miles translating, "What happened?"

"While I led several cohorts of janissaries around the harbor this morning, those remaining in the citadel revolted. Even some of those men who had marched out with me deserted in the afternoon and returned to the citadel. When I returned there, the gates were closed to me. Arrows were fired in my direction, I retreated, first to some friends in the souk and then, on Yusuf's advice, to you."

"Who is leading this revolt of the janissaries? Osman?"

"He did not show his hand. The overt leader is Colonel Ismet, who somehow escaped his confinement. Yusuf's men reported that cohorts of janissaries were scouring the city looking for me on the grounds that I am a traitor to Benbali in attempting to destroy its navy."

Luke had just returned to his residence when he received a summons to see the pasha. Luke was apprehensive. Would he be reprimanded for protecting the dey?

Luke noticed that the atmosphere in the palace had changed. There were Turkish troops everywhere. Was the pasha a prisoner of the new rebels?

As he entered the throne room, Luke was relieved to see that Elif was present. The pasha began a long explanation, which Elif translated as he went. "Ambassador, you are aware that, over the last twenty-four hours, Benbali has faced two coups. The dey attempted a preemptive strike against his alleged enemies by attempting to put himself in a position to seize the fleet and its goods and to arrest Admiral Hasan. A group of janissaries, the more recent recruits from Anatolia, viewed this with alarm, freed Ismet, and took control of the citadel. Most of the troops who had gone with Ahmed to implement his policies, upon hearing of the insurrection, returned to the citadel, deserting the dey. He escaped into the souk and, as you well know, is now being guarded by your troops within the English quarters."

"This is not an action designed to take sides but to protect a person until the situation clarifies, and Your Excellency's wishes are known."

The pasha continued. "I have ordered the janissaries under Ismet's control to remain in their barracks in the citadel, apart from a company of the newest recruits whom I have seconded for my own protection and use. I have withdrawn support from the current dey but have not proceeded to the election of a successor. The situation is too volatile. Yusuf will act as dey until further notice, and Colonel Ismet will command the janissaries and be governor of the citadel."

"What role did General Osman play in these developments, and what is his position now?" asked Luke.

"My answer to the first question is that I do not know. When Ismet was freed, he took a cohort of men to arrest Osman as an ally of the dey. He had disappeared and has not been seen since. I then formally dismissed him as general of the janissaries and governor of the citadel."

"What happened to Hasan and the fleet?"

"Another mystery. I assumed they would anchor offshore in the bay, which until recently held your English ships until the situation here could be clarified. They are not there."

"They could not have gone far. They had several prizes. Hasan would not want to risk these on the high seas."

"But he might risk selling them in another market—Christian or Muslim—if he was unaware that Ahmed has been deposed. He would see selling the prizes in another market as a serious blow against Ahmed and his corrupt merchant allies."

"Did you warn Hasan about Ahmed's intended preemptive strike?" asked Luke.

"No, I knew nothing about it. Ahmed acted covertly. I was probably one of his intended victims," answered the pasha.

"Then who warned him in advance?"

"He was not warned in advance," interjected Elif. The surprised pasha invited Elif to elaborate. "Your Excellency, you are well aware that Hasan and I are friends, in part because of our English birth but also in our desire to remove Ahmed. Hasan told me, on one occasion, that the navy never trusted the troops in the citadel and had developed its own early warning system. If it was not safe to enter the harbor, three of the navy wives would walk along the headland when the ships approached and stand motionless together, holding hands. I imagine that this is what happened."

Luke asked, "Did Hasan tell you what he would do in such circumstances?"

"Yes, but clearly, he has not done it. He planned to anchor in the next bay until the situation clarified."

The pasha turned to Luke. "What do you intend to do with Ahmed?"

"Protect him from injustice."

"But I hope not from justice," replied the pasha sternly. He continued. "I have reconfirmed the treaty you signed with the previous dey and endorsed the list of English slaves to be released into your care for transport home. I understand that Lord Stokey has already returned to England in pursuit of the golden Madonna and that you will not reappoint Sir Ambrose Denton as English consul. I suggest that, on the return of your ships, you leave Benbali as soon as possible."

"With respect, Your Excellency, there are two murders within my community that need to be solved, and there is an inhabitant of Benbali, located in the English quarters or the wider community, who is a murdering killer and who, for the safety of all, must be identified and brought to justice."

"Do it quickly, Ambassador. If you cannot reform your merchant community, I will expel all English residents other than the Goodrich couple, whom I will allow to stay on condition that they cease preaching their blasphemous and heretical doctrines to my people. There is one last request. Lady Elizabeth Scarfe had close relations with the sultan's court. I would appreciate it if you question her on the sultan's attitude to Benbali and his officials here."

The pasha clapped his hands. The entire room, including Luke, exited, walking backward.

Luke had been diplomatically warned. His mission in Benbali was over.

31

Luke was in a dilemma. His current suspect as Lord Morton, Hasan, had disappeared with his fleet. He could not progress with that part of his investigation until the corsair returned.

He needed to gain time legitimately to keep the pasha happy. It came from an unexpected source. Upon returning to his residence, Yusuf—the acting dey—awaited him. Yusuf was relaxed, and Luke congratulated him on his promotion.

With Ninian translating, Yusuf explained, "Ambassador I need your help. I want you to find General Osman and Admiral Hasan. In return, I will pass on to you any information relevant to the murders you are attempting to solve and your search for this nefarious Morton."

"You would know that the pasha has given me limited time to solve those issues."

"Your assistance to me will obviously require you to remain a little longer," said Yusuf with a knowing smile.

Luke suddenly decided to take Yusuf into his confidence. "Finding Hasan is imperative to both our investigations. I suspect Admiral Hasan is my mass murderer, Lord Morton."

Yusuf threw up his hands and proclaimed, "You English certainly weave very tangled webs."

"I cannot see what we can do regarding Hasan, unless he returns. I have no ships available to hunt him down, even if I knew where he went. The practical approach is to concentrate immediately on Osman. Why is finding him important?"

"Osman has never fitted into Benbali. He is a professional soldier whom the sultan has moved about more frequently than the norm."

"For good or bad reasons?"

"I don't know how you define *good* and *bad*, but I suspect Osman has been moved frequently to prevent his ambition overreaching itself. Unlike most in the sultan's administration and army, he is of the Ottoman nobility. He has served on the empire's frontiers both in Persia and the Crimea as military governor. Instead of the expected promotion to the court, he was sent here to an environment where his power was severely limited by the competing authority of the dey, the pasha, the admiral, and myself. I suspect he prefers a military dictatorship with the powers of all but himself abolished."

"That would explain his changing loyalties. Was the dey's preemptive strike that was overtly directed at the admiral, but could easily be extended to the pasha and yourself, part of an agreement to replace you all with the general?"

"It could well be, but upon seeing the dey's plans backfiring, Osman ran."

"Do you have any information regarding his disappearance?"

"Yes, unfortunately, he did not act alone. Ismet has just completed a muster of his troops, and between fifty and sixty men are missing. Worse still, an inventory of the arms and ammunition indicated that a considerable number of both have disappeared."

"Osman therefore has a small well-armed body of men?"

"Yes, some of the men who originally supported Ahmed and then refused to follow him did not return to the citadel but rallied to Osman."

"The janissaries have become the major element of instability. They divided three ways during this crisis. A few stayed with Ahmed, and a large minority went with Osman, but the majority rallied to Ismet. Could Osman and his small army cause Benbali much trouble?" asked Luke.

"Only if it were joined by Hasan and the navy. Hasan and Osman were partners in the earlier conspiracy. Maybe Osman is meeting Hasan farther along the coast. They were both unhappy with the truce you mediated between them and Ahmed. This could be their revenge."

"My ships should return within the next two days. I will immediately join the *Cromwell* and search along the coast between here and Algiers, and the *Wildfire* can do the same between here and Oran. I will leave the *Greenham* here in case you need to contact me urgently. In the meantime, I will continue my investigation of the murders within the English community."

Although convinced that Hasan was Morton, there was still much to be clarified regarding the background and behavior of the English residents. Even if Hasan was Morton and behind the murders, he may have had an accomplice within the English quarters.

The comments that the God-fearing James Goodrich had lived a wild and wanton youth needed probing. He interrupted Lucy, who—because of James's continued absence—was working twenty hours a day. Luke began his probing by gently asking her when and where she had met her husband.

Her reply sent Luke's mind racing. "In prison about ten years ago."

"Which one?"

"It was not in England."

"Tell me more."

"In the late forties, the victorious Parliament imposed a rigid Scots-type Presbyterianism on the nation. My family moved to the Netherlands. I began preaching there, which upset the local Calvinist pastors, who had me imprisoned."

"Was James there for the same reason?"

"Yes, his imprisonment in Holland was due to reasons similar to mine, except it contained a political element—in preaching God's Word, James emphasized the satanic nature of the local burgomaster hierarchy. He was charged with sedition and blasphemy."

"Serious charges. How did he escape?"

"With the rise of the army in England, there was an exchange of prisoners with the Dutch Republic. As a now married couple, we were included but with the proviso that we did not return to England."

"Everybody says that James, by his own confession, had a wild youth. Do you know any details of this?"

"James exaggerates. Much of his wild past is concocted to highlight the wonderful redeeming power of the Lord, although he did seem to know the routine of the ecclesiastical courts quite well. As a young man, he had trouble conforming to the morality of the day."

James was not Morton, but he could be an accomplice. His past could have provided material for blackmail—and the need for a murderous response. Luke hoped that James would return from Oran and not be found washed up in the Benbali harbor.

The next morning, Luke was awakened by the firing of two cannons, the accepted method of informing the citizens of Benbali that ships were approaching the city. He was delighted to see that they were the three English warships returning from patrol.

Within two hours, Luke was aboard the *Cromwell* with Ralph and John and the commanders of the *Wildfire* and the *Greenham*. He updated them on developments in Benbali and decided to send the three ships together in search of the Benbali fleet and its prizes. All three ships were quickly resupplied and ready to sail the next morning.

Luke and Miles joined the *Cromwell*. Luke carried with him a letter from the pasha addressed to Hasan explaining the situation and requesting that he return to Benbali and participate in the reorganization of the government. Yusuf had advised Luke that, should he come across a scenario in which Hasan's fleet and Osman's army were discovered together, he should deliver the pasha's letter and return as quickly as possible.

It was a short journey. Just beyond the bay in which the English ships had anchored, Luke saw the corsair fleet and its prizes riding at anchor. On the shore, he saw a small number of troops. Osman and Hasan had combined as feared.

Luke ignored his instructions and immediately returned to Benbali, seeking an urgent meeting with Yusuf and the pasha. Luke explained that he had acted to give the authorities an opportunity to move their army to contain Osman before he could do much damage and also to put pressure on Hasan who would worry at why the English flotilla had rapidly disappeared after sighting his fleet.

"Hasan could fear that we might return with the full force of the English Mediterranean fleet to do Ahmed's bidding. He has no way of knowing that Ahmed had been deposed. Hopefully, it could force him to return immediately to Benbali to assess the situation."

The pasha sent orders to Ismet to lead an army twice the size of Osman's to bring him back. With the citadel undermanned, the pasha asked Luke to station the *Cromwell* in a position that would control the entrance to the harbor should Hasan return with disruptive intentions.

The next two days did not go well for the Benbali authorities. When Ismet reached the location indicated by Luke, neither Osman nor his troops were there, and Hasan's fleet had moved further out to sea. Everybody waited anxiously for Hasan to act. He did—but in a most unexpected way.

Elif and Luke were sitting on the roof of his residence, sipping spiced cold fruit drinks and eating a pizzalike savory, complete with cooked meats and vegetables on top of a thin pastry base. As the meal progressed, Luke enjoyed his newfound delight—baklavas, with their crushed nuts and honey, and the delicious *lokum*, which the English called Turkish delight. It was now dark, and the couple enjoyed their meal accompanied with several glasses of sweet Italian wine. Both entered a period of mellowness before retiring for the night.

Just as they were about to leave the rooftop, they heard a scuffle on the outside staircase. Before Luke could investigate, two of Elif's bodyguards appeared, dragging an insignificant little Arab up the stairs to confront the two residents. The little man had an overlarge *shemagh*, the typical Arab headdress. This one was poorly tied and covered all his face, except his eyes. The little Arab astonished his listeners when he announced in English, "May I join you?"

It was Hasan.

Elif instructed her servants to clear the roof garden and ordered her bodyguards to stop anyone coming onto the roof by either the external or internal stairs.

"Why are you here?" asked Luke abruptly.

"I want to know what is going on, especially whether I will be received as a conquering hero bringing rich, valuable prizes to enrich hundreds of citizens or as an enemy whose possessions are about to be confiscated and who will be condemned to death."

"How much do you know?"

"I received our traditional signal not to enter the harbor as I approached it, and I anchored several bays along the coast where, if trouble struck, those troops that would support the navy would await me. Osman told me that Ahmed had planned a preemptive strike against the navy, but the troops deserted him. He gathered a few loyalists, fewer than expected, and had no idea what had happened after he left the city."

"The coward fled before the situation clarified," announced Luke bluntly.

"So what has happened? Where's Ahmed? Who rules? Where will I fit in?"

"Ahmed has been removed. He is currently under my protection in the English quarters. Power is being exercised by the pasha, Yusuf is the acting dey, and Ismet commands the janissaries and is governor of the citadel. Osman has been deprived of his command and has a price on his head—dead or alive," explained Luke.

"Where you fit in, Hasan, is up to you. Your enemy, Ahmed, has been defeated, and your most recent ally, Osman, is now officially a fugitive. Yusuf and the pasha, who were your original allies against Ahmed, are in power. Your nominee as future dey, Ismet, is the military commander. On that basis, your allies—apart from Osman—are the victors. They are waiting for you to join them," purred the sympathetic Elif.

"Your return will be well received, and you will have time to influence the election of a new dey, which will be held once the pasha is satisfied that conditions have returned to normal," added Luke.

"It's not that simple. I have made a mistake that the pasha and his allies may not forgive," confessed a contrite Hasan. "I will return only when that error has been rectified." He left.

32

Hasan had second thoughts and returned within a few minutes. "If the Benbali authorities are after Osman as a traitor, those who harbor him could suffer the same fate. Unfortunately, Osman and his men are aboard my fleet," he confessed.

"As an ally? You would not be aware that, the moment the fleet sailed, Osman became Ahmed's right-hand man. He placed his faith in a dictatorial Ahmed regime. It was only when the dey's preemptive strike failed that Osman decided to change sides and meet your fleet. Bring the fleet into harbor, hand Osman over to the pasha, and Ismet will deal with the rebel janissaries," advised Luke.

Hasan was silent for some time as he thought—and filled his mouth with handfuls of Turkish delight. Finally, he announced, "Inform the pasha, Yusuf, and Ismet that the fleet will enter the harbor before sunset tomorrow."

"What about Osman?"

"That problem I will solve."

Just after midday, Hasan's fleet with its prizes entered the harbor. The pasha was waiting on the quayside. He embraced Hasan. Ismet boarded the ships and led out about forty janissaries who would be absorbed back into the citadel establishment without much ado.

Luke was disturbed. Osman had at least sixty men with him. And where was Osman?

Hasan retired with the pasha to his palace accompanied by Yusuf and Ismet. Luke was irritated that he was not invited. Miles was more relaxed. "This is a purely internal matter. The English ambassador cannot to be involved."

It was late afternoon when Elif returned from the palace to bring Luke up-to-date. He noticed immediately that she was pale and had been crying. "What's wrong?" asked Luke.

"I have been here long enough to understand man's inhumanity to man and the constant needless slaughter of young men. Somehow I never thought I would hear a fellow countryman describe with obvious delight a completely unnecessary massacre."

Luke handed Elif a glass of their favorite wine and waited for her to explain. She did. "Hasan told the janissaries who were spread across all his ships that, while he was returning to Benbali, Osman was not. The soldiers had a choice of joining the general and rowing off to a new future in one or more of the longboats or returning with Hasan to the citadel. Twelve men opted to join Osman. They were placed in a longboat from one of the prizes. At the very moment they were thanking Hasan for allowing them this option, a fusillade from the rigging of Hasan's flagship into the longboat killed them all. Before the flagship sailed away from the corpse-laden vessel, Hasan's cannons opened fire and sank it. Osman and those men loyal to him, if not fatally shot, were drowned."

Luke could not conceal his elation. Elif was appalled at Luke's obvious delight in her horrific tale. Luke explained, "My only joy from your story is that Hasan's behavior is consistent with that of Lord Morton—brutal slaughter with no compassion." Luke was now sure that Hasan was the man he had to denounce as a serial killer. It would be so much harder as Hasan was now the hero of Benbali and a leading member of the new administration. But Hasan had lost one previous supporter—Elif.

Miles raised another concern. "I don't believe him. All slaughter has a purpose. The killing of a dozen innocent janissaries may be a cover to enable Osman to escape. People saw the troops aboard the longboat, the fusillade, and the subsequent cannonade, but can anyone vouch that Osman was a victim? You only have Hasan's word."

Luke wanted a further chat with Elizabeth. "She must know more about the sultan's attitude to Benbali and, more recently, what happened around Ahmed before his abortive preemptive strike."

Luke was alarmed to discover that Elizabeth had left his residence early in the morning to visit Ahmed in the English quarters. She had spent the day there and was still with him. He arrived unannounced to find the couple covering up what may have been a compromising situation. Luke did not apologize.

"Ahmed, I cannot guarantee your safety here in the English quarters. Hasan has returned and is demanding your arrest and punishment. I expect I will be asked to hand you over to the authorities, and I do not have the manpower to resist any armed attempt to seize you."

"What should I do?" asked a worried Ahmed.

"Early tomorrow morning is the regular changeover of the troops on board our ships and those on land. You will dress as one of them and be taken to the *Cromwell*, where you will be completely safe. The one weapon I have is the power of the *Cromwell* and, if need be, the might of the English Mediterranean fleet."

While Luke and Ahmed talked, Elizabeth had disappeared behind a screen and eventually emerged fully clad. She said, "Luke, let me say my farewells to Ahmed. I will return to your residence this evening. Perhaps I could join you and Elif for a meal?"

Luke agreed and left. Elif was not pleased, but her jealousy was ameliorated by Luke's account of Elizabeth's relationship with Ahmed. Elif delighted in Luke's gossipy account of Elizabeth's possible affair. Her assessment of Elizabeth as a femme fatale, against Luke's view of a naive young woman, was vindicated. She would enjoy the evening meal.

It would take her mind off her friend Hasan's brutal behavior. She decided to seek from him a personal explanation. Perhaps she would have to concede that Luke was right. Hasan was Lord

Morton. But for the moment, her thoughts were dominated by her continuing seduction of the English ambassador.

But it was Elizabeth who arrived for dinner dressed to seduce. Luke was surprised that, having been caught in a compromising situation with Ahmed, she should arrive at the dinner table of the English ambassador more lightly clothed than Elif and display her physical charms scarcely concealed by her flimsy see-through garments. She sensed Luke's astonishment and Elif's delight in having her assessment vindicated.

"I have not dressed like this to seduce you, Luke, or to rival Lady Elif. The heat is appalling. It is the coolest outfit I have as most of my clothes are still in the citadel. I could claim that it reveals that I would do everything, including risk my virginity, to uncover the monster Morton."

"Such as sleeping with a man old enough to be your father?" replied the hypocritical Luke.

"Sharing a bed does not necessarily involve sexual intercourse. Ahmed was very depressed and needed comforting. I saw this as probably my last opportunity to make sure that Ahmed did not know the identity of Morton, and that he had told me everything he knew relevant to my search."

"And did you learn anything new?" asked Elif, who was enjoying Luke's discomfort.

"Nothing. He simply repeated the lies of Nasim and attempted to depict Hasan as the mass murderer."

Elif's mood suddenly changed. Luke had not previously passed on Nasim's assertions regarding Hasan and his apparent delight in the slaughter of the crew and passengers of the Maltese galley that he seized.

Recent events then flashed before Elif. Hasan's massacre of Osman and his men validated Nasim's assertion. Elif was depressed. She sought temporary relief in enjoying the assorted dishes that had been laid before them.

Luke concentrated on the spiced lamb and goat stew, which he ate with the aid of delicious wheaten bread. The women preferred a *pastilla*—a layered pie with savory meat between crepelike layers of pastry topped with ground almonds, cinnamon, and sugar. Elif waved away the sherbet, a spicy fruit drink, and the mint tea. The sweet red Italian wine and the strong Arabian coffee were continuously replenished.

All three seemed to have lost the appetite to talk. Suddenly, the mutual reveries were shattered by Elizabeth. "Ahmed told me nothing new regarding my search for Morton, but he told me several pieces of information that might help your murder investigations."

Luke, who was on the edge of dozing off, became alert. "What did he say?"

"Ahmed was a confederate, ally, and friend of Sir Ambrose. Ambrose did not hesitate to tell Ahmed of his problems within the English enclave and seek the dey's advice or assistance. Sometimes their conversation amounted to little more than gossip."

"Elizabeth, get to the point." interrupted Luke.

"Don't be so rude," responded an equally inebriated Elizabeth.

Elif, who wanted Luke to herself, chirped in, "It is late. Let us retire. Luke and you can discuss this matter in the morning."

Elizabeth nodded assent to the suggestion, but Luke was not happy. "No, no, no. What did Ahmed tell you that would help me?" insisted Luke boorishly.

Elizabeth, now sensing Elif's desire to retire, decided with malice to prolong the evening. "Ambrose became increasingly alarmed with his partner, Applegarth. Apparently, he has been found wandering around the warehouse, singing bawdy songs in a high-pitched voice, and appearing not to recognize his partner. Ambrose thought he was in a trance, although Ahmed suggested he may have been sleepwalking."

Elif bristled. "Luke has already had that information, which I gave him after talking to Patience."

"The second snippet that may help you is that, because of Ahmed's friendship with Ambrose, Yusuf has had his men deliver a recalcitrant Englishman to the dey on several occasions, to be later rescued by Ambrose without the locals or the English quarters officially knowing anything about it."

"About what?"

"A drunk James Goodrich was picked up regularly by Yusuf's men and in the company of young girls and boys."

"Why didn't Yusuf tell me this himself?"

"Yusuf strongly supports Goodrich as a friend of the Arabs. He, like Ambrose and Ahmed, would wish to keep James's secret."

"You are right. It doesn't help to identify Morton, but it may assist in solving May's murder—an intoxicated James may have made advances." Luke turned to Elif. "Yusuf is close to Murat Pasha. Did not such information filter down to you?"

"Hints and rumors but never any concrete evidence," she replied cagily.

Elizabeth, obviously relaxed by the wine and in her current company, unexpectedly embarked on a general confession. "When Jethro and I arrived here, there were rumors that we were spies of the sultan sent to investigate the local officials. This was in part true. The grand vizier, the sultan's chief minister, had asked the English ambassador Sir Thomas Bendish if Jethro could elicit information during his visit, especially on the loyalty of General Osman."

"Constantinople does not trust Osman?" asked Luke.

"They were very suspicious. That is why the sultan sent one of his favorites, a brilliant officer, here as Osman's deputy—Colonel Ismet."

"So in recent months, the sultan's man on the ground in Benbali was Ismet?" repeated Luke.

"Yes."

"Did Jethro contact Ismet before he was killed?"

"I don't know."

"Did any of the local officials know of Ismet's link with the sultan?"

"The only local official in regular contact with the sultan's court is the pasha. He may have been informed," replied Elizabeth.

"He never revealed such information to me, but it may account for his secondment of Ismet to lead his bodyguard and to protect the English ambassador," interposed Elif.

"Elizabeth, did you obtain any idea from Ahmed that Osman and he were planning to turn Benbali into a semiautonomous military republic, following the pattern of Algiers and Tunis?"

"Yes. Ahmed, Osman, and the English consul Denton could see greater profits for themselves if the annual tribute to the sultan's court was redirected to them."

"Why didn't they act to achieve their ends?"

"They were about to, but their key ally Nasim, who controlled the navy, was overthrown in a move they did not anticipate. Nasim was developing a policy that the Benbali fleet should be at sea twelve months of the year and extend their privateering into the Atlantic and attack Spanish ships from the Americas and Portuguese and Dutch ships from the East Indies. The proximity of the English fleet and your arrival in Benbali forced them to delay executing their plans."

33

"That would certainly increase profits," said Luke.

"But it had two serious disadvantages. It would alienate Morocco, whose warships could do serious damage to Benbali. And above all, it meant that Benbali ships would not be available to join the sultan's fleet on its annual conflict against the Christian fleets of Venice, Spain, and the Papal States. The sultan knew of Nasim's plans," explained Elizabeth.

"So that is why Hasan's coup was assisted by the sultan's supporters in Benbali," Luke commented.

"Both the pasha and Yusuf supported it as you know," replied Elif.

"Why did Yusuf, who has strong links with the local population, support the sultan's men? Would not the locals want freedom from Turkish control—an independent Benbali?" Luke asked.

"Quite the opposite. The Arab sheikhs and urban Arabs of the city believed the distant sultan, represented by the pasha and Yusuf, could protect their interests against an increasingly predatory and greedy local Turkish administrator in the dey and the general. The second move of the sultan to undermine hostile elements in the local government was to flood Benbali with several companies of janissaries loyal to him and ignorant of local conditions and power groups. Ismet was already here to organize them. They replaced troops that had been in Benbali, some for decades. Ahmed and

Osman lost a considerable amount of traditional support among the occupying troops in the citadel with these recent transfers."

"The Ottoman court put into operation a multipronged attack against the separatist elements in its local administration—Ismet, Jethro and yourself as its agents, the placing of the navy into the hands of Hasan who saw his summer service as part of the sultan's fleet as essential, and then the transfer of loyalist troops from Anatolia in place of many who saw an independent Benbali as their future," said Luke, summarizing the situation.

Elif's sympathy with Elizabeth increased as she expressed her support for the sultan. Elif offered an olive leaf. "Lady Elizabeth, you are full of surprises. You are willing to use your feminine allure to gain political information to the extent that you have completely taken in Ahmed Dey. While you pretended to be his friend, if not lover, you were determined to prevent his separatist tendencies from dominating. You should convert to Islam and join the pasha's household."

"I am not that ruthless or unfeeling. Ahmed was a genuine friend when I was a child, and he did protect me here on the death of Jethro—and saved Luke's life. However, when he moved against the navy, when the fleet was absent, to advance his separatist plans, I informed Murat Pasha of all I knew. Ahmed shot Nasim to rid himself of an unreliable ally. It was I who had Ismet released from his confinement, pretending it had Ahmed's approval."

"That seems to explain the recent volatile politics of Benbali, but who committed the murders in the English quarters still eludes me, and Hasan's identity as Morton has to be proved," concluded Luke. "On that issue, Elif, how long have you known Hasan?"

"For a decade."

"So he was not captured from a West Country village at the same time as yourself."

"That is the picture he created to impress the large number of English sailors under his command. I do not know when and how he was first enslaved, but he bears the mark of someone enslaved by the Christians of Malta."

Luke winced as he thought of the situations under which Hasan had revealed his brand to Elif. "It is conceivable that Hasan escaped an English prison ten years ago, made his way to Malta, had himself branded as a slave, boarded a galley, led a mutiny, surrendered his ship and crew to a Benbali privateer, and came here," summarized Luke.

"It is possible," conceded Elif reluctantly. "But it is highly unlikely. No one would willingly enter slavery and be branded in the hope that they could ultimately free themselves. Hasan could not have known that he would be able to lead a mutiny so soon after his enslavement in Malta."

"Nevertheless, I am still convinced that Hasan is Morton," Luke reiterated. Luke turned to Elizabeth. "The pendant worn by Patience Applegarth on the night of our initial reception—have you seen anything like it before? Did something similar ever belong to your family?"

"You already asked me these questions. I was too young to remember any of the jewelry of my parents. When Jethro returned to England, he found an inventory retained by the family solicitor from some decades ago of the furnishings and other items at Scarfe Abbey, but the details, except for large items, was not sufficient to identify items of jewelry."

"Did Jethro have a copy of the inventory?"

"No, as he was no relation and as everybody assumed I was dead, the solicitor was reluctant to release the document to a stranger."

"Was there nothing Jethro remembered from the list that would help?"

"He was impressed that a majority of the jewelry on the list were emeralds." Luke beamed, but before he could express his delight at Elizabeth's information, she continued. "You are the second person to raise the question of Patience's pendant. In that last meeting with Rowland May, he asked me if I had ever seen a pendant similar to it. Do you think it is important?"

"If it could be proved that your family possessed such jewelry, it is proof that Morton has been in Benbali and that, in some way, Patience is involved."

Luke wasted no time. The morning after, he was at the Applegarth residence, speaking to Patience. "Forgive this early visit, but a matter has arisen that forces me to seek some immediate answers. Is the pendant you wore at the reception on our arrival a family heirloom?"

"You are the third person to ask me that question. Rowland May asked me on the night I wore it and Jethro Chatwood the next day."

"Doesn't it strike you as odd that they are the very two men in the community who have been murdered?"

"I had never thought that their questions could, in any way, be related to their murder. Do you think they were?"

"I have no proof yet, but it is a striking coincidence—ask about the pendant and die. What was your answer to their question?"

"No, it is not a family heirloom. It's a recent present from Gregory."

"Where did he obtain it?"

"I never asked. He is in the warehouse at the moment. Question him." Luke did.

Gregory was intrigued. "I have had the same question from two others and a related one from another two. Rowland May and Jethro Chatwood asked me where I had purchased the pendant. I thought it an absolute intrusion into my private life and refused to tell them. You don't think my refusal to clarify the situation led to their death?"

"It could have indirectly contributed in that it probably forced them to raise the matter with others, who became alarmed. Who were the other two who showed an interest?"

"Your lords Stokey and Fyson asked me separately whether I knew the family origins of the jewelry. They had been asked by someone if they could identify the family crest represented by the jewels in the pendant. They thought I might have been told by the person who sold it to me."

"And who was that?"

"I purchased the pendant and a similarly designed ring from an Arab silversmith in the souk."

"Do you know where he obtained them?"

"Yes. Where he obtains most of his European gems and precious metals—from the corsairs who looted them on one of their raids. The sailors keep most for their wives and daughters, but from time to time, some of them need ready cash urgently and sell jewels and coins in the bazaar. My Arab silversmith only obtained the goods a few days before my purchase. He thought he paid too much for them and regretted his purchase. He was delighted that I was willing to pay his price for such a fine example of English jewelry. He was keen to get what he considered a poor buy off his hands."

"Apart from it being corsair loot, did your silversmith know any more about its origins?"

"He did not say, but I doubt it. It is almost obligatory in his trade not to ask questions."

"Nevertheless, I will speak to him and the dealer who sold him the pendant and try to elicit the name of the corsair who sold it to him."

"Not possible. The dealer who sold my silversmith the pendant was murdered recently in a robbery that went wrong," replied Gregory.

Luke was jubilant. The evidence was accumulating. Whoever put the pendant on the Benbali market was covering his or her tracks. The murder of the dealer, Jethro, and Rowland must all have the same motive—to protect the original seller's identity.

On his return home, he outlined his conclusions to Miles. "The situation is clear. Hasan is Morton. Morton looted the gems from Scarfe Abbey and, only in the last year, sold them in the souk. Maybe he needed cash to overthrow Nasim as admiral of the fleet. He could reasonably have expected that the Arab buyer would have broken up the pendant with its multitude of emeralds, sapphires, and diamonds. The pendant surprisingly saw the light of day in its original form when it was purchased by Gregory several weeks ago because he sensed that his wife was drifting from him."

"Your interpretation, Luke, lacks two vital links. You can only link Hasan with Scarfe Abbey if he is Morton, which you have not proved. And you cannot link Elizabeth and her family to the pendant and ring. Another weakness in your thinking is that you assume Hasan knew about the pendant reappearing at the Applegarths. He is not a member of the English community and, at the time, was plotting against the English consul. The occupants of those quarters do not discuss matters with the locals. Ambrose would not have communicated any information to a man he knew was plotting against his ally, Ahmed. He may eventually have heard, but Jethro was murdered the day after the pendant appeared in public. Your theory does not add up."

"I will prove it all. If I don't, I will kidnap Hasan and bring him back to England, where there will be hundreds of people who will confirm his real identity."

"Now you are being absurd. You are the English ambassador. You do not go around kidnapping the head of a country's navy on a whim. You have become obsessed with Hasan because, in the past, he has shared Lady Elif's generosity.

I had heard of your womanizing ways. I did not believe it would affect your professional activities. You are no longer the government's hit man, removing its political enemies."

Luke was taken aback by his deputy's spirited outburst. "Miles, I am obsessed by this matter. What Morton did at Scarfe Abbey denies him any protection by the law. He is a brutal animal, and I will treat him as such. An accidental death will be the most diplomatic solution."

"I will assist you to remove Morton in any way we can, but you have no proof that Hasan is Morton."

Elif entered the room. "I am glad to catch the two of you together. The pasha has asked me to inform you of a major development affecting the English community. James Goodrich has returned but may not survive the day."

34

"Details?" asked the concerned Luke.

"A Genoese merchantman docked earlier today. On board were an emaciated and ill James Goodrich and a Jewish family of four. They had been placed on the boat by a special order of the governor of Oran," explained Elif.

"Was James tortured by the Spanish governor?" asked Miles.

"No, he and his Jewish friends were tortured by the Inquisition. The governor intervened and immediately exiled them. The pasha thought you might wish to question James before his condition deteriorates."

Half an hour later, Luke entered the Goodrich residence, where Lucy was nursing her husband. She left his bedside and ushered Luke to the far end of the bedchamber. "James wishes to speak to you, but he has told me much, which I will relate to you so that you do not need to go over these issues. He finds it difficult to talk."

"What has he told you?"

"He went to Oran at the request of a Jewish family who has returned here with him. They had received word that the Inquisition was about to confiscate all their assets, which they wanted James to move to safety in Benbali. He was arrested on the border as he was leaving the Spanish territory by agents of the Inquisition believing he had the assets of his Jewish friends in his possession."

"The Inquisition is not only responsible for the enforcement of correct doctrine but has the responsibility for border protection," commented Luke.

"He was tortured not because of his Protestant faith but simply to elicit the whereabouts of the Jewish fortune," explained Lucy.

"Did they succeed?"

"No, neither James nor his Jewish friends weakened under torture."

"Where is this Jewish fortune? Did the Spaniards find it?" asked Luke.

"James said it is safe but gave me no further details."

"Thanks, Lucy. Why does he wish to see me?"

"He wishes to confess."

"I am no cleric."

"His confession involves a secular crime, and in his eyes, you represent English law."

Luke approached the bedside, and after Lucy had given James several sips of water, he took Luke's hand and announced, "Ambassador, I murdered Rowland May."

Luke was shocked. The dying man continued. "From my youth, I have preferred men and boys. When I heard that Rowland and Silas had fallen out, I came across the former one night near our warehouse and made certain suggestions to him. He reacted quite violently and tried to hit me with a plank of wood. I wrestled it from him and then, in my own defense, smashed the plank into the back of his head. He fell to the ground dead. I panicked. I dragged the body away from the warehouse and was pulling it toward the river when I heard a shout from the Dutch bank. I ran back into the warehouse. When I reemerged several minutes later to complete my task, the body was gone."

Luke was delighted. He could bring solace to a dying man. "James, you did not kill Rowland. He was alive when you left him on the riverbank. He staggered to his feet and was seen stumbling toward the Denton factory, where someone shot him numerous times at close range. You assaulted him, but you did not kill him."

This news brought instant contentment to James, but in a few minutes, it had turned into anger. "What is it?" asked an alarmed Luke.

"Since that night, I have been blackmailed by a person who saw me hit Rowland. Deal with him for me."

James fell backward onto the pillow, and Luke thought the worst. Lucy came to the bedside, held James's hand, and prayed. Luke made to leave, but Lucy signaled for him to stay.

Sometime later, James regained consciousness but seemed unaware of Luke's presence. "My dear, Ishmael's possessions will eventually find their way into our warehouse disguised as everyday goods. Employ him in the warehouse so that he can reclaim his possessions immediately they arrive. Look after him. Tell the ambassador that the blackmailer was—" Once again, James lapsed into unconsciousness.

Ten minutes later, he opened his eyes and mumbled, "Silas. The Lord protect you all." They were his last words.

James was buried, at Lucy's request, in the small Christian cemetery in a service that conformed to no known liturgy. It was administered by one of Miles's soldiers who adhered to the same brand of Puritanism as the Goodriches. The soldier was a very tall redheaded man whom Miles confirmed to Luke was his senior sergeant and deputy, a Welshman, Davyd Jones.

After the burial, Ambrose—no doubt as part of his campaign to rehabilitate himself in the eyes of the English community—offered one of his properties within the English enclave to the Jewish family led by Ishmael as a residence and place of business—rent-free. Miles was cynical. "It's a ploy to somehow get his hands on their assets. He knows full well that the authorities will not permit it. Jews must live in clearly designated ghettos."

"What do we do with Silas?" asked Luke.

"Hand him over to Yusuf as a blackmailer and the concealer of an attempted murder. You have enough on your plate. Why add to it?"

"If we can put pressure on Silas, he may reveal information that will help us convict Hasan."

"What exactly do you plan?"

"Exactly what he did to James. With a lie, we will blackmail him."

Miles sent his men to Silas's residence and then to the Goodrich warehouse. The blackmailing bookkeeper had disappeared. Miles returned to Luke and asked, "Does Lucy know that Silas had been blackmailing her husband?"

"Yes, he told her in his dying breath. I will go to see Lucy immediately. Given her liking for the young man, she may still have helped him leave Benbali before we or the authorities acted."

Lucy was coping with her loss by working in the warehouse, assisted by the Jewish family. Luke gently asked her, "Lucy, I wish to speak to Silas. Do you know where he is?"

"Leave it in the hands of the Lord. He will exact a just revenge."

"No, Lucy, I cannot allow that blackmailing varlet to escape secular justice. He made James's last few months a hell on earth."

"An agent of the Lord will deliver swift and final judgment. After James's funeral, those of us who hold similar beliefs met for prayer, and the Lord led us to take immediate action to revenge our betrayed brother. One of James's brothers in Christ will deal with Silas."

"Which brother has taken him, and where are they now?" demanded Luke.

"I will not stand in the way of the Lord," replied Lucy, refusing to cooperate.

Luke returned to his residence and summoned Miles. "Any chance we had of questioning Silas may have already disappeared. One of their fellow extreme Puritans has taken him and will execute him in the name of an avenging God."

"Do we know who this avenging angel is?"

"It has to be one of your men or one of our sailors enjoying shore leave."

"Or someone from the Dutch community?" replied Miles.

"These fifth-monarchy-type religious fanatics remained very strong within the army. For a time, one of our generals was their leader. Do you know which of your men has openly avowed this variant of our faith?" asked Luke.

"Yes, the man who conducted the funeral service, my deputy, Sergeant Jones."

"Let's find him quickly."

"My men want to assist."

"Why?

"Jones is very popular and a born leader, and James made himself liked by providing the men on shore leave with the goods they needed for a very small price. This may not be an act of one religious fanatic carrying out God's will. It may be a large number of soldiers righting a wrong. Silas, being a homosexual, will ease the conscience of some of the men. Killing queans was a regular pastime in some units."

"Muster your men immediately. I will get an answer."

Luke explained to the assembled soldiers that he sympathized with those who were involved in the kidnapping of Silas and that none of them would be punished for this act if they handed him over to Captain Oxenbridge or himself. He needed to question Silas about other crimes that he may have committed, and he probably has evidence that will lead to the conviction of others for murder. "Where is Sergeant Jones?" was his final appeal.

Not a single soldier moved. Luke fumed. He eventually calmed down and discussed the situation with Miles. "Finding Jones may not be difficult. Our men know very little about Benbali City. They have been confined to the English quarters or the *Cromwell,* where there are not many places to hide Sweetlace," asserted Luke.

"Not quite the full story. They regularly visit the town to buy goods and relax," Miles replied.

"Relax? There are no alehouses in this Muslim town."

"Don't be naive, Luke. There are places where drugs can be obtained that are far more satisfying than several English ales—and there are many brothels."

"Good. Yusuf's men follow all foreigners when they enter the city. Let's ask him which locations our men frequent."

With Yusuf's elevation to acting dey and relocation in the citadel, his city-policing duties had been taken over by his deputy, Colonel Gamal. Gamal was about to begin his daily inspection of the city and had gathered the captains of the various precincts around him.

Miles explained the problem, and Gamal asked his deputies where the Englishmen tended to gather. "They concentrated in my area of the city and regularly visited four destinations—two brothels, a public bath, and a supplier of Turkish sweets," answered the relevant officer.

Miles asked him, "Did you notice where a very tall redheaded man regularly went?" He was delighted with the reply, which he immediately passed on to Luke. "We are in luck. When his comrades went inside the brothel, Jones was taken by one of the girls to tour the historic parts of the city. The captain named two derelict Roman villas on the southeastern edge of the town as a regular destination for the odd couple."

"Is there anything special about those villas?" asked Luke.

"Yes," replied Gamal. "One of them had an attached early Christian church, under which is a series of caves, used like the catacombs of Rome, to bury the dead." Gamal with several of his men led Luke and Miles to the location.

Arriving at the historic site, there was little to be seen on the surface other than a few almost completely demolished columns and a few concrete bases for walls, whose bricks or stones had been purloined over the centuries for reuse. Most of the mosaic floor had also disappeared.

Gamal talked at length with Miles, who then explained to Luke, "The original entrance to the catacombs was blown up during the initial Muslim conquest, when the Christian church was bombarded and burned. Under an iron grating is a metal ladder that leads straight down into the first cave. The authorities had blocked off access further into the system, so Jones and Sweetlace will not be far from the entrance. They will be close to the ladder because light does not spread far from the entrance shaft. Gamal has sent one of his men to obtain some tapers. Do you want his men to enter the cave, or would you prefer that we descend first?"

"I will go first. Do you know what weapons Jones has?"

"Pistol, sword, and dagger."

"So one man descending the ladder at a time would be easy pickings for someone such as Jones," concluded a concerned Luke.

35

"Yes, but he will not shoot either of us. Just identify yourself," replied Miles.

"I'm not so sure. As soon as we are in the shaft, I want a cover thrown over the top to exclude all light. If we descend in total darkness, it will make any attack on us more difficult," Luke ordered.

As soon as Luke and Miles were on the ground and had moved away from the shaft, Gamal—followed by one of his men—allowed light to penetrate the cave. Luke called out, "Put down your weapon, Sergeant. This is General Tremayne and Captain Oxenbridge."

After a moment of absolute silence, Miles announced, "There is nobody here."

"There is," countered Luke.

Gamal moved farther into the cave with a lighted taper. All three men saw a body propped against the far wall. "We are too late. Jones has delivered God's vengeance," Luke announced.

"No, this is not Sweetlace—it is Jones," said Miles.

"And he lives. His chest is moving in and out," added a relieved Luke.

Gamal assessed the situation and gave orders to his man, who ran to the ladder. He explained to Miles, who translated for Luke. "Jones has been bitten by a scorpion. The two or three that Gamal has seen are yellowish fawn, identifying them as the deadly Algerian southern scorpion. On the other hand, we are in luck.

Gamal has sent for an expert in reptile and snake bites from one of the inland Arab tribes that he saw at prayers earlier in the day. Gamal suggests we carry the victim back into the daylight before anyone else is bitten."

As they waited for Gamal's scorpion expert, Miles summarized what he thought had happened in the catacomb. "Jones tied the kidnapped Sweetlace to the bottom of the ladder while he prayed over his soon-to-be-departed victim. I noticed in the dust near the ladder knee marks. Perhaps he decided to sleep on his decision to kill the man, and during the night, he was bitten by a scorpion. It would take hours for the symptoms to develop, but in essence, the critical problems are that the toxin affects breathing—he thinks his throat has constricted—and it creates palpitations, and the heart can develop irregular rhythms. Incredible pain, nausea and vomiting, muscle ache, and fatigue are present. With Jones incapacitated, Sweetlace freed himself and escaped up the ladder."

Luke welcomed the scorpion expert. He was the same Arab who had cared for Luke after his snakebite in the desert. Accompanying the expert was his chieftain, Sheikh Ibrahim. "It is good to see you so well," he said in greeting Luke. "While we were riding up to Benbali yesterday, several people along the way warned us that a troop of Abbasids were an hour or so ahead of us, riding in the same direction. The witnesses picked up the information that they were on a special mission to Benbali to avenge the death of one of their own and to deal with people who had frustrated their activities. You certainly frustrated their activities when you rescued my sister and me."

"Thanks for the warning," replied Luke. "Have they been sighted within the city?"

"No, but there are extreme elements associated with the mosque who might hide them in a part of that sprawling edifice. When they are on a mission, the Abbasids are quite happy to replace their black habits and red bands with something inconspicuous," explained Gamal.

Miles, after chatting with the healer, announced, "A few drops of the potion in this phial, administered hourly until exhausted, with rest and lots of fluids will have Jones back to normal in a couple of days."

"It's been a good and bad day," summarized Luke as they made their way back to his residence. "Jones has been prevented from killing anyone, but Sweetlace has escaped."

"Don't worry about Sweetlace. There are not many places he can go. Gamal's men will soon track him down," replied the optimistic Miles.

Later that day, Luke, Elif, Miles, Ninian, and Ralph gathered on Luke's rooftop to eat and drink. It was an extremely hot day, and the usual cooling late afternoon sea breeze had not arrived. Ralph held forth on the idiocy of northern Europeans who continued to wear clothes more suitable to colder climates. Miles agreed as he looked along the shoreline and added that the Arab boys who could be seen swimming in the harbor had the best answer to the heat.

"We English do not swim nowadays, except for the man who would be king. Charles Stuart has scandalized the French by swimming naked most days," observed Ralph.

"As children, my brothers and I swam in both the river and the sea," contributed Elif.

"Medieval knights were trained to swim to enable them to cross moats and rivers in pursuit of their causes," added the emerging pedant Ninian.

"Can you swim, Luke?" asked Elif.

"As a boy, I too swam in the sea. And in early days in Holland that ability was useful in crossing the many waterways there. But as an adult, I have not. Most diseases and illnesses seem to have their origin in water. It is not safe. I never put my head underwater and always stroked from the breast outward, not like those Arab boys who spend much of their time under the water," replied Luke.

"Not safe for the soul either. The church has convinced many that if you can float in water, you must be aided by the devil. Many an old woman has died because of her ability to stay afloat," said Ninian.

"Whatever, at least those boys are keeping cool. This climate is intolerable," repeated Ralph.

"Stop complaining, and do something about it. Adopt Arab dress, and replace warm wool with cooling Egyptian cotton. Follow the Turkish officials here and visit the local hammam," advised Elif.

"What is that?" asked Ralph.

"It's a public bath similar to that of the ancient Romans. You are cooled, then heated to a high temperature, and then cooled and massaged," answered Elif.

"Being heated doesn't sound like a way to keep cool," grumbled Ralph.

"The pasha tells me that he feels so much better after such treatment. The excessive heat seems to bring out the cooling agents in the body, and after the massage, you are cool and relaxed. If any of you would like to try it, I shall arrange it," said Elif.

"I do not feel like hopping out of cold water into hot and then back into cold," said Luke.

"No, it is not like that. In Benbali, the hot rooms are created by steam, and the cooling process is obtained by splashing cold water over you. There is no immersion. Water is too precious to waste," explained Elif.

"Anything else I should know before I decide?" queried Luke.

"Most of the time, most people in the baths are naked."

"Surely, they must quickly descend into dens of iniquity?" said the moralistic Ralph.

"The fundamentalist Muslims have insisted that people have the option of wearing a towel. The Turks cannot see the necessity, but the Arabs have prevailed. Are you interested, Luke?" Elif persisted.

"Given the heat, a cleansing massage and wash appeals to me rather than any overall cooling effect. Rubbing oil over my body and scraping it off with a bone knife is not that effective in this climate. Yes, make arrangements for me to visit the hammam tomorrow afternoon."

"Which means I, as your interpreter, will have to go as well," muttered Miles.

"No one else?" continued Elif.

"No, but if you could find a guide to bring me to the souk to buy Arab clothes, I would be grateful," answered Ralph.

"No need. I will take you. We can both buy ourselves some more appropriate clothing," replied Ninian.

It was late the following afternoon when one of the pasha's attendants led Luke and Miles to the public baths. The servant explained to the manager that these men were guests of his master and must receive special treatment. Miles was apprehensive about what special treatment might mean.

They were led into a changing room where they undressed. Luke was delighted to be thrown a thin towel. They were directed into another room where they sat on a wooden bench. Neither men spoke as they experienced very cold air circulating over their bodies.

Luke was happy to stay where he was for the duration of the visit, but the manager then led them into an adjoining compartment. Here, the heat was noticeable upon entry and increased rapidly as they sat together perspiring. They began to feel very uncomfortable.

As the room filled with steam, Luke became distressed and muttered that he had to leave before he fainted. Before he took such a step, the manager returned with two athletic, well-muscled, seminaked men. He apologized. Someone had tampered with the hot water facility, which was sending overheated steam into the cubicle.

Luke and Miles looked at each other, realizing they were very vulnerable to any assailant. The manager sensed their anxiety and placed each of them in the hands of a personal attendant who would see to their well-being and protect them from any outside intervention.

The two Englishmen were separated and led into adjacent rooms. Luke was relieved to have containers of very cold water dribbled over him. He lay face down on a marble bench as the attendant with a coarse cloth and a soapy liquid gave him what he afterward remembered as a thorough scouring. After this wash, he was rubbed with perfumed oil, and the attendant began to massage him. It was so relaxing that Luke dozed.

Half-asleep, he heard a gasp and then a thud. A few seconds later, the warm hands of the masseur were replaced by cold, rough hands that moved to Luke's throat. Luke tried to turn over and force the hands away, but the assailant was now sitting on top of him. He could not breathe. He lost consciousness.

Luke came to, to find Miles and the manager pouring cold water over him as he lay motionless on the bench. He slowly took in his surroundings and saw two bodies lying beside the marble bench. One was his attendant. The other was presumably his assailant. Standing beside Miles and the manager was Colonel Gamal.

Miles explained, "You are lucky to be alive, Luke. If your assailant had broken your neck, as he did to the unfortunate attendant, instead of trying to strangle you, you would be dead. If Colonel Gamal had not come looking for you to report the capture of Silas Sweetlace, your attacker would have succeeded. Gamal entered the room, assessed the situation, primed his pistol, and shot your would-be killer behind the ear."

Luke expressed his thanks to the colonel and asked about Silas. "He is currently in the city dungeon, and Gamal will have him transferred to us in the morning. We could have been collecting a dead body," explained Miles.

"Did Silas try to commit suicide?" asked Luke.

"No, Gamal's men were taking him to their prison when a group of armed men approached, and two of them threw javelins at the troop. Initially, Gamal's men thought it was an attempt to free Silas, but a third assailant ran into the troop and tried to spear Silas. They were out to kill him."

"Given our earlier conversation with Sheikh Ibrahim, were the assailants Abbasids? And what could Silas have done to offend them? Was my assailant here also an Abbasid?" asked Luke.

Gamal replied, "They were Abbasids, but I do not know whether Silas and yourself were singled out because of past actions against them. More likely, it was a squad of Abbasids running through the town, killing any infidels they could find. Your European dress attracted their ire."

36

Luke's interrogation of Silas began simply. "Why did you run? Are you guilty of some heinous crime?"

"Not at all. I ran because, with the murder of my partner, Rowland, I did not feel safe."

"No, you ran to avoid punishment for blackmailing James Goodrich and murdering Rowland," declared Luke.

"Rubbish. You have the facts upside down. James was blackmailing Rowland and me. He threatened to have his friend Yusuf invoke sharia law and have us executed. He said he would make available to the authorities precise times and places of our indiscretions with local Arabs that would have forced Yusuf to act. If that failed, he would inform the Abbasids, who would have cut our throats after a succession of exquisite tortures."

"Is that why the Abbasids tried to kill you yesterday?"

"Why else would they single me out?"

"I was attacked also. We were random Europeans whom they came across in their search for infidels—betrayed by our European clothes," answered Luke.

Miles intervened. "Your story is implausible. Why would James blackmail you on the very grounds that he could equally be found guilty? His behavior with young Arab boys is identical with that to which you confess."

Silas did not answer.

Luke continued, "Did James murder Rowland?"

"How would I know?"

"James thought he had murdered Rowland, and you saw his assault on your partner. That is why he claimed you were blackmailing him."

"As I have said, absolute rubbish. If you have trouble deciding which of us is a liar, you can forget the petty squabble between James Goodrich and me. I know who killed Rowland, and I know the identity of your mysterious Lord Morton."

Luke was convinced that Hasan was Morton, but it would be useful to get confirmation from Silas.

It was not forthcoming. Luke was disappointed in Silas's assertion. "Gregory Applegarth is Lord Morton—and he killed Rowland."

"What evidence do you have?"

"Rowland told me he once acted as attorney for a descendant of a Viscount Thames whose family's coat of arms consisted of green, blue, and green columns with a white horizontal strip clearly depicted in the emeralds, sapphires and diamonds that made up the pendant worn by Patience Applegarth. An earlier Viscount Thames presented his three daughters with an identical pendant each."

"How do you relate this to Morton and Scarfe Abbey? According to Lord Stokey, Elizabeth's mother was not a Thames."

"True, that is what Rowland found out when he questioned her, but Lord Fyson recalled that there was a link between the Thames and the Scarfes. He was not sure, but he thought that Elizabeth's grandmother may have been one of the three sisters who would have passed it on to her eldest daughter, who married a Scarfe. The pendant was most likely part of the Scarfe treasure that Morton ransacked."

"Why kill Rowland?"

"He was asking too many questions about the pendant. Applegarth feared that his real identity as Morton would be uncovered. When Rowland stumbled into his warehouse after being hit by the predatory James, it was too good an opportunity to miss."

"But why would he completely destroy Rowland's face? He was already dead from a shot through the chest."

"Maybe some psychological quirk. Morton was hiding his identity. His pursuer must lose his. Maybe it was a warning to Lady Elizabeth to stop her quest."

"An interesting theory, but I don't accept it. If Applegarth is Morton, why would he allow his wife to wear such an incriminating pendant in public—and why suddenly reveal it after ten years of keeping it hidden? Gregory's explanation that he bought the jewelry recently makes more sense. Your story does confirm that Morton was and is probably in Benbali and disposed of the incriminating gems some time ago. The real Morton, not Applegarth, was horrified to see them on public display," concluded Luke.

"Who is Morton then? There are not many options left if you reject Applegarth—only Ambrose and myself."

"That is, if you limit your options to the English community."

Silas smiled—a gesture not lost on Luke. "What is going to happen to me?" asked Silas.

"You will leave Benbali as soon as you can get your affairs in order. You should talk to Ambrose. He may have similar plans. Do not leave the English quarters without a military guard. If you are seen alone in the city, Gamal's men may kill you on sight."

Later, Luke discussed the situation with Miles. "If only Silas were right, we could leave for England tomorrow. He believes that Applegarth is Morton and killed both Jethro and Rowland because they were getting close to revealing his identity," commented Luke.

"He does not convince you?" asked Miles.

"No. Facts and intuition. Why would a man worried that his real identity might be revealed allow his wife to display jewelry that would lead others to the truth? And intuition—you are a soldier, Miles. Morton was an efficient and ruthless professional. Can you imagine Applegarth in that role? No, the man does not have it to be a successful soldier, let alone a ruthless killer. Morton does," concluded Luke.

"That only leaves you with Ambrose, Silas, and your obsession with Hasan."

"It only leaves me with Hasan" was Luke's obstinate reply.

"You are wrong. Applegarth fits the bill for both Morton and the murderer better than Hasan. Your argument about not showing off the pendant does not hold up. On the night of the banquet, Applegarth was incandescent with rage when he saw his wife wearing it. We all thought, at the time, that it was because she was revealing too much of herself, and all the males in the room were ogling her breasts. Patience may have been given that pendant on the condition that she did not wear it in public. From what you have said about her behavior, she may have deliberately flouted this instruction, not realizing the repercussions. Morton's identity will be discovered because his wife wanted to humiliate him in public. Their marriage is very shaky."

"I will question Gregory and Patience again," Luke announced.

"And you cannot dismiss Ambrose as a suspect. What is the terrible sin that his wife constantly seeks forgiveness for? Can it be her husband's atrocities committed in England? His past history fits the Morton model even better than Applegarth," added Miles.

"We need a breakthrough in the next few days. The pasha has virtually told me I have outworn my welcome and should depart immediately. They have their treaty and their change of government. The one card I have left in dealing with the local authorities, other than our naval power, is that I still have Ahmed as a bargaining point."

They were interrupted by the unexpected arrival of Ralph Croft. "The last thing I can cope with today is a crisis aboard our ships," muttered a depressed Luke.

"Not a crisis, but some information I thought you would like to have," replied Ralph.

"Does it contribute to finding Morton and the murderers?" asked Miles optimistically.

"Probably not. It relates to the recent coup and change of government. Several days ago, we were sent to find Hasan's missing fleet. It was only a bay or two along the coast, and you and I returned in the *Cromwell* to give its location to the authorities. While returning, one of the lookouts thought he saw a large fleet on the horizon. I sent the *Greenham* and the *Wildfire* to investigate. They were to follow but not engage. They have only just returned."

"Was there a large fleet lurking off the shores of Benbali exactly when an internal revolt was under way?" asked Miles.

"Yes, it was the whole of the Algerian war fleet, some twelve to fourteen sail. Upon seeing our ships, the Algerians turned for home. They had no intention of taking on the English, although with their superiority of numbers we would have had to use our faster speed to escape undamaged."

Luke was intrigued. "Was the Algerian fleet there to assist Hasan, help Ahmed, or progress their own agenda? Were they forewarned of trouble in Benbali, or was their location just offshore during the internal conflict a coincidence?" Luke turned to Ralph. "Return to the *Cromwell* and send Ahmed back here under guard. Have him disguised. I do not want the local authorities recognizing him."

Ralph had no sooner left than Ambrose arrived unannounced.

"Luke, I need your help. Rose has disappeared."

Miles poured Ambrose a glass of red wine as Luke waited for him to explain. "As you know, apart from meals, we lead completely separate lives in different parts of the house. When she did not appear for the early afternoon meal, I sent a servant to fetch her. He returned with Rose's personal maid, who was distraught. The maid claimed that Rose was very depressed and threatening to take her own life. The maid left her to pray in a small annex off her bedchamber, which she has turned into a private chapel. When the maid returned, Rose was gone. She took nothing with her. All her clothes and jewels are still in place, although her precious and very valuable rosary beads are missing. We are both Papists, but I am sure your investigation had already discovered that."

"Would she kill herself? Suicide is a mortal sin," asked Miles.

"Possibly. She has always been unstable, and up until now, her faith has helped her maintain some semblance of normality. Without it, I would have placed her in an institution years ago. I won't elaborate on some of the manifestations of her condition. Simply put, she is not right in the head."

"We must find her as soon as possible. Miles, organize our men, and send one of them to alert Colonel Gamal, who is policing the area adjacent to the English quarters. Where might she go in such a state?" Luke asked.

"The obvious place is the Catholic chapel in the Genoese precinct to receive solace from Father Battista. I sent a servant there immediately she was missed, but Battista has not seen her."

"Has she any particular friends whom she might visit?"

"Not that I know of."

"Surely, over the years, you must have been alerted to where your wife went when out and about in Benbali City?"

Ambrose thought for some time. "I can only recall Father Battista, the Genoese enclave in general, and the slave market. And years ago, she did visit the merchant Wasim regularly over a few months."

"Why does she visit the slave market?"

"I am not sure exactly what she does, but she is heavily involved with Father Battista in freeing female slaves."

"And visiting Wasim?"

"To gain an insight into the slave market, and Wasim had slaves at the time whom Rose wished to free. I deliberately ignored such activity. It ran counter to my slave-selling operation."

"Did any of these freed slaves become Rose's friends? They may be helping her."

"Not likely. Rose freed Italian girls who invariably returned home. I doubt if any remained in Benbali."

"It seems that Rose's flight has its origins in her religious state of mind. Is there anyone in your household who can give us a clearer picture of that?"

"Yes, the undermaid. She is a young girl in her early teens. Rose took a great liking to her as she has a similar overdevotion to our faith. They regularly prayed together."

"Is she a former Italian-born slave whom Rose had freed?"

"No, she is a young girl sent from England by an acquaintance of mine. Apparently, it was a choice of a Spanish convent or service in a Catholic household abroad."

The young girl, who had obviously been weeping, was gently questioned by Luke. "I know you are very upset by your mistress's disappearance. Sir Ambrose and I think you are the only person who can help us find her."

"How can I help?" asked the distraught girl.

37

"Lady Rose has been led by her faith to leave this household. When you prayed together, did she reveal any particular anxiety or indicate what she might do when she left? Did she indicate to God her intentions?" questioned Luke gently.

"She prayed that she would have the strength to do for Christ what he had done for us."

"What did she mean?"

"Simple," answered the naive young girl. "Christ died for us. Her Ladyship will die for him."

Luke was sure that the girl did not fully comprehend the import of her statement. "How would Lady Rose die for Christ?" he asked.

"I do not know, but over the last few weeks, we have prayed for the help of all the saints who had been crucified. Crucifixion has dominated our prayers."

"You cannot crucify yourself," remarked Ambrose cynically.

"Did she ever ask you to help her obtain this end?" asked Luke.

"No, Lady Rose would do no such a thing. It is horrible," answered the maid, who relapsed into uncontrolled weeping.

Ambrose remarked, "I agree with the girl. Rose is a gentle person. All these prayers about crucifixion were probably symbolic or a code concealing her real concerns. The whole idea is impractical. You need others to crucify you. Where would someone like Rose find such people, even if they exist?"

"I must talk to Father Battista. Does he speak English?" asked Luke.

"No, but he has an assistant who does," answered Ambrose.

Half an hour later, Luke and Miles were with Father Battista. Luke explained, "Lady Rose is about to do herself great harm or even take her own life. It is possible that she could seek crucifixion as a response to Christ's sacrifice for her. Did she reveal any such tendencies to you?"

The young novice translated Father Battista's response. "She is obsessed with her faith and increasingly determined to do something dramatic to justify herself to Christ. She carries an immense guilt, which she has never explained. Crucifixion is not her solution. Who would help her? The mother church opposes such action, and our Muslim brothers, apart from the Abbasids, have similar views."

"If crucifixion is out, what form would Rose's self-imposed penance take?"

"Rose led a very narrow life. Her faith was everything, and the most important manifestation of it was freeing as many slaves as she could. Something related to slavery may be her solution. Talk to Wasim. He initially advised her when she became traumatized by the slave trade."

"Why did she go to Wasim?"

"He was known to treat his slaves well, and Lady Rose wanted to question them on their experiences. She then discussed with Wasim how they could be freed. As her husband was often the dealer selling these girls, Wasim bought and freed many of them on Rose's behalf," added Battista.

Wasim was horrified but not surprised to hear that Rose had disappeared. "She still visits me regularly to organize the purchase of slave girls to be freed. On her last visit, she bemoaned the fact that freeing these girls was not enough. She needed to do more to justify God's gift to her. I have known for some time that she is a very unstable person. I alerted Father Battista to her condition."

"Anything else that might help find her?"

"I did not think much of it at the time, but she asked me some weeks ago who was the cruelest slave master in Benbali."

"God's blood! That's it. She is going to offer herself as a slave. How would she go about it?" exclaimed Luke, who was now confident he had discovered her intentions.

"There are a number of ways. She could offer herself for sale at the next slave market, which is tomorrow. There are enough dealers who could see a great profit in adding Rose to their lists. Or she may have approached one of them—her work with Battista means that she knows many of them personally—and had herself added to a caravan of slaves already heading south."

"We are well aware of such caravans," muttered Luke. "I will inform Gamal immediately. Rose only disappeared today, so his men will be able to catch and search all relevant caravans. Where are the women awaiting sale tomorrow being housed?"

"In numerous places. It would be better to await the sale. If she does appear there, Gamal's men will rescue her."

"Wouldn't she be immediately recognized? Dealers would be taking a risk selling the wife of the former English consul."

"They will cut her hair, and she will appear half-naked. Most would not recognize her as the English gentlewoman."

The next morning, Gamal's men were in their usual positions to supervise the slave auction. They were instructed to stop proceedings, free Rose, and hand her over to Luke and Miles, who made no effort to hide themselves from the multitude of sellers and potential buyers. Ambrose did not attend.

The women in the first batch were fair-haired, from northern Europe, and followed by Africans from Niger. Then came an assortment of Mediterranean girls captured by a returning corsair. At last, Luke thought he saw Rose, although he found it hard to visualize the dowdy, morose, taciturn matron as an almost appealing half-naked slave. He was about to signal Gamal to intervene when Miles pointed out that the woman concerned was missing an arm.

Slave after slave came up for auction. After two hours, it came to an end. Rose did not appear. Hopefully, Gamal's investigation of caravans already on the road would yield better results.

Later in the afternoon, Gamal informed Luke that Rose was not in any of the caravans leaving Benbali. Luke now feared that the woman had killed herself somewhere within the city and that her body remained to be discovered. He feared that the search had ceased to be one of rescue and was now concerned with the retrieval of a corpse. Miles added to Luke's difficulties by suggesting that Rose could have walked into the river or the sea and that her body might not surface for weeks, if at all.

The next day, late in the evening, Elif announced that the Genoese and Dutch chaplains urgently wanted to see Luke. Jan Claasen announced that he accompanied Father Battista to act as interpreter. He translated the priest's confession. "Ambassador, please forgive my delay in informing you. I had to buy time for Lady Rose. Just after you left yesterday, she appeared in the confessional and sought my help. She is alive and has been taken to Oran by my assistant. She will return to Italy and join a convent, which I am sure will be able to return her to full health."

"Thank god she is alive, and her plans seem to proffer hope for a happier future for the conflicted soul," uttered a relieved Luke.

"Before she left, she commented on the behavior of her husband. She claimed he is guilty of a heinous crime, which caused her troubled state and which eventually forced her to flee. Question Sir Ambrose about his role in his wife's mental decline. Discover his crime that had such a traumatic effect on Rose," suggested the priest.

"Thank you, Padre. I will see Ambrose as soon as possible."

The following morning, Luke sent Miles to bring Ambrose to him. He returned alone and flustered. "Ambrose has disappeared."

Luke was not too concerned. "He is not under arrest. His only restriction is my request that he not leave Benbali until I solve the murders. Until the priest's information, I had cleared Ambrose of any involvement in the murders and of being the notorious Morton."

Miles noticed his sergeant Davyd Jones running toward Luke's residence. Miles met him at the door and then turned to Luke with alarm written all over his face. "Ahmed has escaped."

"How?" asked Luke.

"Ambrose approached Ahmed's guard waving a piece of paper that he claimed was from you authorizing him to escort Ahmed here."

"Didn't your man read the note? He would have seen it was a forgery."

"If it was a forgery, my man would have no way of telling. He has never seen your signature. But it did not involve such complexity. The guard concerned cannot read. He simply complied with Ambrose's request."

"Why would Ambrose free Ahmed?"

"Obvious. Ambrose's only hope of remaining in Benbali lies in another change of government. Both men have a common cause in restoring their past influence and power."

"Would Ahmed forgive Ambrose's betrayal so easily? He was very bitter at the conclusion of the failed coup against him."

"Desperation creates new friends," announced Miles with great satisfaction.

"I will visit the acting dey, Yusuf, immediately and inform him of the unfortunate news. He will not be happy."

He was not. He was incandescent with rage. "I will alert all our agencies. They are two dangerous men who could undo the reforms we are bringing to Benbali. When they are recaptured, I will deal with both of them as traitors."

"How could they be any real danger? You control the janissaries, the navy, the local militias, and internal security. Your men—Admiral Hasan, Colonel Ismet, and Colonel Gamal—occupy all positions of power."

"True, and any residue of support for Ahmed based on his professed aim of a more independent Benbali would disappear when his real intentions are revealed," added Yusuf.

"What were they, and how do you know?" asked an interested Luke.

"Let my source tell you himself." Yusuf spoke to an attendant who reappeared a few minutes later with Hasan. "Admiral, inform the ambassador of the nature of the former dey's treachery."

"Before General Osman met his unfortunate accident at sea, I was determined to elicit all the information I could from this serial turncoat. I need not go into the details of how my men reduced the general to a weeping child, willing to tell all. As a former intelligence officer, you will be well aware of our techniques."

"And was this information very different from what you already knew?"

"Incredibly so. Ahmed Dey had fooled us all for a long time. None of us had any idea of his real intentions," commented Yusuf.

"And what were they?" asked Luke again.

Hasan continued. "Ahmed was facilitating an Algerian invasion, and in return, he was to be appointed as the first governor of the Algerian province of Benbali with absolute power. Osman was part of the plot, having served years ago in Algiers and being on close terms with its dey. The ruler of Algiers was having trouble with his current military commander, and after requests to Constantinople to replace him had been ignored, he offered the position to Osman."

"How was the Algerian invasion planned?"

"While the Benbali fleet was at the sea, the Algerian fleet would enter the Benbali harbor with sufficient troops to remove any resistance. Ahmed, whose control of the citadel was assumed, was to assist this invasion by turning the citadel guns on the city and not the incoming Algerian fleet."

"My ships sighted the Algerian fleet on the horizon at the time of the coup," contributed Luke.

"Yes, that is why they turned back."

38

"Surely, they were not put off by three English frigates?" asked Luke.

"No, Osman got cold feet. He believed an Algerian takeover would negate the treaty you had signed with Benbali. You would feel double-crossed and direct the wrath of the whole English Mediterranean fleet against Benbali. And the Algerians received the same message. Their participation in anything that might undermine the Benbali treaty with the English might bring the full force of the English naval power against them."

"Did Osman reveal anything else that would interest me?"

"Yes, it was Ahmed who ordered your abduction."

"But why? He appeared very concerned for my welfare and convinced me that he was a friend. He saved my life."

"Ahmed is a very clever politician," admitted Hasan. "He believed that your abduction and disappearance into deepest Africa would provoke a massive English naval response against Benbali that would destroy my fleet. The Algerians would offer to bring Benbali into line, presenting themselves as England's greatest ally in the region. Your successor would sign a treaty with them. Algiers would appoint Ahmed as the new governor of their Benbali province. Apparently, Nasim was to be appointed as admiral of a flotilla of the Algerian navy based in Benbali. In essence, Ahmed and Nasim would still hold the positions they held for a decade as representatives of Algeria, without having to answer to anyone in Benbali—or in Constantinople."

"My disappearance was to be a signal for an Algerian invasion?" asked Luke.

"Initially yes, but the location of both the Benbali and English fleets delayed the implementation of the plan."

"Did Osman explain why Ahmed saved my life and killed his ally Nasim?"

"Nasim was a blabbermouth. The reason why Ahmed hid behind the partition was to ensure that Nasim did not tell you too much. He may have panicked and thought that the admiral might let drop some reference to Algeria, which would have removed considerable local support from Ahmed, which at the time he desperately needed."

"No, that explanation does not make sense. Why would Ahmed organize my abduction with all the possibilities of it not leading to my enslavement or death when all he had to do was delay his intervention a few seconds? Nasim would have killed me, and England would have retaliated along the lines he anticipated. Osman lied to you on this matter, probably getting his own back on Ahmed for his success in fending off the initial coup," Luke suggested. He kept to himself the thought that this lie was not Osman's but concocted by Hasan, who was smarting from what he saw as the Ahmed-Luke partnership that defeated the original attempted coup.

Luke returned to safer ground. "Did Osman say anything concerning the murders in the English quarters or the identity of Lord Morton?"

"As those matters did not concern the Benbali state, I never raised them with him," Hasan confessed.

Luke turned to Yusuf, the interim head of state, and asked, "Where would Ahmed and Ambrose go?"

"They cannot leave the city. Ismet's janissaries and Gamal's men have the city completely blockaded. They will be hiding, awaiting some external development that would give them a chance to escape," suggested Yusuf.

"Ahmed ruled the city for so long that, despite everything, there are many who would give him shelter," commented Hasan.

"Gamal will conduct a house-to-house search, but I am not optimistic of finding them," announced Yusuf.

A janissary entered the room and spoke to Yusuf and Hasan. They were elated. "The external event that Ahmed might have prayed for, or more likely had planned, is about to happen. An Algerian ship flying a white flag has entered Benbali waters. Ismet has sent one of his officers to ascertain the purpose of the visit," reported the acting dey.

"Why has it come?" asked Luke.

Hasan replied, "To find out what happened to their overall plan and to their agents Ahmed, Osman, and Nasim and the current location and strength of the English and Benbali fleets."

"And to combine this high-ranking political visit with creating an avenue of escape for Ahmed," added Luke.

As Luke made his way home, he was of two minds. He was happy with the information that Yusuf had advanced but was concerned with Hasan's key role in the new administration. If he was Morton, as Luke believed, it would be very difficult to bring him to justice.

Miles added to this concern when he commented, "Even if you can prove that Hasan is Morton, the Benbali administration will consider it irrelevant to his current position. Why should what a man did in England over a decade ago be of any concern to them? Morton is not part of your mission. Solve the two murders, and let us return to England."

Half an hour later, Elif arrived, accompanied by an elderly man in Arab clothes dragged along by two Nubian slaves. "Luke, this man was found trying to enter your courtyard." The man threw back his elaborate headdress. Elif gasped. It was Ambrose.

"What are you doing in such a ridiculous disguise?" asked Luke.

"Throwing myself under your protection. I made a mistake in being tempted by Ahmed's offer of a brighter future for both of us. I am now a fugitive whose capture, dead or alive, has been shouted throughout the marketplace and at the mosque."

"That is an understatement. The current administration has all its resources devoted to capturing Ahmed and yourself."

"Yes, that is why I seek your protection. I have no intention of having myself shot or stabbed by a patriotic Benbali."

"Ahmed's offer no longer looks inviting?" Luke snarled.

"I was mad to be tempted. All about a better future when he regained control of Benbali. But he refused to tell me his solution to our immediate problem. How were we going to change from fugitive to restored dey and his merchant ally?"

"Ahmed has no chance of returning to power. You are in danger as Commander Yusuf has made it clear that he considers your assistance to Ahmed an act of treachery against Benbali and claims jurisdiction over the case."

"Can't you help?"

"Rest assured, I will not allow an English subject to be dealt with by a foreign power. However, my hands are tied legally. Nevertheless, Miles will bring a platoon of his men here. You, dressed as one of them, will accompany the group back to the *Cromwell*, where you will stay until we leave Benbali."

"Thank you, Luke. May I gather a few of my personal possessions?"

"No, it would be unwise to return to the English quarters. You can send messages to Gregory regarding your business and personal needs from the ship. Officially, as far as we are concerned, you are still with Ahmed."

"What has happened to Rose?" Ambrose asked, almost as an afterthought.

"She has left you and Benbali for good and is to be accepted into an Italian convent. Father Battista implied that, initially, it was for the sisters to nurse Rose back to health, and later, she would be able to realize her dream of becoming a nun."

"A satisfactory ending" was Ambrose's surprising response.

"Not quite. Battista puts Rose's condition down to something horrendous that you did in the past that preyed on Rose's mind, which became worse over the years. Are you Peregrine, Lord

Morton, who slaughtered innocent women and children over a decade ago?"

"Of course not."

"Then what was Rose on about?"

"We were never married in the eyes of the church. She felt she was living in sin, and the pretense of being Lady Denton became too much for her as did the circumstances of our coming together."

"Why didn't you marry her?"

"I did. We were married by a priest in Livorno. Her father, and initially Rose herself, thought we were married. Let me explain. I am a second son and not expecting to inherit the title or lands, I became a merchant. I married a wealthy woman in London, but she ran off with a peer who persuaded the ecclesiastical courts to give her a divorce on the grounds of some trumped-up evidence she and her friends presented. The situation was so humiliating that I moved my commercial enterprise to Livorno, where I went into partnership with a rich Italian ship owner. His unmarried daughter Rosa got herself pregnant and had an illegitimate child who was immediately sent to a convent. My partner felt humiliated, and his daughter now had no possibility of a good marriage.

"It was around this time that I received my appointment as consul here. My partner, believing I was single, proposed that I marry his daughter who spoke almost perfect English and take her with me to Benbali. He offered an immense amount of money to sweeten the deal, which enabled me to establish a position of dominance very quickly among the foreign merchants. At the same time, my elder brother died childless, and I inherited the title and lands, becoming Sir Ambrose."

"You were married by a priest to Rosa, who adopted the more English-sounding name Rose?" summarized Luke.

"Yes, but the problem was that, as a Catholic, I was still married to my first wife. This did not worry me initially. Rose and I never consummated our marriage because of issues stemming from the birth of her illegitimate child. She was reasonably happy believing she was married and beginning a new life, although guilt about the child seemed to stay with her."

"How did she discover the truth?"

"An old friend arrived from England and was surprised to find that my wife was not the woman he knew I had married in England. One of the servants overheard his comments and passed them on to Rosa, who was traumatized by the thought that I had another wife back in England. I explained that, in English law, I had no such wife, but her ingrained Catholic beliefs were too strong. In the eyes of God, she was not married. That, Luke, is the horrendous crime of which I am guilty."

The next day, Luke was summoned to the citadel by the acting dey, Yusuf. The Algerian envoys wished to meet the English ambassador. Seated on large soft cushions were Hasan, Ismet, Yusuf, and two strangers whom Luke and Miles took to be the Algerian mission.

Hasan explained, "Our Algerian brothers have suggested that our two fleets combine for joint missions in the Mediterranean. I pointed out that this might jeopardize our treaty with you."

Luke responded strongly, "England's interests would not be served by an alliance with the largest and strongest North African state that has a reputation of unpredictability. My instructions were to deal only with loyal outposts of the Ottoman Empire. Benbali's loyalty to the sultan is at the essence of our agreement. An independent Benbali or a Benbali subjected to Algeria or Morocco would render any agreement null and void."

Yusuf and Hasan were delighted with Luke's forthright statement. Yusuf followed it up with further information that shattered any Algerian thoughts of expansion with or without English help. "The pasha has just received information from Constantinople that, as a reward for our loyalty, the sultan is sending five of his most modern ships to join our fleet to protect his western frontier. If we combined that augmented fleet with that of the English, we have the largest navy in the western Mediterranean."

39

Luke was amazed that the Benbali officials seemed determined to provoke the Algerians. One of the latter, who spoke fluent English, responded, "Ambassador, I understand your attitude, but some of your comments are based on a misunderstanding of our position. I formally invite you to visit Algiers on your way home so that we may present to you a more accurate picture of our situation and the advantages of an alliance between us."

"I will consult my government, and if I have a positive answer before I leave Benbali, I will accept your invitation," Luke replied diplomatically.

"Word has spread rapidly across North Africa that you command a modern frigate that outsails and outguns all its rivals. May we inspect it? If impressed, we would order several from your shipyards. It would be an extremely valuable contract for your government."

Luke did not miss Yusuf's look of concern, which disappeared with Luke's reply. "It is not England's intention to strengthen the fleets of states that continue to prey on English merchantmen, no matter how rewarding contracts for new vessels would be. Unfortunately, gentlemen, I decline your request."

Luke could not resist the temptation to stir the pot further. "Gentlemen, why was your whole fleet lurking just offshore a few days ago?"

"We were not in the area to prey on European shipping. We had received an invitation from the previous dey to visit Benbali.

When we heard of the change of government and not sure whether a visit would be welcomed by the new government, we returned home. Our current visit is designed to establish relations with the new government—and to invite you to Algiers."

Hasan went for the throat. "And to rescue the former dey, who we have discovered is a very close friend of Algeria."

The Algerians were excellent diplomats. They did not miss a beat. "The previous admiral and dey were close friends of Algeria, and if they had remained in power, there would have been even closer collaboration. And there are some in our administration who believed we should not neglect friends who have fallen on hard times. If you felt free to hand Ahmed over to us, we would be happy to remove him from your territory."

Yusuf was surprised at their honesty. "Part of your mission is to rescue the old dey from our jurisdiction?"

"Only with your approval," was the cautious reply.

Colonel Gamal entered the room and spoke to Yusuf, who informed the group, "We have just received some sad news. Half an hour ago, two disreputable-looking Arabs were seen by Gamal's men climbing up a rope ladder on the seaward side of the Algerian ship. Anxious to protect you, our visitors, from any unexpected disturbance from local troublemakers, Gamal's men fired at the potential intruders, who fell back into the water. The corpse of one has since been recovered. It is Ahmed. The other was probably his accomplice, the English merchant Sir Ambrose Denton."

Only then did the Algerian mission lose their bland expression. Its leader announced that the meeting was at an end and that they would seek permission to sail on the next high tide. He turned to Luke and repeated the invitation to visit Algiers.

Luke offered to inform Elizabeth of Ahmed's death. He found her with Elif in the reception chamber of his residence. Luke was momentarily concerned about how to break the news as one of the women would be deeply saddened by the event, the other jubilant. "Ladies, I have some sad news. Ahmed, disguised as an Arab, has been shot dead trying to board the Algerian ship in the harbor."

Elif, sensitive to Elizabeth's closeness to Ahmed, merely smiled at Luke. Elizabeth remained silent for some time. Finally, she commented, "I cannot shed a tear. He was not the Ahmed I knew years ago. He planned to betray the sultan and bring Benbali under the control of the almost independent Algeria."

"Elizabeth, what will you do now?" asked Luke.

"I had intended to stay here until you found Jethro's murderer and Lord Morton and then return to Constantinople to the couple who adopted me. However, events of the past few weeks have led me to change my mind. For the time being, I will stay in Benbali."

"What is that situation?" asked a surprised Luke.

But before Elizabeth could answer, she was interrupted by Elif. "The pasha wishes you, Luke, to be informed immediately that new instructions have been received from the sultan. Commander Yusuf, as a reward for his role in keeping Benbali on a steady keel during these troubled times, has been appointed to the sultan's court and leaves for Constantinople as soon as a new dey is elected. Ismet, now promoted general, has been confirmed as governor of the citadel and commander of all troops in the country. Gamal takes over Yusuf's old position, responsible for internal security and tax collection. Murat Pasha has been confirmed in his role as the sultan's representative. The sultan has endorsed Benbali's treaty with England."

Luke turned to Elizabeth. "I hope I can solve Jethro's murder and discover Morton before I leave, but my options are running out. It is not Ambrose, and despite Silas's obsession, it is not Gregory. James and Rowland are dead. If I focus only on the English merchant community, it has to be Silas or Gregory—and both of them are highly unlikely."

"Perhaps Morton never came to Benbali," sighed Elif.

"Or he has concealed himself outside the local English community. Unless he can convince me otherwise, I suspect that Admiral Hasan is Morton."

"No, you are wrong. I will invite Hasan here, and he can exonerate himself," replied a visibly upset Elif, despite her recent concern at Hasan's brutal execution of General Osman.

Elizabeth changed the subject. "Who will be consul? There is only Gregory left, and he wishes to take his business to London."

"Ninian hopefully will stay on in the post. He spent a lot of time with his uncle who was consul in Aleppo and has done a good job over the last few weeks. He has expressed no desire to return to England and take up his position as the Marquess of Fyson. His affection for Nour may be another reason why he wishes to stay in Benbali."

"Don't rely on the last factor," announced Elif.

"What do you mean?"

"Nour—with the approval of her father, the pasha, and Lord Fyson—is to marry another," Elif replied.

"That is hard to believe. I will go to see him now, formally offer him the permanent position as consul, and find out exactly what has happened to his relationship with Nour."

Elif gave Elizabeth a knowing look.

Luke found Ninian in Ambrose's old office in the Denton warehouse. "Ninian, I will soon be gone, and before I leave, I am obliged to appoint a consul. You have been doing an excellent job, and I would like you to accept the position for a five-year term."

Ninian was delighted. He accepted the position with alacrity. "Don't be too hasty. You are the Marquess of Fyson. The role of English aristocrat and landowner might be a more suitable future for you than consul in the Maghreb," advised Luke.

"No, I was never intended to succeed my father. I know more about trade than running landed estates. I have already transferred enough assets from the Fyson estates to set myself up here as a wealthy merchant. I gave Applegarth a bill of credit as payment for the warehouse from which I will operate as both consul and trader. I may renounce my title and estates in favor of my first cousin who is the closest male relative, although recent events have given me more options for my long-term future."

"And married to Nour," asked Luke, pretending he knew nothing of any recent developments.

"No, Nour is about to marry General Ismet."

"What went wrong? You were both deeply in love."

"We were, but reality set in. I could only marry Nour if she became a Catholic or if I became a Moslem. Neither of us would or could budge on such a matter of faith. Her father and the pasha acted quickly to ensure we did not have second thoughts."

"I am sorry to hear that."

"Don't be. I have since found a woman that I love and whom I will marry."

"Who is that?" asked a surprised Luke.

"Don't tell me you have no idea. A budding and rapidly developing romance has occurred in your own residence. I have not been coming to your evening meal every night for the last fortnight to enjoy your company. I came to woo Lady Elizabeth Scarfe."

"I am delighted, Ninian. Given this relationship, I would not renounce your title. In years to come, Ninian, Marquess, and Elizabeth, Marchioness of Fyson, may find the life of a landed English aristocrat more pleasing than the commercial life of North Africa." Luke then asked, "Is Gregory still here?"

"He went to his residence just before you arrived."

Luke found Gregory and went straight to the point. "I have just appointed Ninian as consul on the assumption that you had decided with Ambrose's coming departure to relocate to London."

"That is correct. There is nothing here for me. Everything has changed. Apart from Lucy Goodrich, the English community that existed when you arrived is gone. The Benbali administration with which we worked so well has been overthrown. There are new brooms everywhere. And I have just been told that Ambrose is dead, shot while trying to board an Algerian warship."

Luke decided not to tell Gregory, at this stage, that Ambrose was still alive and safe aboard the *Cromwell*. Instead, he asked, "Surely, you and Patience could have adapted to these changes?"

"Patience has left me, refusing to return to England. She has moved into the pasha's palace."

"I am sorry to hear that," replied Luke, now determined to visit Patience immediately.

On his way to the pasha's palace, Luke changed his mind. He would ask Elif to arrange a meeting as he did not know Patience's new status and did not wish to upset the pasha by visiting women of his household uninvited. He was a little confused. Surely, Patience must be a governess to the children of the household, rather than a new member of the harem. He must clarify this with Elif before he met Patience.

Luke dropped in on Lucy, the only remaining English trader until Ninian set up his operation. "Lucy, I have just appointed Lord Fyson as the permanent consul. You and he will be the only English merchants in Benbali, at least for the short term. Are you able to carry on without James?"

"Yes, the Jewish family who escaped Oran with James are my new partners. They will have to live in the Jewish ghetto within the city. We will be forced to have two retail outlets, one in the ghetto and one here. Has that rogue Silas been dealt with?"

"Not yet."

"He has hardly missed his old partner, Rowland May. He has been entertaining a dissolute-looking Arab over recent days. It is his new lover. How could I have been taken in?"

As Luke walked home, he wondered what sort of commercial enterprise a fanatical Christian and an urbane Jewish family would develop.

40

The next morning, Elif ushered Patience into Luke's reception room. Luke confessed, "My visit has obliterated the English trading community that I was sent to reform. Only Lucy Goodrich remains. James, Rowland, and Jethro are dead; Ambrose is assumed so; and Gregory and Silas are leaving. Rose has moved to a convent, Elizabeth until recently was returning to Constantinople, and you have joined the pasha's household."

"I could not see myself growing old as the neglected wife of a London merchant. Here, I can help educate the women of the household and, at the same time, expand my knowledge of the Muslim world and become fluent in both Turkish and Arabic. Elif and I have become close friends."

"And both of you have lost Ismet," said Luke teasingly.

Elif changed the subject. "I feel sorry for young Ninian. He lost Nour, but there could be no compromise within households. It can either be Christian or Muslim, not half of each."

"Does this mean, Patience, that you will become a Muslim?"

"Yes, with Elif's help, I will adapt to my new environment very quickly. I must return to the palace now to teach the English-born slaves how to read and write. I must not be late." She gave Luke a quick hug and left the room. Elif followed her, picking up a shawl that Patience had inadvertently left behind.

Luke followed Elif to the door and was astounded. Elif and Patience were in the next room, kissing and fondling each other passionately. It had never dawned on Luke that two of the women he was attracted to were in love with each other. His male ego was shattered.

Elif returned. Luke had hoped for an amorous interlude, but the situation with Patience dampened his enthusiasm. Elif's mind was also elsewhere. "Luke, I have invited Hasan here to prove he is not Morton. May I call him in?" Luke nodded approval.

Hasan arrived and confronted Luke. "Elif says you believe me to be the notorious lord Morton."

"Prove that you are not." demanded the discomforted Luke.

"At the time of the massacre at Scarfe Abbey, I was a slave on Malta. I have the brand of my Maltese Christian master, the three-pointed star within a circle, and I have a document that lists me, John Dodds, with my past history. It states that I was a slave on the ship that we slaves seized from our master and surrendered to the Benbalis. These documents were on that ship."

"How do I know you are the John Dodds referred to in the documents?"

"Each Maltese slave was given an additional brand for identification purposes. This was a number, expressed in its Latin form. If you look at the document, John Dodds is listed as XV."

Hasan removed his shirt, revealing brands showing a three-pointed star within a circle and the number XV. Luke perused the documents, which showed that, when the Morton massacre was occurring in England, John Dodds was a slave on Malta.

Elif could not resist commenting, "Are you satisfied now? Hasan is not Morton?"

"Not quite. These documents could be forgeries. I will show them to people who could vouch for their authenticity—Wasim and Father Battista, who in different ways have handled hundreds of slaves and their papers."

Hasan handed them over, remarking, "They will prove my innocence. I do not want to start my new position with such an accusation hanging over my head."

"Your new position?"

Elif answered before Hasan. "The pasha has altered the rules for election of the new dey. Candidates at alternate elections will be drawn from the navy on one occasion and the army on the next. With General Ismet content with being military commander and not wanting the new dey drawn from his junior officers, the next dey will be Hasan."

Luke congratulated him. "I hope these documents prove your innocence because, if you are Morton, we both know that there is little I can do, especially if you are the dey. And I hate to fail."

Elif and Hasan left.

Luke took the documents first to Wasim and then to Father Battista. Both men had seen many similar documents and vouched for their validity. Luke returned to his residence quite depressed. Perhaps Morton had never been in Benbali.

Miles entered the room with a young English officer whom Luke had never seen before and who looked totally exhausted. The young man addressed Luke directly. "Lieutenant Davidson, courier for the Lord Protector. I am to deliver this to you personally."

"No English ships have entered the harbor. How did you get here?" asked a surprised Luke.

"I took an Italian merchantman from Livorno as no English vessels, military or commercial, were docked there, and I had orders to get these to you as soon as possible."

"Miles, take the lieutenant to get a good meal and lingering bath, and we shall dine together tonight and catch up on what is happening in England."

Luke was left alone with a large leather satchel. Its contents included letters from the Lord Protector and military intelligence and copies of witness testimonies from the Middlesex assizes.

He first opened the letter from Oliver Cromwell. It contained his new instructions. He was to return home as soon as possible after acting on the additional evidence provided in the attached documents.

He opened the second letter from military intelligence. Its pertinent passages were most interesting.

Thurloe did not seem to be particularly interested in uncovering the past of the various members of the English community, but when the name Lord Morton was mentioned, he left no stone unturned. Apparently, Sir Everton Scarfe had been a mentor to him in the early days. The materials sent to you are witness accounts presented at Morton's trial that may give a clue to the uncovering of his new persona. Thurloe told me to emphasize that, although Peregrine was a brutal mass murderer, his younger brother Lancelot was even worse. Lancelot was Peregrine's deputy during the slaughter at Scarfe Abbey. Thurloe believes that it was Lancelot who engineered Peregrine's escape from the Tower. Neither brother has been seen since. Hope the detail in the court records help.

By the time Miles returned, Luke had divided the court documents into two piles. "We are looking for any detail that might help us identify Morton," he explained.

After a couple of hours of reading, Luke asked whether Miles had come across anything that he thought relevant. Miles informed him, "Peregrine was not the eldest son. As the second son, he trained in the law and only succeeded to the title on the death of his brother in the first battle of the civil war. His third brother, Lancelot, was a merchant and moneylender based in Italy who only returned to England at the outbreak of war."

An elated Luke asked, "Miles, will you repeat what you have just said?" Miles obliged. Luke jumped to his feet and threw his papers into the air. "Eureka! Your simple summary has solved the mystery. I know who Lord Morton is—or rather was."

41

"You are ahead of me," confessed Miles.

"Think! Have you met two men who were close associates, one a lawyer and one involved in commerce?"

"Rowland May, the lawyer, and his partner, Silas Sweetlace, the bookkeeper. Damn it, we have wasted our time! If Rowland May was Lord Morton, his death deprives us of administering justice," replied a disappointed Miles.

"Yes, but if Lancelot was a greater criminal than his brother, we can at least return him to England for trial and execution."

"And it would follow that if Rowland and Silas were the Morton brothers, then they were almost certainly the murderers of Jethro," proclaimed Miles.

"But who murdered Rowland?" emphasized Luke.

"So close yet so far from an answer that solves all our problems," muttered Miles.

"Keep a close eye on Silas. He is not to leave Benbali except aboard the *Cromwell*. That may give us time to prove our suspicions and discover who murdered Rowland."

That evening, Luke dined with Miles and Lieutenant Davidson, who looked remarkably better than he had been earlier.

The next morning, Luke and Miles resumed their reading of the court documents. Luke commented, "Right at the beginning when she was Chantal, Elizabeth said that Morton had a disfigurement that might help identify him. You would think that such a disability would be one of the first things referred to by the witnesses, but there is nothing that I have read indicating anything distinguishing."

"I have found one small item. One witness said that when Peregrine was stressed or tired, he slurred his words. Apparently, he had been wounded in the tongue, which if he was concentrating did not affect his speech. But if his concentration lapsed, he could appear by his speech to be drunk."

"Damn! I have never heard Silas or Rowland slur their words," replied a disappointed Luke.

"Don't totally despair, Luke. I have a vague recollection someone told us one or other of our suspects was drunk when it was obvious that he had not been drinking too much. God, if only I could remember who it was."

Luke and Miles completed their reading, and Luke suggested they now read the pile that the other had read to make sure nothing was missed. All of a sudden, Miles hit the table with his closed fist several times. "I remember. It was Strad. After that welcoming banquet when Ninian collapsed, he commented that May also might have been poisoned. He was slurring his words but he was not poisoned and he did not drink alcohol."

"And he would have been stressed because their intended victim, Jethro, had escaped. I am now certain. The late Rowland May was Peregrine, Lord Morton, and Silas Sweetlace is his brother, Lancelot."

Their celebration was cut short by the arrival of Colonel Gamal. "Silas Sweetlace, accompanied by an Arab male, against your specific orders, has boarded a Moroccan coastal trader, which will leave at high tide in about an hour."

"Thank you, Colonel. With your permission, I would like to have my men board the ship and remove Silas and his friend."

"Only my men have the authority to the board the ship. You may accompany them, and while they search the ship, you can remove Silas."

The ship was a small sloop that, Gamal explained, would sail to Oran and onto a number of Moroccan ports. Once on the deck of the ship, Gamal asked the crew and passengers where the

Englishman and his friend were. The ship's captain, anxious to avoid any trouble from the Benbali authorities, sent his men below deck.

They soon emerged, dragging Silas and his companion with them. Silas was distraught to see Luke and a platoon of English troops. He was soon shackled.

His companion, who hid his features, was dragged off the ship. In the process, his elaborate headdress fell off. Luke and Miles were astonished. The Arab companion was Rowland May.

Rowland and Silas were taken immediately to the *Cromwell*, where they were placed in the brig with their feet tied together and their hands shackled. Luke gave orders that the ship would sail for home early the next day.

Luke spent his last day in Benbali paying courtesy visits to the Benbali authorities and the women who had been part of his life for the past months. He was delighted to inform Elizabeth that the murderers of her family and Jethro were in custody. He wished her and Ninian well. His farewell to Elif was an amorous and surprisingly happy affair.

The next morning, the *Greenham* and the *Wildfire* left at dawn to rejoin the English Mediterranean fleet. In midmorning, the *Cromwell* left its anchorage and sailed close to the citadel, whose guns delivered a salute to the departing English warship, which returned the courtesy with an impressive cannonade.

On the north tower, the Benbali authorities had gathered; and among them, Luke was pleased to see three couples—Elif and Patience, Ninian and Elizabeth, and Ismet and Nour. It was a happy ending.

Gregory Applegarth was delighted to find that his old partner, Sir Ambrose Denton, was alive—and a fellow passenger. Denton would disembark at Livorno. Applegarth would be taken on to London. They agreed to continue their commercial partnership, with Gregory the English and Ambrose the Italian agent—hoping eventually to involve Ninian in Benbali in their network.

When the ship was well out into the Mediterranean, Luke and Miles began their interrogation of the Morton brothers, who had masqueraded successfully for years as the homosexual couple Silas

Sweetlace and Rowland May. Peregrine Morton was interested in how Luke and Miles had identified them. He was amazed that his small tongue wound and the slurring of his words during the welcoming banquet, after their first attempt at murder had failed, had contributed to his capture.

Luke asked the obvious question. "Who was the body whose face was so disfigured that you, Lancelot, could identify it as Rowland?"

"It was the bargeman Kareem, who knew we had murdered Jethro," replied Lancelot.

"Why kill Jethro?" asked Miles.

"He knew a lot more about us than he told his adopted sister, Chantal. He reached the conclusions you arrived at a day or so ago, months before you," said Lancelot with a tinge of spite.

"Did the emergence of the Thames pendant force you to act?" probed Luke.

"No. It was a surprise but not a problem. I sold it recently in the bazaar. I expected, as is the custom, that it would be broken up and its parts reassembled into entirely different pieces of jewelry. When it reappeared on the night of the welcoming banquet, it was disconcerting, but I knew it could not be traced back to me because I used a third party to sell it, and he was killed by Kareem soon after the transaction," explained Peregrine.

"Jethro had to go simply because he was getting too close to uncovering our real identity," added Lancelot.

"That is why we arranged for your abduction. Lancelot forged a number of documents so if anyone did follow back the money trail about who paid the kidnappers, it would lead to Ambrose and Ahmed," explained Peregrine.

"What are you going to do with us?" asked the younger brother, who was beginning to show signs of anxiety.

"You, Lancelot, will be handed over to the authorities in London to be brought before the assizes, charged with multiple murders. Your elder brother will be returned to the Tower of London to be hanged, drawn, and quartered and his head placed on a pike outside the castle, according to his original sentence."

Both men seemed relieved. "We thought you might make us walk the plank," half joked Peregrine. Both brothers were confident that, as long as they remained alive, their chances of escaping justice remained strong.

Luke had a similar thought.

He later dined with Miles, Ralph, John, and Lieutenant Davidson and raised the issue. "Our legal system remains corrupt, and persons of influence can sway decisions. The Lord Protector's appointments to the judiciary have yet to prove themselves. The only certain way to ensure justice *is* to deliver it ourselves."

The English officers gave one another knowing looks and drank a toast to the Lord Protector.

The midnight watch was alarmed by two shots followed by a loud splash. Captain Croft recorded nothing in his log. Later Luke's formal report suggested that the two brothers had committed suicide by hurling themselves into the sea.

Meanwhile back in England, Simon, Lord Stokey, brought his obsession with the golden Madonna to a satisfactory conclusion. Unknown to Luke, Ninian—as the Marquess of Fyson—had given Simon letters, one to Charles Stuart and one to Oliver Cromwell, claiming that neither government had a right to the Madonna, if it were recovered in the Tamar estuary. Legally, it belonged to him, but he would return it, through Simon, to its moral owners—the Cistercian monks in Spain.

For two weeks, Simon—with a large group—dredged the river under the close supervision of Sir Evan Williams and military intelligence. Cromwell had no intention of allowing the valuable icon to be returned to the papist church.

Late one evening, against all the odds, the Madonna was found which Simon immediately handed to Sir Evan; and half an hour later, the carefully wrapped icon was dispatched by military courier to Whitehall, escorted by a heavily armed posse.

By the time the object sent to Whitehall was unwrapped and recognized as a worthless bronze imitation, Simon had left Truro with the real Madonna aboard a fishing boat bound for Spain.